NIPPED

in the

BUD

NIPPED
in the
BUD

Susan Sleeman

BARBOUR
PUBLISHING

ISBN 978-1-60260-573-2

This book is a work of fiction. Names, characters, places, and incidents are either products of the author's imagination or used fictitiously. Any similarity to actual people, organizations, and/or events is purely coincidental.

For more information about Susan Sleeman, please access the author's Web site at the following Internet address: www.susansleeman.com.

Cover design: Faceout Studio, www.faceoutstudio.com

Published by Barbour Publishing, Inc., P.O. Box 719, Uhrichsville, OH 44683, www.barbourbooks.com

Our mission is to publish and distribute inspirational products offering exceptional value and biblical encouragement to the masses.

ecpa Member of the
Evangelical Christian
Publishers Association

Printed in the United States of America.

DEDICATION

In memory of my parents Rodney and Geraldine Becker
who taught me the value of hard work and perseverance.

ACKNOWLEDGEMENTS

Special thanks go to:

Becky Germany of Barbour Publishing for bringing
the Hometown Mysteries series to life.

Editor Ellen Tarver for her keen eye and flexible spirit.

Susan Downs who took a chance on an unpublished author and
contracted *Nipped in the Bud*. And to my critique partners Elizabeth
Ludwig, Janelle Mowery, Sandra Robbins, and Jessica Ferguson whose
experienced hands helped shape the book. Thank you to all of you for the
special surprise when I received my first book contract at the
ACFW annual conference.

My husband Mark for understanding the crazy life of a
writer and always, always, always being supportive of my dream.
To my daughter Emma for the title of the book, and daughter
Erin for her graphic design help.

And, of course, to my heavenly Father,
without whom I could do nothing.

CHAPTER ∥∥∥ ONE

"This is Harly Davison, your host of KALM's exciting new show, Wacky World of Motorcycles, *hoping you'll join us every Wednesday morning at ten and reminding you that Hogs, not dogs, are man's best friend. Now we return to the locally acclaimed show,* Through the Garden Gate, *with host Paige Turner."*

Weed Whacker! You can't possibly want to kill your husband!" I yelled into the boom microphone and looked for advice from my producer and best friend, Lisa Winkle.

Tucked safely in her little booth adjoining mine, Lisa shrugged and twirled her finger in our signal that meant I should say something before dead air killed the show.

I shook my head. Her finger picked up speed as if she possessed the power to spin me around and force words from my mouth. But what could I say? What could an unmarried gardening expert know about killing a husband?

"Paige, are you there?" Weed Whacker's tone bordered on desperation, elevating my concern.

I gave up on Lisa offering any assistance and punched the mute button then searched through the middle drawer of the ancient metal desk. If I could locate the station's talk show schedule, I could refer Weed Whacker to the self-help program.

"Paige," Lisa said through my headset. "What are you doing? We can't have dead air like this."

"You're not helping," I said. Words from my mother with her many years of advice, my pastor's weekly sermons, and God, already fought for space in my head. I had no room for anything Lisa was saying. I punched the button again and adjusted the mike. "Perhaps you would like to call into our self-help show. If you hold on, my producer will give you the broadcast time."

"Please, Paige. I can't wait. I need your advice."

"Don't do anything drastic," I blurted before she changed her mind, disconnected, and did something crazy. Eyes on the drawer, my fingers fumbled around for the laminated schedule. If I gave the wrong advice, how would I recover from being implicated in a murder? "There has to be an amiable solution to your problem."

She sighed. "We're way past working things out. It's bad enough I have to do all the yard work myself, but to face the same thing inside the house? I'm losing it, Paige. I tell you, I'm losing it. I'm so tired of my husband sprouting up every Sunday in the same place, just like the weeds you described."

I gave up on the search for the schedule and closed my eyes to think. Weed Whacker needed a counselor, not someone like me who only knew how to handle a plant's 911. Wait. . .counselor. I was a peer counselor in college. If I remembered right, I should repeat what I heard the distraught person saying so she'd know I was listening.

I cleared my throat, a no-no on radio, and charged ahead. "I can certainly empathize with your concerns, Weed Whacker. I understand that your husband pops up in the recliner every Sunday and watches football games. And yes, technically, this type of sprouting in an unwanted place week after week, no matter the effort you put in to stop it, sounds like most weeds." I raised my fist in the air and shook it in victory over my professional counselor speak.

"Paige, please. I called for advice, not to hear you repeat everything I say."

I slowly lowered my arm and gave in. If my suggestions ended with my incarceration, so be it. "If you need my advice, then I must caution you. This morning we've discussed two successful methods of removing weeds. The first is digging a hole the width of the crown and pulling roots and all from the soil. The second is applying one of the many available herbicides on the market. We both agree your husband might be exhibiting weedlike tendencies. Still, I must ask you to think long and hard about removing this particular species. If you have no other choice but to act, I recommend the plucking method, as the use of herbicides in this particular application could be misconstrued as murder."

As my words aged on the airwaves like a pile of compost, I cut my gaze to Lisa. She slashed her hand across her throat, either telling me I was dead or to wrap it up. I chose to believe the second one. Barely able to contain my joy over the end of this Monday morning disaster of a show, I nearly shot up like a daffodil on a warm spring day. Weed Whacker was our last caller, and if another show tanked like this one had, she could be the last caller—ever. I needed to stick with plants. They didn't conspire to kill each other. Sure, some of them were more aggressive than others, choking out their neighbors, but unlike Weed Whacker, their wayward tendencies were never premeditated.

Oops, right. Weed Whacker. I needed to close the show.

"Thank you for calling, Weed Whacker. I hope my advice has been helpful. Unfortunately we're out of time." I stifled a sigh then dug deep for my cheery broadcaster's voice. "Thank you for listening. Join me again tomorrow at nine as we take another trip *Through the Garden Gate.* Be sure to stay tuned for *Success Serendipity Style,* where host Tim Needlemeyer brings you up to date on all the exciting activities planned for this weekend's Pickle Fest. But first, Ollie Grayson and the *Farm to Market Report.*"

I flipped the switch that kicked off the prerecorded agriculture show and tossed my headset onto the desk.

"And we're clear," Lisa shouted, like some big-time producer, though it was just the two of us in a closet-sized studio.

On my feet, I charged toward her and kicked open the door separating our work spaces. "Where are all these wackos coming from, and why aren't you screening them out?"

"Maybe it takes a wacko host to attract wacko callers," Lisa said with a slight shrug of her perfectly postured shoulders. She turned away and shoved a manila folder titled LIABILITY into one of the many file cabinets lining the walls.

Mouth hanging open, I watched her work. She'd effectively called me a nut job but seemed oblivious to my rage. The space was so small she had to stand to the side of the open file drawer to wedge another folder into the back. Perspiration sprinkled her face from an hour spent in the airless room. Her mouth wasn't puckered in a sneer or flopping open in a big goofy laugh.

Lisa was serious. She really *did* think I was as wacky as my callers. I sighed much like Weed Whacker had. Lisa looked up.

"What?" She laughed and slammed the drawer. "All I'm saying is if you didn't give such flaky advice, we might attract a different kind of listener."

"*We?* I'm the one who has to come up with something to say on the spur of the moment when these nut jobs phone in. All you do is sit back and make gestures with your hands." I yanked my backpack from the shelf behind her and pulled out my lip balm. Between the hours I spent gardening and licking my lips in nervousness for the last thirty minutes, they were as rough as my show had been.

"I do my job the best I can, and if you don't like it, fire me." Lisa pulled her crisply ironed jacket off the back of her chair and flicked me an irate look before exiting. My five-foot-three dynamo of a friend rushed down the long hall to the front entrance as fast as her fuchsia colored flip-flops allowed. I tromped behind, wondering how the two of us were going to get through the next three hours working on my landscaping job if all we could do was bicker.

I'd decline her free labor and send her home, but this was my first big project since I included landscape design in the services offered by my shop, The Garden Gate. I'd just landed a big fat juicy contract with the city of Serendipity, Oregon, to renovate the play area and otherwise spruce up the park. Once the Pickle Fest visitors saw my professional work, they were sure to sign up at my booth for a little renovation of their own yards.

No. No way I'd let one of our many little tiffs blow my big opportunity.

I caught up to Lisa, who studied a chipped fingernail as she tapped her flip-flops in a snapping sound on the asphalt beside my Ford 150. I unlocked the passenger door and waited for Her Highness to slide onto the seat before slamming the door. From a Frendi, Schmendi, or whatever they called those designer purses with the squiggly little marks etched into the material, she pulled out a bag of sunflower seeds and attacked the tiny morsels.

I climbed behind the wheel and nudged her elbow. Eyes downcast, she ignored me and chewed a seed. Maybe I really had hurt her feelings. I'd been a bit testy since signing on to do this job with such a short deadline. The park renovation had to be completed by sundown on Thursday to set up for the opening of Pickle Fest. The whole community was counting on me.

So, testy or not, I needed my friend more than ever right now. That meant I needed to apologize. "Sorry for getting so mad at you. It's not your fault these people end up on the air."

"Don't you know it!" She snapped her fingers near my face then popped another seed into her mouth and grinned like the Cheshire cat.

"You weren't really mad, were you?"

Her grin widened, giving her the impish look that her twins had when they were up to no good. "So, did I tell you about the problem at the girls' preschool?"

"What problem?" I shifted into drive and hoped Lisa's kids weren't implicated in the current disaster. Last week her daughter Lori sneaked into the bathroom with the class hamster to see if he could swim. Fortunately, he could, but the teacher wasn't too happy about returning a toilet-bowl-swimming hamster to the classroom.

"Well, don't tell anyone, but they've got lice. A big ole breakout of lice." She graphically described the painstaking process of shampooing then using a fine-toothed comb to remove the little nits from her daughters' lovely blond hair.

I stifled a groan and said, "uh-huh" in all the right spots as she talked, but really, her fixation with these gross childhood stories was getting to be too much. The entire drive to the studio she'd yammered on about potty training mishaps and ear infections. A single, thirty-four–year-old woman like myself should never be subjected to these gruesome topics. Not if there was any hope that I would aid in the future population of the human race.

"Once you have the little buggers free," Lisa said in a tone she usually reserved for BOGO sales, "the rest is simple. You just drop them in the liquid medicine and flush it all down the toilet."

"Aw, c'mon. Please tell me they're dead by then? Or do they live on and on, waiting to pounce on some unsuspecting person?" I stabbed my ragged fingernails into the spot right below my ponytail and scratched away.

She swatted at my arm. "You're not taking this seriously. You can't imagine the trauma of discovering your child has lice."

"I can't even imagine the trauma of discovering I have a child." I gave one last scratch then turned left at First Avenue and pulled the truck into the empty lot at the park. The lot rarely held many cars, as most businesses, including The Garden Gate and the radio station were within five blocks of the town center, where the park was located. Lisa and I would have walked to the park if the job hadn't required a ton of tools. Tools we needed to move to the job site if I was going to meet the deadline. "How about forgetting your Lice Capades for a while and helping me unload the tools?"

Without a word, but with copious sighs, Lisa changed into beat-up sneakers then trudged alongside me, hauling shovels, rakes, and clippers to the play area. Whenever my hand was free, I pawed at the back of my head for imaginary lice. I needed to get the creepy crawlies out of my mind and get to work.

Today we would remove the old mulch from under the play structure. Tomorrow I would enlarge and deepen the fall zone. Despite my rush to get started, I could still appreciate the typical Northwest setting as we entered the playground section of the park. Tall swaying pines dotted garden beds that lined three sides of the area, hiding it from the traffic on Oak, one of the main retail streets in town, and home to my apartment located above the pharmacy.

After I applied my loving touch, the neglected garden beds filled with native Oregon plants would be more in keeping with the healthy lawn adjoining the play area. A quaint old refreshment stand and picnic tables sat in the center of the clearing. Of course, Serendipity, home of the annual Pickle Fest, couldn't resist sprinkling bright green trash cans in the shape of dill pickles across the park. They were stamped with the slogan, LISTEN TO BRINY. KEEP OUR PARK SHINY. Briny, the town's mascot, showed up not only at the annual celebration, but at other events as well. I found it rather odd to see a child snuggle up to a giant pickle, but my fellow residents loved him.

"Hey," I said as we made our final trip. "Did you do that?"

"Do what?"

I pointed at the heavy zip ties I'd used to secure the temporary fence after I installed it around the play area yesterday. They were scattered on the ground in tiny neon fragments. "Did you cut those?"

"Don't look at me."

With fingers once again wiggling over the back of my head, I stared at the gaping hole as if looking at it would clear up the mystery.

"Are we here to work, or are you just gonna stand there scratching?" Lisa pulled on her gloves and walked through the hole I was gaping at, grabbed my short blue-handled shovel, and started tossing mulch onto a tarp.

Normally, I would have rushed into the enclosure and hefted my shovel before she did, but I couldn't get past the cut ties. I glanced around the park as if I would find the scissors-wielding culprit. I found a culprit, all right, but probably not the one who cut the ties.

"Check that out." I pointed through the trees toward the Main Street entrance. "Today's topic on weeds was right on target. Here comes the two-legged variety." I said weed, but technically, I'd dubbed our city manager, Bud Picklemann, a globe thistle.

Not that he was special or anything. I gave everyone I knew a plant name. Case in point, Lisa, my perfect little Shasta daisy, rested her shovel and swiveled around to watch Bud storm across the lush green grass. If divided regularly, Shastas could be counted on to flower season after season. Plus their creamy white color complements most flowers around them. Like the Shasta, Lisa's personality is a perfect complement to mine, and I counted on her for the support I lost when my mother passed away.

Lisa looked up and rolled her eyes. "Great. Wonder what our fearless leader wants?"

"If his body language is any indication, I'm in for it." To me, Bud's clenched fists and red face were just outward signs that he was living up to his globe thistle name—a prickly, troublesome weed, whose painful barbs kept people at a distance. But I hadn't a clue what set him off today. "He can't be mad about this project yet. All I've done is put up a fence. That's not enough to cause this kind of reaction."

"If you'd listened to me, *for once,*" Lisa's face grew smug, a look I'd learned to fear yet rarely reacted appropriately to, "you'd have expected this. I told you it's never a good idea to work with a man whose wife would do anything to get back at you."

"And if you'd listened to *me*, you'd know that Rachel has forgotten all about our little misunderstanding."

"Hah!" Lisa pointed a gloved finger at me. "You don't steal Rachel's prom date and not live to regret it."

"I did not steal Todd from her. He didn't even ask her to the prom. She just thought he was going to take her."

"As did the whole school."

"So what? That was seventeen years ago. Water under the bridge." I glanced at Bud. Wearing a short-sleeved white shirt cinched at the neck with a narrow black tie, he surged toward me like a bamboo shoot on a garden-conquering rampage. Was Lisa right? Was Bud planning on taking revenge for his still-embarrassed wife? Nah. No way.

I turned back to her. "Even if Rachel wants Bud to fire me, he can't. The city council signed my contract."

"He can make things difficult for you."

"How? I could do this job in my sleep." After twelve years in the landscaping business in Portland, I'd hoped my first job in Serendipity would be more challenging, but I believed this was only the first step. I pointed at the playground. "This project is cut and dried. How can Bud mess with that?"

"Okay, Miss Know It All. If everything's so simple, why's he glaring at you?"

"Doesn't matter. I'm doing this job no matter what. It's going to get me the public exposure I need." Bud picked up speed, and I hoped I'd be able to stand behind my words when he arrived.

My eyes locked on Lisa's. We stared at each other as we often did when we hit an impasse. She was shorter by a good seven inches but made up for her height impairment in attitude. We frequently found ourselves nearly duking it out until something happened to make us laugh it off.

Bud wouldn't be the source of our humor today. His huffing and puffing arrival, as if he intended to blow my house down, guaranteed that. "Take a hike, Lisa," he grumbled. "I need to talk to Paige. Alone."

Lisa wrinkled her nose at him and stabbed her shovel into the soil. The bright blue handle pinged back and forth as she came over to me and leaned close. "Watch your back," she whispered. "Or you might be exposed in ways you never dreamed." In full voice, and with a glare for Bud, she said, "I'll head over to your shop and get a cup of coffee. Call me when he's through."

"Thanks for the help." I glanced at my watch. Ten thirty. If I was lucky, Bud would only snipe at me for a few minutes, and Lisa and I could get back to work.

As if he'd read my mind, Bud didn't wait for Lisa to get far before he turned on me. "Well, you've done it, Paige, just like I predicted you would. I knew you'd mess up. Just didn't think you'd mess up this fast."

Caught off guard by the vehemence in his tone, I mouthed, "Huh?"

"Yesterday, someone saw kids playing inside this poor excuse for a safety fence." He grabbed the top slat of the orange plastic and shook it until his face turned red from the exertion. Unfortunately for him, all he succeeded in doing was making his long comb-over flap up and down. "We can't have kids on a construction site."

I took a few deep breaths and thought. Not about Bud's unique hairdo, as that took few brain waves. I was more interested in his notoriety for jumping to conclusions. And I wasn't about to take the fall for something he couldn't prove. "Are you sure whoever told you about the kids isn't making it up?"

He ripped his hands from the fence and crossed spindly arms. "Don't try to squirm out of this, Paige. You chose this flimsy fence instead of chain link. You'd best upgrade it if you hope to keep this job."

I stared at him, his puckered lips, his closed stance. He wasn't going to listen to me at all. I could say almost anything. He'd have the same comeback and we'd have the same result—I'd be shelling out big bucks for a chain link fence.

Bud came close and clapped his hands in front of my face. "Don't just stand there staring at me. What're you gonna do? If a kid got hurt on your job, the liability'd kill us."

"You know, Bud," I said, stepping back from his barbs and trying to infuse a level of calm into my tone that I didn't feel, "I think you're overreacting. I'd like some proof before making any changes."

"I have pictures."

Now we're getting somewhere. "Mind if I look at them?"

He yanked a photo from his back pocket and waved it like a decorative garden flag blowing in the breeze. "Here. See? Kids inside the fence."

"I'd like a closer look."

He shook his head, settling the last of his wayward hair back into place. "You know all you need to know. Now, what are you gonna do about it?"

"Picklemann, you big old scammer," a husky male voice called from behind us. "I want to talk to you."

We both turned and watched pharmacist Charlie Sweeny stomp our way. He wore a white lab coat over black pants that looked as old and fashionable as men's double knits of the eighties. His reading glasses hung around his neck on a frayed red cord, dangling below a crimson face and eyes filled with rage.

Bud, dense as usual, must not have noticed the threat I saw in Charlie's eyes as he glared back. "I have nothing to say to you, old man. I'm busy. Take a hike."

Charlie sneered. "Oh, you'll talk to me all right, or I'll blab your secret to everyone in town."

I stood in the war zone, wondering if I should risk hanging around as they hurled bombs at each other just so I could learn Bud's big secret. If a fight broke out, exposure to their fallout could be deadly. I saw Charlie as a foxglove, and that meant you didn't cross him. The genus name for foxglove was *Digitalis*, the medicine still used today to treat heart problems. The plant was pretty, but deadly, and as the local pharmacist, Charlie could end someone's life with one simple mistake.

Since I leased one of the few apartments in town from Charlie, I didn't want to make him mad. I smiled at him with so much syrup dripping from the corners of my mouth that I had a sudden craving for pancakes. "We're almost done here, Charlie," I said, followed by a quick lick of my lips. "Do you mind if I finish with Bud, first?"

Charlie kept his heated gaze fixed on Bud. "I'll be back, Picklemann, when a little bit of a girl isn't protecting you." He turned and marched away in a gimpy cadence.

I glanced at Bud to gauge his reaction to the turn of events. It seemed his full attention rested on Charlie's animated departure.

What's that saying about opportunity knocking? I inched toward Bud and snatched the photo.

"Hey, give that back," he shouted.

I studied the picture on my way to the other side of the fence. "You sly old dog." I flicked the picture back and forth. "These are your kids. You cut the zip ties and let them into the play area to get me in trouble."

"Doesn't matter whose kids they are. The council agreed with me. You've got to put up a more secure fence, or we'll pull the contract."

I resisted the urge to stomp my foot like Lisa's preschoolers and decided to beg or maybe even whine. "Renting a chain link fence will take time I can't afford to lose. Then I'll have to hire laborers to do the work I planned to do by myself just to catch up and meet the deadline. I might get done on time, but I'm sure to lose money."

"You should have built a contingency into your bid."

I snorted. "Right, and come in as the highest bidder. Even

as the lowest bidder, the council had to force you to give me the job."

"You want to stand here all day arguing or get to work before time runs out?" His snide smile dissolved the last of my manners.

I picked the first thing that came to mind to use as a weapon. "This is about Rachel, isn't it?"

"What? What could my sweet Rachel have to do with this?"

Sweet? Hah! "Seriously, Bud Picklemann, you were the densest boy I knew in school. If it's possible, you've gotten worse. Your wife has you doing her dirty work. Man up and admit it."

His mouth fell open and flapped about. I guess no one had ever confronted him with his puppet status before. I snapped my own mouth shut before more offending words flew out, and offered a quick prayer for guidance. I wasn't known for my subtlety, and I was close to losing it. Only God could help me keep a lid on it when my inner child took over.

"C'mon, Paige," I mumbled under my breath. "Stop. There will be other jobs."

"You say something?" Bud snapped.

I had no other jobs lined up. Still, the wisdom of giving in before this became more personal seeped into my brain. "Fine. I'll get the fence."

"About time. Remember, no more work until it's up." He turned and charged toward the parking lot.

His dismissal grated on me as if a real globe thistle had brushed against my skin, and the little bit of wisdom I had found took a hike. "You do anything else to interfere with this project, Bud Picklemann," I yelled at his back, "and so help me, you'll wish you hadn't."

"Ohh, I'm shaking in my boots." He laughed in a tone that

fully released my wrath.

"I mean it, Bud. You do anything, and I mean *anything* else, and I'll have your. . .your job. . .and your. . .your head on a plate."

I cringed as the last words passed my lips. The morning had come full circle. If I had a spray bottle of pesticide with me, I'd be as tempted as Weed Whacker to douse the human weed in my life.

CHAPTER TWO

"And now, enjoy the best of Through the Garden Gate *with your beloved host, Paige Turner."*

"Hi, Paige. This is Edna in Portland. I heard Friday's show when you shared the list of essential clothing to wear in the garden. I've ruined more clothes while gardening than I care to admit, so I took your advice and ran right out to the store. I bought a cute pair of green gardening clogs, a big white floppy hat, and even found a pair of the gardening gloves that you like so much."

"Wonderful, Edna. I love it when I can be helpful. Would you care to share with our listeners how these items are working for you?"

"I have to say it took me a little while to get used to the feeling of freedom, but now—"

"Edna, being married to you is gonna kill me."

"Sorry, just ignore my husband yelling in the background."

"Edna, I mean it, get back in the house and put some clothes on. What are the neighbors gonna say if they see you like that?"

Hoping physical labor would help still my fuming soul and shut my big mouth, I turned my back on prickly old Bud and tossed equipment into the enclosure with a little more force than necessary. Normally when I left a job site, I took my tools with me, but after I located a fence, I'd need these tools when I came back to replace the plastic one.

Gate secured again with more zip ties, I set off for my shop on foot with the hope that exercise would calm my residual anger. I spotted Charlie Sweeny, red-faced and gesturing wildly, this time talking with Uma Heffner, the local beautician. I was too far away to hear their conversation, but Uma's hands were clamped on her ample hips and her legs planted wide, radiating tension.

I picked up my pace, glancing back at the duo as I went. Charlie's screaming was old news. Still, this argument seemed more intense than usual. Charlie argued with everyone after his son died in Vietnam. Most people had tried to understand the change in his personality and cut him some slack. A few thought he shouldn't continue to take his grief out on others and gave back as good as they got.

Uma was one of them. Although she claimed twin status with Uma Thurman, our Uma had little in common with the actress other than her name. Our Uma had a personality as big as the beehive hairdo she wore and was as likely to erupt as the thighs she had packed into her spandex pants. I'd dubbed her the showy shrub rose named "Betty Boop". Enough said.

The sound of squealing brakes ripped through the streets. I whipped around. A city refuse truck screeched to an angled stop seconds before nailing Rachel Picklemann. She must have darted out of one of the stores and tried to cross Oak without looking.

"What are you trying to do, kill me?" she screamed at the driver. Her normally tidy blond hair hung in her face as she skirted the truck and ran into the park.

Her frantic behavior seemed odd for the usually cool and calculating Rachel. In fact, everyone was acting extra weird today. We locals had our share of quirks, and I wasn't one to say anything, what with my habit of assigning plant names to people, but today their behavior was a little too bizarre. Maybe there was a full moon or something.

The truck took off. I remained locked in position, allowing my gaze to follow Rachel's movements. My cell chirped in text message mode.

From Lisa, it said, "P. FORGOT LUNCH. TAKING IT TO HIM. CUL8R."

I turned my focus back to Rachel, who, sans Uma's awful spandex pants, took over where Uma left off shouting at Charlie. She inched forward and stabbed her index finger at his chest. He backed up, but I could have told him it was useless to try to get away from Rachel Picklemann.

To me, Rachel was a petunia, pretty and innocent on the outside. When you got close and nipped off the dead flowers, your fingers came away sticky and hard to clean. When you came away from beautiful Rachel, no matter how hard you tried to get rid of the painful things she often said, they stuck to you for the rest of the day. As much as I wanted to find out what was going on, I didn't want dirt from another Picklemann to wash off. Besides, the new fence was my priority. I turned left and headed down Poplar, a street with fewer distractions. As I entered the alley behind The Garden Gate, I saw torn black garbage bags, soggy paper scraps, Styrofoam coffee cups, and various other items I could no longer identify courtesy of last night's rain.

"Yuk, yuk, yuk. Why'd I come this way?" I mumbled and picked my way down the alley.

Velma Meyer, owner of the Scrapbook Emporium, had done it again. Put her trash cans out for pickup and failed to set the lids on tight. *Argh*. I so wanted to scream over the interruption when I needed to focus on getting a fence, but Velma needed my help. I called Velma an Oriental poppy for her similarity to the flower's flamboyant color and messy self-sowing habit. Velma was one of the flashiest seventy-five–year-olds I knew, and messy? Well, look around.

She did the best she could with her arthritis. No way she'd be able to clean this up. I would have to do it, and do it now to keep from attracting varmints to my city gardens. The trash wasn't scheduled to be picked up for several days.

"Why today, of all days?" I punched my code into the electronic lock of the rear entrance to The Garden Gate.

In the hallway, I listened to Hazel Grimes, my full-time employee, as she explained the difference between sun and shade gardening to a customer up front. I'd scheduled the staff to free up my time for a full day of work at the park, so I didn't bother letting her know I'd come in but went straight to my office, flipping on the light as I entered.

"First name Mister, middle name Period, last name T," Mr. T, my inherited Amazon parrot, squawked from his cage in the corner.

"Shh, you silly bird." I was always surprised by my affection for the mostly green feathered bigmouth, whose full name was Thunderbird. His bright blue head tilted to the side, portraying a simple innocence coupled with a haughty superiority. He was nearly thirty years old, but I'd had the dubious pleasure of Mr. T's company only for the year I'd owned this building.

My shop had lived its first life as a service garage. The previous owner kept Mr. T to entertain the clients as they waited for their cars. The television, always on in the waiting area, had expanded Mr. T's vocabulary. He randomly spouted bits from commercials, songs, and shows, especially his favorites like *The A Team* and *Jeopardy*. When his owner died, Mr. T went into a deep depression. I bought the shop and agreed to let him stay in his familiar surroundings to see if he would perk up. He didn't just perk; he boiled over with enthusiasm.

"'I gotta be free, I gotta be free,'" he said in a singsong tone, his way of telling me he wanted out. We let him out of his cage daily for exercise. This required vigilance, as many plants are poisonous to parrots.

I didn't have time to watch him, so I did my best to ignore his continual talking and surfed to Portland Construction Rentals' Web site. With specifications listed on the screen, I sketched a quick layout of the fence sections my job required and tallied the cost.

"Three thousand bucks," I grumbled then leaned back and threaded my fingers into my hair, loosening my ponytail. Maybe if I pulled it out from frustration, I could sell it to help pay for the fence.

"'I'll take Fun Facts for five hundred, Alex,'" Mr. T said.

"Nothing fun about this, old buddy." I tapped out a quick message to Ned Binski, owner of Portland Construction Rentals, with my detailed fence needs, as Mr. T watched in silence.

Where was I going to come up with the three thousand dollars to pay Ned? Easy answer. I wasn't. I'd need to convince him to bring the price down to free. He owed me for my part in getting the largest landscape design firm in Portland to sign an exclusive rental contract with his company, and it was time to call in a return favor. I never wanted to use his business as a bargaining chip, but I had no choice. Failing on this highly visible job was not an option. What was I saying? Failing at anything was never an option in my book.

"See you later, buddy," I said to Mr. T and seated my wireless headset on my ear.

"'Y'all come back now, ya hear?'"

Laughing at his departing phrase, I went to the workroom and grabbed some large black garbage bags and rubber gloves. I dialed Ned's number, sent up my second prayer of the morning, and rushed outside.

"That you, Paige Turner?" Ned asked after the third ring.

I cringed as he read my full name off his caller ID. *Thanks, Mom.* A librarian, of all people, should have known better. She didn't realize her mistake until after she signed the birth certificate, or so she claimed.

"Paige, you there?" Ned asked.

"Hey, yeah, hi, Ned." I put a cheerful lilt in my tone as I tugged the form-fitting gloves over my fingers then took out my frustrations with my crazy morning on a mound of soggy paper.

"So how's business in the boonies?"

"Booming. At least the store is. I bought an old gas station with three service bays. Turned them into greenhouses and planted gardens all around the place. The weekend tourists can't seem to get enough of it."

"That sounds. . .ah. . .what do you chicks say? Quaint. . .yeah, quaint, that's it. I never thought you'd go all girlie on me like that and give up landscaping."

Girlie, right. If he could only see me now. "I didn't. That's why I'm calling."

"So, what do you need?"

Play it cool. Warm him up first. "Who says I need anything?"

He laughed, a big Santa Claus booming chortle, which is why

I'd always thought of him as a thick Scotch pine, deeply rooted, sturdy, and towering over me. "I know you, Paige. You don't call for a year, then out of the blue I hear from you. You need something."

"Actually, I have a huge favor to ask. I just e-mailed an order for a chain link fence. I need to rent it for next to free."

"For you Paigey-girl, I'll give you my friends' discount, 50 percent off."

I stood up straight like a staked dahlia, taking strength from my posture while explaining my dilemma. "I'd never ask, Ned, but I just started the landscaping part of my business, and the city manager's trying to kill it before it gets off the ground. I know I'm asking a lot. Is there any way you can let me have it for nothing and get it here by the end of the day?"

"Hold on," he said reluctantly. "Let me pull up your e-mail to see what you need."

I resumed trash picking while listening to his fingers click on a keyboard. I felt as trashy as the hunk of dripping paper I scraped off the concrete. Why was I doing this? Using Ned this way? Was a little business worth it? True, my back was against a wall, and I had no choice. All my profits from The Garden Gate were reinvested in equipment and supplies for this first job. I didn't have any liquid assets, other than the small stream of water with scrapbook rejects floating merrily into a puddle at the end of the alley.

I shoved a large coffee filter into the bag. The tiny grounds clinging to the paper reminded me of Lisa's lice situation. My fingers crept toward my head. I forced them down. No more scratching. My hands were filthy, and I had to focus on my own problem. I could pay Ned back. Yes, that was it. Once the landscaping business was up and running, I'd send him a check for the full amount.

"You're in luck," Ned said. "One of my drivers just came in. Give me a chance to load the truck, and I'll drive out while he takes an early lunch break. Does that work for you, princess?"

"Yes, thank you," I squeaked out, my voice wavering from his willingness to make the hour-long drive from Portland, not to mention forgiving the huge price tag associated with a rental fence.

"Ah, c'mon now, Paige. You really are going all girlie on me."

"Sorry, this just means so much to me."

"Still no need to act like that, if you ask me. Next thing I know, you'll be wearing dresses and all that other girlie stuff." He chuckled, perhaps at the vision of me dressed in anything that slightly identified me as a female. "Look, I gotta run if I'm gonna get the fencing out there. I'll call you when I'm a few miles out."

"Use my cell number. I'll be at the park waiting for you, and I can give you directions."

We said good-bye, and I looked up at the startling blue sky to thank God for the break. Okay, so my methods for getting the fence were creative and manipulative perhaps, but God still came through. I didn't deserve the fence. Face it, I didn't deserve anything, but God still provided and put joy in my heart.

Enough joy to make the rest of my cleaning seem to speed by even though it took nearly ninety minutes to scrape up every tiny piece of soggy paper. There. The last can was righted with the lid firmly settled. I took off my gloves and sighed over a big blue blotch right in the center of my uniform top. I couldn't let the stain set in, or it'd ruin the fabric. At the cost of these custom-embroidered polos, I had to go home and toss it in the wash.

For the first time that morning, I easily succeeded in my plan. I rushed down the alley that ran behind the main businesses on

Oak Street. Fortunately, none of the employees at either of the antique stores, the Bakery, or the Crazy Curl were outside to spot my disheveled condition. I cut left at the pharmacy and charged up the outside stairs to my apartment, where I kept a spare key under a variegated hosta on the back landing. The jade and lime colored leaves should still be rolled and barely above ground this early in the season, but the height of the staircase, coupled with the warmth of container gardening, had the plant's giant leaves open, completely concealing the container.

Once inside, I tossed a frozen sandwich into the microwave for lunch and set off for the bedroom. I ripped off my shirt as I walked over the aged oak floors and then pulled a fresh polo from the closet. After slipping into the soft yellow cotton garment, I dialed Little Susie Homemaker on my cell and pushed my headset back onto my ear.

"Hey, Lisa," I said and snatched up my dirty top. "How do you get a dark stain out of clothing?"

She sighed, her usual reaction to a question that she thought I should know the answer to by this point in my life. "Depends on what caused the stain and the fabric it's on."

"Blue dye from scrapbook paper I spent the last ninety minutes cleaning up. It's on my work shirt." I set out for my stacked washer and dryer in the kitchen.

"Velma strikes again, huh?" Her tone lacked any real sympathy for my plight with my absentminded neighbor.

"She had that big scrapbooking party last week, and there was a huge mess. This is happening too often. I think I'll start going by on Sunday when she puts out the garbage to make sure the cans are closed." At the large picture window in my living room, I stopped walking and peered through the tall swaying pines into the park. Something. . .something white was moving through the bushes. "Are you at the park waiting for me?"

"No, I'm at Mom's house, why?"

Wishing I had binoculars, I squinted and searched through the thick foliage. "I can see someone inside my fence. Looks like they're wearing something white."

"How can you see them? Where are you?"

"At home. Washing my shirt."

"Well, I'd use a basic stain spray," she said, as if the stain were more important than another break-in on my project. "Then soak it and wash like usual."

I looked at the shirt then back at the park one last time. Seeing no further movement, I went into the kitchen. "I wonder if someone is over there messing with my things."

"It was probably just a plastic garbage bag blowing around. You know how those things show up everywhere. Hold on a sec, Lacy is giving Mom a hard time." It sounded like she placed her hand over the phone to cover a muffled conversation in the background.

I located the right bottle in the cabinet and sprayed the stain before tossing the top into the washer to soak. At the microwave, I pulled out the ham and cheese sandwich and waited for Lisa to get back to me.

"Sorry about that." Lisa let a long sigh escape. "The girls are always so tired after preschool on Mondays for some reason. I need to get them down for a nap. Oh, but before I let you go, you've *got* to tell me what happened with Bud."

As I wrapped up the sandwich to eat on the run, I replayed the meeting in great detail. "Even though I got a few good licks in, he was clearly the winner."

Lisa snickered. "I wonder if he ran right home to report to his wife."

"Nah, I think she was shopping or something." I stepped into the front stairwell and told Lisa about the dump truck nearly running over Rachel.

"Do you think she was at the park to check up on you and Bud?" Her voice held the first excitement of the day. Nothing like some nice juicy gossip to perk her interest.

"I think Rachel checking on me is kind of a stretch, but much as I hate to admit this, I think you were right about Bud and Rachel holding a grudge against me."

"What? Wait. . .let me get some paper." She laughed. "Mom! Mom!" she shouted. "Can you hand me that notepad and a pen? Paige just said I was right about something, and I have to document it."

"Funny, Lisa. Very funny." I ran down the steps.

"So what are you going to do about the fence?"

"My friend Ned is giving it to me for free. Soon as he gets the truck loaded, he'll be on his way. Don't s'pose your mom would keep the girls longer so you could come back?"

"Seriously, Paige, you need to hire somebody."

"I don't have enough time to find someone now. C'mon, Lisa, you're always whining about still having excess baby weight. Think of the great exercise you'll be getting."

She groaned but in a tone that said she'd caved. "Okay. But this is the last time. I'll be there as soon as I can."

I exited the front of my building and stepped onto the sidewalk. Hazel came out of the Bakery, her head down, hands digging into a tote bag emblazoned with Led Zepplin in faded letters. I employed a part-timer to fill in at the shop during our lunch breaks, so Hazel never missed her daily gossip fest at the Bakery.

"Hey, Hazel," I called out. Her head snapped up, exposing her wrinkled face and cracked skin. My hardworking employee was a native Oregonian through and through. She loved the outdoors, no matter the climate, and to me that spelled the sedum plant. Rugged, durable, rock-hardy, often described as tough as nails, sedum fit Hazel perfectly.

We strolled toward each other and met in front of the Crazy Curl.

She pulled a toothpick from her mouth and stabbed it in my direction. "Well, haven't you been a busy girl this morning. I heard all about your big blowup with Bud. Everyone in the Bakery was yakkin' about it. Especially about the end, when you threatened him. You didn't really, did you?"

"Maybe. . .a little, but I didn't mean it. I was just mad." My face got hot. I thought about the whole town gossiping about my weak moment and took a bite of my sandwich. "Hey," I said with my mouth full, "how'd those people know about it, anyway? Bud and I were alone."

"Ernie Hansen was lookin' for pop cans in the park, like he always does on Monday morning. Said he heard you givin' Bud what for."

"Of course he has to go and blab it all over town." I ran a hand around the back of my neck, stopping to massage a muscle that had tightened. "Just what I need. No one is going to want to hire me to do their yards when they hear this."

She tossed the toothpick into a nearby trash can. "Relax. No one pays much attention to Ernie. He's always telling stories."

"Then let's hope people think this is another one of his stories." We chatted about her morning at the shop while we walked toward the park. At the corner of Main and Oak, Hazel kept walking toward The Garden Gate to return to work, and I entered the park by the front entrance.

While traveling the distance to the play area, I ate the last of my oozing sandwich and plotted out my afternoon. I didn't like surprises when it came to my schedule or my life. Control of my day was priority to me, and I didn't react well when things didn't go as planned. Case in point, the sight before me. I *was* right. Someone had been here. The zip ties once again peeked from resting spots in tall blades of grass. And someone had shoveled Lisa's mulch into a mound on the vinyl tarp.

"Bud," I said under my breath. Probably let his kids pile up the chips so they could add to my work. "No matter." His trick would not ruin my day. I'd recovered from his fencing demands, I could recover from this with some fast work.

I picked up my favorite shovel and threw my frustrations with Bud into digging. The spade penetrated the mound and stopped short on something. The reverberations of the wooden handle sent a tingle up my arm.

"What did that prickly old globe thistle do now?" Exasperated, I moved to the other end of the mound and tried again. This time, my shovel went deep but came up holding something heavy. Like roots clinging to a tree stump, whatever I'd found was connected to something that wouldn't budge.

I strained the muscles in my arms and shook the shovel, sending bark flying.

"What in the world?"

I sucked in a breath. The air seemed to swirl around me like a vortex.

I was mistaken. There was no way Bud made this mound because. . .Bud *was* this mound.

CHAPTER ⛩ THREE

"And now, enjoy the best of Through the Garden Gate *with your beloved host, Paige Turner."*

"Hi, Paige. This is Bamboozled in Beaverton. Several months ago you talked about selecting the right type of bamboo."

"That's right, Bamboozled. I mentioned there were two main types of bamboo, clumping and running. Clumping spreads very little as it grows, while running sends out shoots that invade everything nearby."

"We're looking for that nice clumping kind, but we're new to gardening and don't want to ask stupid questions at our nursery. So we've been spending a lot of time at the nursery, watching the bamboo. Every time we go, the containers are sitting in orderly rows. We haven't seen even one container of bamboo running around, so we don't know how to choose."

Careful not to jiggle the blade and reveal more than the shoulder-up view I had of Bud's body, I lowered the shovel to the ground. My gaze locked on his face. My brain scrambled for my next move. This was all wrong. I was used to dealing with dead plants—tugging them from the heavy clay soil after careless clients forgot to water them, but I wasn't prepared to find a dead body.

I wasn't prepared at all.

I'd need to report this, but who to? 911? Or should I just run to the police station a few blocks from here? Wait, police? Did I need the police or a doctor? Was Bud still alive?

"Think, Paige, think." I looked around.

Maybe it would be faster to get Doc. But if Bud was dead, fetching the good doctor would be a waste of his time. I had to check—lay my fingers against his neck and see if blood still coursed through his veins.

I reached out my hand. Snapped it back. I couldn't do it.

"His wrist. Use his wrist. Pretend it's a plant runner, not an arm." I knelt in the moist mulch with my back to his face and dug into his chip blanket until I found his hand. I positioned my fingers at the wrist. The clammy skin told me what I needed to know.

"Sorry I'm late," Lisa called from outside the fence.

I dropped Bud's hand as if she'd caught me in the act of killing him.

"Lacy didn't want to go down for her nap. Wow! You've really been shoveling—" Lisa stopped on the other side of the fence, her mouth hanging open, eyes wide. "Oh my gosh! Paige! You didn't? Did you. . .did you kill him?"

The two of us were tainted by murder for the second time today. This one was real. Someone had died. Right here on my project. Someone I had an argument with and threatened earlier. Someone even my best friend thought I'd killed.

"I didn't kill him," I said, forcing calmness into my voice and fighting the desire to snap at her. "But he's dead. I found him under this pile."

"Oh, oh, oh, what are we gonna do?" she wailed and looked around in frantic sweeps of the area. "We should call someone. Yes, that's it. Call. We need to call. Who should we call? Maybe Perry. He's a lawyer. He'd know what to do, wouldn't he?" Our gazes locked, and her eyes displayed my inner turmoil in vivid Technicolor.

One thing we had to do. Get away from Bud and fast. I stood and rushed to the other side of the fence. Slipping my hand through the crook of her arm, I directed our steps to the nearest picnic table. Ashen and perspiring, Lisa dropped onto the bench in a plop. I leaned against the tabletop, resisting the urge to climb on and curl into a fetal position. Both of us turned our faces from Bud and stared at each other without speaking. We had to do something. It was my job to take charge. Keep calm for Lisa.

"I'll call for help," I finally said and flipped open my cell.

"911, what's your emergency?" The perky female voice that should never be allowed for a 911 operator answered on the third ring.

"There's a body. I mean, I found a body." I was surprised by how stilted and lifeless I sounded.

"Who is this?" the operator asked in a far more fitting tone for her job.

"Paige. . .Paige Turner."

"Paige. Oh, hi, Paige. This is Janice Engler. You might remember me as Janice Baker. We went to school together. You helped me with my algebra."

"Right, yeah, school together. . .algebra."

"Yes, good, now how about telling me where you are."

"Oak and Main. The park playground."

I heard her fingers clicking on a keyboard, tapping into a computer and most likely onto a screen for others to see that Paige Turner found a dead body.

"You say there's a body at the playground?"

I glanced across the grass to be sure it wasn't a bad dream. I could see the mound, not Bud, yet I knew he was still there. "Yeah, I'm working on a landscaping project here, and I found a body."

"Is this person breathing?"

"No, no, he's. . .ah. . .no pulse. I touched his wrist." My tone zoomed high like a rocket with its sights set on the moon.

"Okay, okay, Paige. Calm down. You're doing fine. We already have a unit on the way. They're just down the street. Listen. You might be able to hear the siren already."

Willing my stomach not to empty onto the ground, I slumped against the table and planted my hands on my knees. Blood. My knees were covered in blood. Bud's blood.

"Lisa, look." I pointed at my legs.

She leaned forward and groaned. Our gazes met. Her eyes were vacant and scared. Mine likely held triple that emotion as it dawned on me that I could be considered a suspect in the killing of Bud Picklemann. No way he just up and died and mounded chips over his body. No, he was clearly murdered. But by who? And why?

"Paige, are you there? Paige?" Janice wasn't nearly this persistent with her algebra homework.

"Yeah."

"Stay with me now. Listen. Do you hear the siren?"

Nearly in a trance, I listened for what seemed like hours until the wail that told me help was on the way rang through the air. "They're coming. Thanks for the help." Afraid Janice would decide to catch up on old times while we waited, I hung up and handed my phone to Lisa. "This has nothing to do with you. I'll talk to the cops. You should go home. Call Perry to come and get you. You're too upset to drive." I tried to give her a supportive smile, but when I realized I had no one other than Calgon to take me away from all of this, I scowled.

And I kept scowling while she sobbed our story into the phone. Kept scowling while watching the police car fly down the street and screech to a stop on Main. Kept scowling as Police Chief Mitch Lawson rushed across the grass with his hand firmly planted on his unclipped holster.

I jerked my head toward Bud before Mitch could say anything. "He's over by the opening in the fence," I said, feeling as if I, too, were dead.

"You two okay?" Mitch asked, his tone more commanding than concerned.

I nodded and watched him charge away, crossing the grass toward Bud's body. I hadn't seen Mitch this close up since I'd been back in town. He hadn't changed much since high school, except for the touch of gray at his temples. Stout, built like a football linebacker, he didn't have the large-hanging-over-the-belt belly that I'd found to be prevalent in the other males from our class. He still sported a slight limp from when he jumped off a bridge into the river and blew out his knee in high school.

I peered at Lisa and tipped my head in Mitch's direction. "You think he's ever gotten over our little misunderstanding?"

Lisa swiveled on the bench. "I don't know how he feels about your part in all of it, but he won't ever get over missing his senior year of football."

"But surely he doesn't still blame me. He was the one who bragged he could jump off that bridge. I just called him on it." I watched him for a few minutes. "Look at him. He still seems just as cocky."

But instead of lingering on Mitch, an approaching ambulance and several squad cars drew our attention. One by one their sirens wound down and they parked behind Mitch's car. The first EMT bolted out of the ambulance and headed for Mitch. The second raced behind and stayed to minister to Lisa, whose face was as white as the fluffy clouds circling overhead. He draped a blanket around her back and checked her vital signs. He asked if I needed help. After extracting my phone from Lisa's clawed fingers, I told him to take care of her. I remained in a vigil-like stance, watching the surreal action whirling around me.

Mitch and the EMT talked for a while, making wild gestures with their hands then came back across the clearing. The EMT returned to his rig while Mitch instructed his officers to fan out and control the growing group of onlookers. He barked orders to the crowd, his fingers pointing with his demands.

A satisfied look on his face, he strutted toward our table, looking Lisa and me over as if trying to decide something. "You both find the body?" he asked.

I shook my head and explained how I found Bud and when Lisa showed up, adding that Lisa should be allowed to leave as soon as Perry arrived to take her home.

"You, come with me," he said.

You? Did he just say you? Didn't he recognize me? Or was he still miffed after all this time? "Paige. My name's Paige Turner."

"Don't worry, I remember you. How could I forget? Come on." He latched onto my elbow and plodded across the open area to another table. "Sit."

I slowly lowered myself onto the bench. "Why'd you drag me over here? I need to stay with Lisa. She's really upset."

"And I need to keep the two of you apart until we get both your statements."

I stood. "That's just crazy. Lisa had nothing to do with this."

Mitch held out his hand. "This isn't optional, Paige. Like it or not, your friend is part of this investigation. If you talk to her about what happened, one of you might change your story. Not on purpose, but it happens."

I gave Lisa one last look then settled onto the splintered bench. "What do you need?"

He asked me a series of rapid-fire questions. First about Bud and exactly how I found him then about my whereabouts during the day. Though I was distraught, I calmly handled all of them until he chastised me for disturbing evidence. That's when I finally snapped.

"I already told you about that. I didn't know he was under the chips until I used the shovel. The only other thing I did was feel his wrist for a pulse."

"Right, you did mention that." Mitch's face tightened, and his eyes narrowed in what must have been his practiced bad-cop glare. "I found several shovels inside the fence. All of them yours?"

"All the tools are mine. I told you that before, too."

"When's the last time you touched the shovel with the blue handle?"

There were several shovels in the enclosure, but I knew exactly which one he meant. "I don't know. Maybe when I put it in the truck or carried it over to the playground. I brought it along for Lisa. Since it has such a short handle, I don't tend to use it much."

He studied my face, his eyes becoming hard and appraising. "You and Picklemann get along with each other okay?"

"Where's this coming from?" I stared at him until he shifted his feet and looked down at his oversized boots while I tried to classify him in the plant world, the only world that made sense to me most of the time.

No doubt, he was bamboo—not the neat clumping variety I loved to have in my gardens, but the treacherous running type. He was stiff and wooden like bamboo stalks, aggressive and unstoppable with his questions running like roots through my life. Like a surprised mole in the garden, his head popped back up, a patronizing look planted on his face. "Let me rephrase my question. Any reason you might want to see Picklemann come to any harm?" The words were innocent enough, but his tone was loaded with accusation.

Was this residual anger from high school or did he know about my fight with Bud this morning? If he'd talked to anyone in town, he surely heard. I couldn't admit to fighting with Bud. Couldn't form the words. Wait. Oh my goodness. Mitch knows I threatened Bud, too. He thinks I killed him.

Unable to make my mouth move, I panicked and looked around.

Mitch cleared his throat. "I'll take your silence to mean you might have wished Picklemann some harm."

I jumped up and glared at him. "Who in this town didn't? In fact, Charlie Sweeny was in the park today, too. He interrupted my conversation with Bud and threatened him."

"Now that's what I need from you, Paige. Helpful information like that."

Whew! Maybe he didn't think I did it. I relaxed a bit.

Mitch ran a hand over his head, leaving stray hairs sticking up like a bristle brush that would work really well to sweep fall leaves from the driveway. I stifled a smile over the thought of using him as a broom, and he forced one at me. "S'pose you could help me with one more thing?"

This was better. He was asking for my help. I released a smile, a peace offering. "What?"

"Seeing how all those shovels are yours and you explained how Picklemann's head ended up on the one, maybe you could explain how what I'm pretty sure is his blood and hair got all over the blue-handled one."

"How would I know that?" I drew back from the intensity in Mitch's eyes. "You think I killed Bud."

He stepped closer. "You had motive. Everyone in town knows about your argument this morning. Then we have the shovel. Yours to be exact. And you were the one who called 911. So, yeah, if I were a betting man, I'm sure I'd hit the jackpot if I put my money on you."

"Well I'm not a betting woman, so your odds don't mean a thing to me. This conversation is over." I turned to leave and spotted Lisa's husband, Perry, shoving through the curious onlookers surrounding the park. Perfect. He was an attorney. He could advise me. "If you have any other questions for me, you'll have to ask them in the presence of my lawyer."

Shoulders back, heart racing, I stormed away from Mitch.

"Fine! We'll take a break for now," he shouted after me, "but don't leave the park until I give you permission to go."

I kept going, ignoring his snap judgment of my guilt. Clearly, he still blamed me for his rash behavior in high school.

Even as I rushed away, I could feel his anger burning into my back. I picked up speed, nearly running, as if putting distance between us could solve the problem. Maybe it could. What was that old saying that goes something like, "you can't run from the long arm of the law"?

Well, watch me.

CHAPTER FOUR

"And now, enjoy the best of Through the Garden Gate *with your beloved host, Paige Turner."*

"Hi, Paige, this is Moved Out in Portland calling. I really liked the show where you compared plants to people."

"That's right, Moved Out, people can find themselves in places or situations where for some reason they don't thrive. If they move out of the smothering environment, they flourish. Plants also require different settings in which to thrive. So if you find a plant not growing as well as you hoped in one location, move it, apply more fertilizer, or change your watering schedule."

"Well, I tried that with a clump of irises. I thought they needed more sun so I found a perfect sunny location, dug them up, and I'm ready to move them. Before I send them all the way to Tucson from here, I hoped you could recommend a mover. We used a rental truck when my daughter went to college, but maybe you have a better idea."

By the time I returned my attention to Lisa, Perry had taken the seat next to her. His arm settled over her shoulders like a trailing vine. Perry merely had to sit beside Lisa and color returned to her face. Must be from the feeling of security he gave her—that he was watching her back.

I sighed, long and loud. With the passing of both of my parents and my limited ability to find a mate, I had no one watching my back.

At my arrival, Perry stood, concern filling his eyes. "You okay?" he asked.

I smiled at the man I'd dubbed yarrow. Sure, I could have easily attached the obvious name of periwinkle to Perry, except he wasn't at all like the aggressive ground cover. No, he was yarrow through and through. The yarrow plant has been valued since ancient times for its ability to stem bleeding, and that's essentially what Perry did for Lisa. Her first husband died in an accident on their one-year anniversary, and Perry helped staunch her pain and loss. Plus he was undemanding and as sturdy as the plant, rarely wavering in the face of blowing turmoil.

Maybe he could stop the mess I found myself embroiled in. "I need your legal help, Perry. Mitch thinks I killed Bud." I plopped onto the tabletop and shared Mitch's brutal interrogation with the two of them. "It's just a matter of time before he pounds me with more questions."

Eyes curious, Perry peered at the play area where Mitch talked with an officer who seemed a smidgen too enthusiastic about stringing yellow crime scene tape.

Perry gave his head a solemn shake and locked gazes with me. "This is serious, Paige. I don't handle criminal matters. If Lawson is convinced of your guilt, you need an attorney with the right experience."

"But I don't know any criminal lawyers." I glanced at Lisa, whose eyes looked haunted. This was my fault. I put her in the middle of a murder investigation. The last thing I wanted to do was to involve her husband, but I had to. "Couldn't you help me out for now? Until I find someone?"

Perry looked in Mitch's direction. "Fine, I'll do it, but just for today. I have a friend in McMinnville who specializes in criminal law. Once we're done here, I'll call him."

"Thank you, Perry." I smiled my thanks.

His acceptance didn't come any too soon. Mitch stormed across the grass with a sour look consuming his face. I pointed at him. "Since you're officially my attorney now, do you think you could handle that?"

Perry and Lisa pivoted toward the lawman, who seemed intent on setting a speed record. Long strides, hands swinging in cadence, brought him to us faster than I would have liked. Breathing deeply, he halted short of the table. "Winkle, don't tell me you agreed to represent her without hearing the facts?"

Perry pulled back his shoulders and eyed up Mitch. Perry, narrow and string-beanish, weighed a third of what Mitch did, but the fierce look in his eyes made up for the weight difference. "Afternoon, Lawson," he said as if we were at a garden party and not a murder scene. "What, exactly, do you need from my client?"

"Aw, Winkle, come on." Mitch scrunched his eyes. "We're all friends here. No need to get on your legal high horse. As the person who found the body, I need to ask her a few questions."

"So she's not a suspect?"

He scowled. "She's definitely a person of interest. We'll know more after we've had a chance to investigate."

Perry stepped closer to him and pointed at the body. "Exactly.

You haven't compiled enough facts to ask Paige the right questions. The medical examiner isn't even here. If you don't know how or when Picklemann died, can you really detain Paige? Why don't you give her a chance to get over the shock of finding Picklemann and have her come to your office tomorrow morning around ten?"

"I can't be there until ten thirty because of my show," I said with caution, as I feared I might interrupt the negotiations turning in Perry's favor.

"Okay, ten thirty, then," Perry said. "How about it, Lawson?"

Mitch glanced at the body then back at Perry. "I'm holding you responsible for making sure she shows up."

"She'll be there." Perry gave me a demanding look, and Mitch followed his gaze.

"Before you go, I'll need the clothes you're wearing," Mitch said matter-of-factly, as if he asked women to strip in front of him every day.

"Can I go home and change?"

"I'd rather not have the clothes leave the scene. Winkle can pick up a change of clothes for you while I take Lisa's statement. You can use the bathroom here."

"You'd rather, or that's what I have to do?"

"Send someone." He made a half pivot toward Lisa then turned back. "Oh, and we'll be taking your tools as evidence."

I opened my mouth to ask what I'd use to complete the project then snapped it closed. Why bother to ask? With the implication of being a murderer hanging over my head, the city council would likely fire me in the morning anyway.

"Fine," I said.

Mitch looked at Lisa. "Ready to give your statement?"

Ack! What was with the cooing tone all of a sudden? Why did

Lisa get the good cop when all I saw was the bad one?

Perry put his hand on Lisa's shoulder. "I'm not leaving Lisa alone. We'll get your clothes once this is finished."

Mitch pointed toward the far side of the park. "Wait over there."

"Since you put it so nicely." I let my sarcasm float over Mitch then gave Lisa a reassuring smile. "I'll wait by the concession stand."

"You better." She offered me the same look her twins received when trouble befell them, which might I say was far too often for Lisa's liking.

I shot across the clearing. I was going to owe Lisa big time for involving her in another one of my messes, and she would make me pay. Not this minute. No, now that she'd worked through her initial shock, she'd move on to mothering me. But later, oh yes, much later, when this day was a bad memory, she'd pounce, and I'd be helpless.

I moved to a table farther away from the onlookers hanging at the park perimeter. Seated, I watched Mitch question Lisa. Even at this distance, I could see the softness in his eyes. This was the Mitch I knew. The Mitch before our falling out. Now here he was accusing me of murder and heaping kindness on my best friend. He was playing the good cop, bad cop routine all by himself. Why didn't he offer me a smidgen of that respect?

An officer's threatening voice coming from the fence area snapped my gaze in his direction. "Fence, oh my gosh, Ned!" I'd forgotten all about him. I glanced at my watch. Why hadn't he called? I snatched my cell from the clip and frantically clicked to his number.

"Hey, Paigey girl," he answered on the third ring. "Sorry I'm not there yet. I'm running a little behind. Just loading the truck now."

"Don't bother with the fence." In short, choppy sentences to keep my tears at bay, I told him about Bud.

"Man. . .seriously? Killed. . .that's rough. I don't know what I can do, but I'll come over if you need me."

What a nice guy. See, Paige. You do have people who care about you. How many people would offer to show up at a crime scene to support you? "Thanks, Ned. I appreciate the offer. Perry and Lisa are here, and there's really nothing you can do." His kindness made me want to cry, but I couldn't afford to feel that way right now. "I'm sorry I put you to all this trouble. And even more sorry for trading on our friendship like this."

"Hey, no biggie. I'm still raking in the dough from the contract you got me. Feel free to call if you change your mind about needing the fencing or needing me to come over there."

It's not often you made lasting friends in the business world, but I was proud to call Ned my friend and hoped he'd be one for years to come. I stowed my phone and spotted Lisa shaking hands with the traitor, Mitch. We would definitely have a talk about that. My best friend should not be cordial to the enemy. Perry stood, braced his slim hips against the table, and pulled out his cell, hopefully calling his lawyer friend.

Lisa charged my way, her face changing from irritated to tender as her feet pummeled the grass. She reached out and folded me in a hug that I so desperately needed.

"You doing okay?" she whispered.

"I guess. How about you?"

"I won't forget seeing Bud for a long time." She pulled back, searching my face with concerned eyes. "You sure you're okay? You don't look so good."

I snorted. "Neither do you, and it's all my fault. If I weren't so focused on getting this business off the ground, you wouldn't be here. Sorry I got you into this mess."

"Don't be. The only time I ever have any excitement is when I hang out with you." Her eyes sparkled.

"And who's to blame?"

"I know, I know. I should loosen up, but hey, now's not the time to work on my issues. You're the one in trouble." She moved back and tipped her head at Perry. "Perry's calling his lawyer friend, Adam Hayes."

"Good, if Mitch has his way, I'll need all the help I can get."

"First thing we have to do is get out of here. I'll go get your clothes."

I pulled the spare key to my apartment from my pocket. "Bring something comfy. Maybe some sweats."

"Not hardly. Perry is asking Adam to come over to the house tonight. No way I'll let you meet your lawyer in sweatpants." Even flustered over a murder, Lisa had to do the socially correct thing, and I was too exhausted to argue.

Apprehensive about being alone, I watched her go. As much as I wanted her to stay with me, I couldn't bear the thought of Perry rifling through my personal belongings. When she slipped into the crowd, I lowered my head to my knees and finally let the tears drip in one giant pity party. In the distance, I heard Mitch hail the arrival of the medical examiner as heartily as the crowd did. I tuned them out until much later when Perry's voice brought my head back up.

"Lisa's mom will keep the kids for the night. Adam'll meet us at the house around dinnertime." Perry's eyes were alive, probably from the legal challenge I presented.

"So is he a decent attorney?"

He gave a clipped nod. "We went to law school together. He's one of the best."

"No offense to your friend, but what is one of the best criminal defense attorneys doing in McMinnville?"

Before he could answer, Lisa returned and handed me black jeans, a multicolored knit top, and sneakers. "Here you go."

Perry looked at her. "Your mom is keeping the kids. Adam can come."

"Excellent." She snagged my hand and tugged me to my feet. "Hurry up so we can get out of here."

I did as she said. Hurried to the dank bathroom and changed my clothes. When I returned, I handed my shirt, shorts, and boots to Perry, who'd offered to save me from another altercation with Mitch and deliver my clothes.

Though strong willed, some might say ornery, I let Lisa lead me down the sidewalk with her arm wrapped around my back as if I were her toddler. And that's how I felt. All blubbery inside. Wanting to snuggle up to my mommy for comfort. Walking, yet not sure if my feet remembered how to maneuver. Listening to Lisa coo soft words of encouragement offered to displace the sight of Bud's face from my mind. Or was it Mitch's face?

One last glance at the stubborn set of Mitch's jaw, and I climbed in Perry's SUV with the need to protect myself and prove my innocence solidified in my mind. Mitch thought I was guilty. He'd proceed along those lines. It was up to me to find the real killer. The question, the big question, the really big question was, did I possess the skills to do so?

CHAPTER FIVE

"And now, enjoy the best of Through the Garden Gate *with your beloved host, Paige Turner."*

"Oh, Paige, this is Desperate. I'm so frustrated I don't know what to do."

"Go ahead and tell me your problem, Desperate, and I'll see if I can help."

"For starters, I listen to you every day, and I try to implement your suggestions, but I'm one of those people who like the feel of the soil on my hands. Still, everything else you've said about gardening has worked, so I thought, why not give that brand of gardening gloves you recommend a chance."

"Oh, I'm so glad you did. I, too, used to garden barehanded. Now I try to wear the gloves whenever possible. Still, you haven't told me your concern."

"Well, you said I could find these gloves at most nurseries, but I haven't found them yet. Believe me, I've tried. I've stopped by the hospital three times already, and the nurses say they don't know what I'm talking about. They only have those latex exam gloves."

We arrived at Lisa's house, and she gave me hot tea. Then she sent me to a steaming shower in a spotless bathroom and tucked me into the designer bed in her spare bedroom. I took a surprisingly long nap but when I woke, I realized the first shower hadn't erased the sticky feeling of Bud's blood on my legs and the snooze did nothing to rid my mind of his face in the mulch. I showered again to no avail. Perhaps meeting my new lawyer would do the trick.

Anxious about his arrival, I padded across the thick carpet in Lisa's upstairs hallway. A balcony overlooked the family room where Perry and Lisa sat on the leather sofa. Lisa rested her head on Perry's shoulder, accentuating the differences in their coloring. Lisa had baby-fine blond hair like corn silk while Perry's unruly mop resembled a brown thatch of Astroturf.

What a sight—Lisa finding love again after Ben, especially when I couldn't locate it even once. For me, a long-term relationship was as elusive as the perfect garden. Like a new plant hybrid, I'd find an exciting guy that I couldn't wait to add to my life. Before long, a natural disaster ripped the budding relationship from the soil and plunged it into the compost bin. Unlike Lisa and Perry. They attracted each other as salvia drew a hummingbird.

As if Lisa felt my watching eyes, she lurched upright and stared at Perry. I felt like a peeping Tom, but I didn't let her know I was listening. "You do think Paige'll be able to prove her innocence, don't you?"

"I don't know, babe. We need to wait for Adam."

"But you know the law. Do they have enough to charge her with murder?"

Perry inhaled through his nose and noisily released it. "If the forensic evidence confirms the shovel as the murder weapon, they'll likely have a strong case. Even if Paige didn't smack

Picklemann, her fingerprints are bound to be all over the handle. Lawson already has it out for Paige. Couple that with her threat to Picklemann, and she has a rough road ahead. If they don't find other prints on the shovel, I'm sure she'll be charged."

I stepped back as if Perry had slapped me. He was right, and I knew it. The same thoughts continued to shoot through my mind. I tried to find something positive to think about, anything in my favor. I kept coming up empty. My only hope was in this Adam guy. Maybe he was a genius.

No, Paige, he is *a genius. He will restore your life. Better than restore, he'll revitalize it. Rejuvenate, remodel, or even reinvent it. Yes, that's it, keep up the positive thinking.*

I made my way down the steps, positive *R* words rushing through my mind. The doorbell rang, chiming out Oregon State's fight song. Maybe that's what I needed. A fight song. Now if I could only come up with a melody other than the theme to *Rocky* that slipped into the *R*'s still prancing in my head, I'd be all set.

Oblivious to my return, Perry jumped up and made purposeful strides toward the door. "That's either the pizza or Adam."

"I vote for Adam," I said at the bottom step. "I'm not all that hungry."

Lisa, motherly frown in place, gave me a quick once-over. "At least you look better. Feel better, too?"

"Some." I strolled into the room and plopped onto the beige leather sofa opposite her. The shower didn't wash away the dirty feeling. It did allow me to sit comfortably in her immaculate house without worrying about contaminating the place.

"Adam's here." Perry took a step back from the opened door. "And he's got the pizza."

Adam entered, a large box in one hand and a leather binder in the other. "Found the delivery guy outside. So. . ." He glanced around the room. "Where do you want this? On the coffee table?"

Lisa popped up. "No! Oh, no! The kitchen. We'll eat in the kitchen." She charged across the space she'd decorated herself and snatched the pizza. "I'll just take that for you." She raced past us. Her grimace reflected her worst nightmare, a red stain on a light-colored, porous surface.

Shaking my head over her obsessively clean habits, I went to greet my only hope of avoiding incarceration.

Perry rushed through a basic introduction. I leaned toward Adam and whispered, "Don't feel bad about the pizza thing. We've all tried to eat in here at one time or another."

"Anyone ever succeed?" He looked around the design-magazine-worthy space.

I frowned and shook my head. "There're rumors of a guy who successfully ate one bite of food in here, but—" I slashed a hand across my neck.

"Come on, you two." Perry clapped his hands on our shoulders. "Give Lisa a break. She just likes to keep things neat."

I laughed. "You're telling me. She made me shower before I could come in here."

Adam peered around as if confused. "So, where do I find the shower?"

"You two are regular comedians." Laughing along, Perry pushed us into the kitchen.

While the family room was off-putting, the kitchen's warm tones and huge granite island with surrounding stools invited guests to sit and stay awhile. Lisa, sweating pitcher of iced tea in hand, filled tall glasses. My cohorts piled their plates with pizza. Not interested in eating, I took tea from Lisa and chose a seat at the end of the island. While I sipped my drink, I checked out the man who held my freedom in his hands.

When Adam came in the door, his rather ordinary looks didn't grab my interest. His nose was a bit too big and off-center, his mouth larger than it should be, and his eyes were saucer size. In fact there seemed to be little room on his face for anything else. But when Perry cracked a joke, and Adam revealed a full and dazzling smile, everything moved into place to create a deliciously handsome face.

If I were to attach a plant species to him after this superficial introduction, it would have to be a lily, of any variety really. At first, lilies shoot jade green blades from the soil, drawing little interest. But then. . .oh then. . .when the flowers opened and bloomed, no plant was more splashy. Adam was the same, arriving on the scene not drawing attention. When he smiled, his face literally bloomed.

His body wasn't half-bad either. He wore a nubby sweater in a deep green color over a crisp white shirt—a true boyfriend sweater. The kind a girl might borrow on a long walk in the park or when she hiked along breathtaking Oregon trails. The bulky sweater would not only keep the cold out, it would softly caress her skin. Yes, soft. How nice it would be to just rub my cheek against the yarn, snuggle in, and forget all about Mitch Lawson and Bud Picklemann.

"Earth to Paige." Lisa jabbed me. "Are you listening?"

"Hmm, what?" I rubbed my side.

With a frown rivaling the size of an eyebrow on Mount Rushmore, she grabbed my elbow, pulling me from my stool. At the counter, she plopped a greasy slice of pepperoni pizza onto a paper plate and shoved it at me. "What are you doing?" she demanded in a whisper.

"What do you mean?"

"You're drooling all over Adam. He's here to defend you, not date you."

I glanced at him. "Oh, but he's cute, don't you think?"

"What? . . . Maybe. . .look, you have to concentrate on the murder. Mitch isn't playing around. He's serious. He thinks you killed Bud. And he's already got it out for you."

"Shoot, I know. I was just trying to lighten things up and enjoy the view. Give it a rest, already." I took my plate and returned to my stool.

Perry glanced between Lisa and me. "Something going on that we should know about?"

I snorted, and instead of a simple little sound, it came out in a loud, utterly obnoxious way. "Lisa was just scolding me for admiring Adam's good looks."

"Paaaige," Lisa said. "You're being too forward again."

"So sue me. I think he's cute. Why can't I say so?" I smiled at Adam. He blushed, looking like he'd completely lost his lawyer's edge. His mouth opened and closed a few times like a Venus flytrap. I'd embarrassed the poor fella. Time to move on. I turned my attention to Perry, who sat grinning. "So, you two went to law school together, huh?"

Perry clapped Adam on the back. "The dynamic duo, right bro?"

Visions of the pair in tights surfaced. Not a vision I wanted to dwell on. I did wonder if Adam held the starring role as Batman. I'd always had a thing for the Batmobile and caves, but I was too afraid of Lisa's reprimand to pursue further questions of that nature. Instead, I asked Adam, "Was Perry a bookworm like he is now, or did he have a good time in college?"

"Paige, what a thing to say." Lisa seemed ready to pour tea over me for my lack of manners. Good thing I'd opted for the safe route.

"That's okay," Perry said. "I have nothing to hide from my

darling wife. He can answer."

Adam described a more carefree Perry, one who overslept and arrived at class in his jammies, my term not Adam's. Adam sat back and chomped a huge bite from the tip of his pizza.

"So which one of you finished higher in your class?" I asked.

"Okay, Paige, you need a refresher course in tact before I let you out in public again." Lisa crossed her arms and scowled at me. "I'm moving on to a safer topic." She turned to Adam and initiated a conversation about his law practice in McMinnville.

I turned to the most interesting thing in the room—Adam. What was with my preoccupation with the man? Was it due to my dateless year in Serendipity, a distraction from my impending incarceration, or was I really attracted to the guy?

He looked up, caught me staring, and grinned. I returned the smile with confidence until a rush of heat surged onto my cheeks. I don't blush and the feeling left me unsettled. I took my glass to the counter and refreshed the ice. Adam came up behind me. I considered dropping a few of the cubes down my shirt to cool down.

"No need to be embarrassed." He poured cola into his glass. He took a step away, stopped, and said, "You're not hard on the eyes either."

Ohh, he thinks I'm cute. My face heated up again, and I felt like I'd traveled back to eighth grade. But I wouldn't let a little blush stop me. I let the warmth of his words settle in as I watched him saunter back to the island.

I sipped my tea and wondered if I should have tried harder to keep things on a professional level. My parents always told me honesty was the best policy, and I certainly embraced that concept, sometimes to my detriment. Still, I could no more stifle my thoughts than I could quit gardening.

I returned to my stool. "Sorry if I seemed too forward, Adam," I said in a conversational lull. "Sometimes I forget to filter my thoughts before I speak. I didn't mean any harm. I just wanted to get to know the man who holds my life in his hands."

His smile disappeared. "If what Perry tells me is true, we're going to have plenty of time to get to know each other." His gloomy tone sent a wave of alarm crashing over my body.

Lisa reached over my shoulder and slapped another piece of pizza on top of my untouched slice. "Eat. You're gonna need your strength to battle Mitch."

"Yes, Mom." I rolled my eyes. She probably just wanted to keep my mouth full so I couldn't say anything else to embarrass her guest.

I stuffed my mouth full of pizza and looked across the island.

Adam was still staring at me. His eyes were no longer playful. "So, you want to talk about the murder now or wait until we're done eating?"

I swallowed. Hard. "Now, I guess, if you can give me good news."

"Let's hope I can." He smiled, but it didn't reach his eyes.

I looked square into those deep brown eyes that had changed colors several times. "Before we go any further, I want you to know I'm not a murderer. I didn't kill Bud."

"I didn't think you did." He blotted his mouth with his napkin.

"Good. I wouldn't want you to represent me if you thought I was guilty." I set my plate down and leaned forward. "There's one more thing I need to tell you. The police chief, Mitch Lawson, and I aren't the best of friends. In high school he bragged that he could jump off a railroad trestle. I kind of called him on it. He jumped and blew out his knee. Didn't get to play ball most of his senior year. Seems like that's making it easier for him to think I'm guilty."

Adam chewed and flipped open his binder. "We can deal with that. Won't be the first angry officer I've run across. For now, let's focus on today's events. Why don't you start by replaying what happened with Picklemann?"

"Well," I said as I tore off a bite of pizza. "It was really pretty simple." I explained every little detail of our encounter, including my closing threat.

Adam looked up from his pad, now decorated with copious notes. "Your departing shot at the man certainly speaks to a motive. Still, Bud was the only witness to your threat, so the police won't have that bit of information to use against you."

I swallowed a bite that felt like a lump of the thick clay soil found in Serendipity. "Not exactly. Ernie Hansen overheard me when he was picking up pop cans from the weekend."

"So all he heard was the threat at the end?"

"I don't know. My employee, Hazel, told me about him." I turned to Lisa, whose face readily displayed her anxiety. "You're always one of the first to hear what's going on. Anyone talking about the rest of my conversation with Bud?"

She shook her head. "Not yet, but if Ernie was listening, it'll be all over town soon."

"I'll talk to him tomorrow." Adam jotted a note on his pad then looked up. "So what did you do after Picklemann left?"

"I put the tools inside the fence and secured the opening. Then I walked to my shop, The Garden Gate."

"Any idea what time you got there?"

"I looked at my watch when Bud came to the park. That was ten thirty. By the time we finished arguing, I cleaned up the tools, and got back to the shop, it'd be close to eleven."

"Anyone at The Garden Gate who can verify your whereabouts?"

At the thought of my alibi, I laughed. "Only Mr. T."

Lisa and Perry smiled. They knew Mr. T.

Confused, Adam glanced at us. "Think this Mr. T will be willing to testify if it comes to that?"

"Well, sure, but you better let me tell you about him before you put any stock in what he has to say." I explained Mr. T's feathered heritage.

Instead of acting like a stiff lawyer, Adam laughed. A lawyer with a sense of humor. This guy was special. What that meant for my case, who knew? At least I would enjoy getting to know him in the process.

"So," he paused and gave me a silly grin, "any people that could provide an alibi?"

I thought through my day. The people I didn't see. I had no alibi. Why didn't I think of that before? A surge of panic rushed in. "I guess it depends on when Bud was killed."

Adam swiveled on his stool to face Perry. "Any way you could find out the time of death?"

"I could call Lawson, I suppose," Perry said. "But I doubt he even knows yet. This is a small town. Our police force isn't used to this kind of investigation."

"Why don't you call anyway?" Adam asked. "They might have preliminary findings, and we'll all rest easier tonight if Paige has an alibi."

"I'll see what I can find out." Cell in hand, Perry pushed off his stool and walked toward the family room.

"Okay." Adam looked at his notes again. "Other than Mr. T, who did you see after leaving the park?"

I ran the day through my filter again. "I suppose someone

might have seen me. The only person that talked to me was my employee, Hazel, outside my apartment around one o'clock." I told him about the mess in the alley, my communication with Ned, and the trip to wash my shirt.

Adam set his pen on the pad and stretched. His eyes were wary. "This isn't good, Paige. Hazel can only give you an alibi for the time she saw you. If you're right about seeing someone in the park, Picklemann was probably dead before you talked to Hazel."

"But I didn't kill him. Maybe someone else saw me."

"We can do some checking. I wouldn't put a lot of faith in the search. You moved around a lot. It will be hard to find anyone who can provide an alibi that covers a long enough time span. Then, we have another problem. What, exactly, did you tell Lawson about going home after cleaning up the alley?"

"Just that I went home before going back to the park."

"And he didn't ask why?" Adam's eyes narrowed.

"No." I peered at his tightening expression. "You're starting to scare me with the way you're looking at me."

"Sorry, but obviously you haven't realized that Lawson will think you washed your shirt to get rid of any evidence of killing Bud."

I jumped up. "I had a reason for washing it. A good one."

"I know you did, but think about this from the police chief's point of view. You fight with Picklemann, no one sees you for a few hours, and when someone does, you've changed your clothes. While your dirty clothes are spinning away in the washer, Picklemann is found dead."

"So we don't tell him about it."

"By tomorrow, he'll have had time to think about what you've already told him, so he'll be certain to ask about it. You can't lie to him."

"But it makes me look guilty and I'm innocent!"

"I believe you, Paige, but the police aren't going to take your word at face value. You'll need proof of your innocence."

"How about the e-mail you sent?" Lisa came around the counter and laid her hand on my shoulder. "We can get your laptop. That'll prove you were in your office."

Adam held up a hand. "Don't bother. Even if the e-mail is on your hard drive—might not be depending on the type of account you have—it'll only prove you were there for the few minutes it took to send the message." Adam looked at Lisa. "How long would it take Paige to get from her shop to the park and back?"

"Ten, fifteen minutes at most," Lisa said.

"Wait, are you saying I went back to the park and killed Bud?"

"I'm saying we have two hours to account for and a five minute e-mail won't cover it all." He looked at his notes. "How about the phone call for the fencing? Did you use the landline?"

"No, I have free long-distance on my cell."

"A call you could have made from anywhere," Adam said, letting his tone fall off as if he was thinking.

"I was at The Garden Gate then." My frustration over not being able to prove where I was spilled out, and I pounded on the counter. "They have to believe me."

"Wait," Lisa shouted. "I talked to you, remember?"

"I used my cell again."

"Like I said," Adam's brow furrowed, "the only time you have a concrete alibi is when you talked to Hazel, roughly one o'clock. You better hope Picklemann was killed around that time."

As if God sent down an answer, Perry returned. "I struck out with Lawson. He told me it was none of my business."

"Technically, he's right," Adam said. "This isn't the sort of information the police release early on in an investigation."

"Oh, they released it," Perry said with a coy smile. "I called a buddy of mine on the force. This is off the record, and he'll deny saying it if we go public, but according to him the body temp indicates Picklemann had been dead for an hour or two when Paige found him. Looks like they'll place the time of death between eleven and twelve."

I looked from one person to another. The very thing I was thinking lay on their faces like a case of black spot invading my prize roses. I was cleaning up the alley during that time. No one could vouch for my whereabouts. I had no alibi.

CHAPTER SIX

"And now, enjoy the best of Through the Garden Gate *with your beloved host, Paige Turner."*

"Paige, this is Solitary. I was wondering if you stood behind your advice."

"I'm afraid I don't understand your question, Solitary."

"Well, say you gave a caller advice about using native plants—"

"Oh, I hope they listen. Native plants do so much better in the climate and soil conditions they were meant to grow in. Even though they might become aggressive and you'd have to dig them up and pry them apart later, often that's the only work they require."

"Right, well, say the caller agreed with your advice and went out to dig up native plants at the Grand Ronde Reservation. Would you provide legal representation if the person was then apprehended for theft and trespassing?"

At eight o'clock Tuesday morning, I approached the park entrance, pondering Adam's words from last night. Not the sweet little bit where he admitted I wasn't bad to look at, but the nasty, ugly parting words he uttered as we climbed into our respective cars—to be prepared in case I was arrested today at my appointment with Mitch.

Be prepared! What did that mean? It wasn't as if after the birds and the bees talk, my mother ticked off a lengthy go-to-jail list. The only thing I knew about jail preparation was what I learned playing Monopoly. At least there, you could get out for free.

Jail.

I couldn't fathom it. A scary place filled with guards toting guns much like the uniformed cops swarming the park. Any one of them could haul me in and make sure I stayed behind bars. Would that stocky, balding officer carrying a plastic bag to the trunk of his car make the arrest? Or would the conspicuously absent Mitch do the honors himself? I voted for Mitch and his eagerness to prove my guilt.

Not that he was the only one whose face displayed disdain. The growing group of onlookers milling outside the yellow tape gave me harsh glares that screamed their belief in my guilt. I resisted the urge to put my head down while I rushed toward the earthy smell of my shop that always brought comfort. On the toughest of days, when I was unable to bolster a positive attitude on my own, I just had to step across that threshold, and my problems melted away.

Today was different. The gaping faces at the park made me feel like an outsider in my own town. Their guilty verdict was likely only the beginning of what I would face from the other residents. Would I get over this? Stay out of jail? Get the death penalty?

Stop it, Paige. Pity is not allowed here. I gave myself a mental slap. If I couldn't come to grips for myself, I had to put on a good front for Hazel.

I found her stuffing seed packets into a rack beside the front counter. Her braids flopped as she bent over a box of reserve stock. She was dressed in the shop uniform of polo shirt and khakis, but I couldn't help remembering the day she came in for an interview wearing worn, but clean jeans and a well patched blouse. This wasn't the look I wanted my shop staff to have, but I knew about her past, and my compassion for the underdog urged me to give her a chance.

Her father had been in and out of jail for various crimes when she was young, and the family subsisted on welfare and handouts. Even when her father finally cleaned up his act, no one would hire him and they lived in squalor.

Hazel had been teased as a child, and as an adult the stigma lingered. She married a man who abused her, and people couldn't understand why she stayed with him. It wasn't until he got drunk and drove his truck into a lake that she'd gotten a break. That was when she met her current husband, who'd moved to town when the pickle factory opened. He didn't care about her past, but others weren't so willing to open their arms to her.

I didn't want to be guilty of the same treatment. I interviewed her and found a woman knowledgeable about gardening and plants in general. I hired her on the spot and from that day on, she'd proven herself a capable and loyal worker.

I often had other business to take care of, and Hazel worked hard even when unsupervised. Like today, she was already at work replenishing stock by carefully picking through packets and then hanging the seeds on the display pegs. I watched as she found one of my favorite bean varieties. I could almost feel the snappy texture and taste the nutty flavor of the beans. Would I be a free woman to plant them this year?

I let out a long sigh at my inability to get a handle on my

emotions and walked toward Hazel.

"Who is Paige Turner?" Mr. T called from his daytime cage behind the checkout counter.

"Who is Mr. T?" I yelled back in his *Jeopardy* format.

"'Don't give me no back talk,'" he said, mimicking the real Mr. T. Freer to move about in the larger cage, he hopped from his swing to a limb and bobbed his head.

"Crazy bird. Don't know why I bring you up here with me," Hazel said with affection then dropped the packets and came forward in a rush of energy. She flung out one arm.

What was she doing?

Awkwardly, she slipped the taut arm around my shoulders and squeezed hard. "I can't believe what people are saying. How could they think you killed that man?"

Her hug sent tears pricking at my eyes. If Hazel Grimes thought I needed a hug and was willing to step out of her comfort zone to give me one, I was in trouble. I extricated myself before I moved on to crying like an infant and went to the register to set down my bag.

Willing the tears to dry up, I stared at the auto shop counter-top with names engraved in the wood by previous customers. Hundreds of names decorated the stained oak from who knew how many years. On her first day at work, Hazel had whipped out a pocketknife, scratched her name in a tiny space in the corner, and offered to do mine as well. Shocked that I had hired a woman who carried a knife, I refused. Now as I looked at the concern in her eyes, I wished I had let her carve away and engrave my name next to hers for posterity.

"I appreciate your support." I rubbed my finger over her name. "Means a lot to me."

She tromped across the polished concrete. Her footfalls

reverberated from the high ceiling, sounding like an advancing army. Cali, a stray calico cat that had adopted us, shot out from a favorite hiding place in the corner and ran for the side door.

Hazel opened the door and let her out. "Well, I'm not gonna stop there. The police chief called. Asked me to come in after work. I'm gonna tell him that you were here, with me, all day."

My jaw dropped open from the offer. Much as I wanted to accept, I couldn't let her do that. "You can't lie for me, Hazel."

"Shoot." She waved a hand as if she lied under oath every day. "It's the least I can do for you. People around here don't have any idea what a great person you are. Not only did you give me a job when everybody else looked down on my clothes and manners, you pay me far more than you need to."

Hoping to lighten the mood that was feeling oppressive, I laughed. "I guess I'll have to cut your salary then."

She crossed her arms. "I'm serious, Paige. You trust me. Leave me in charge. Let me help run the business. That's more'n anyone else has done in my whole life. I won't see you go to jail. Even if I have to lie."

"I don't want you to lie."

Her eyes tightened, surprising me with the intensity I saw burning. "Fine. I'll do what you say, but I have to help look for the real killer. Already told Zeke not to expect me to make his supper every night, in case something comes up. He didn't like it, but I don't care. He can get his own supper for once."

I had no idea how to respond. In fact, I was a little unsettled by her unbridled display of devotion. Hazel wasn't the brightest bulb in the garden when it came to detecting subtleties underlying many conversations, and I didn't want her to get into trouble over me. I patted her shoulder. "Just be careful you don't get Mitch mad at you. He has a nasty bite."

"'I pity the fool,'" Mr. T said, and I laughed at his timing while pitying Mitch for his upcoming meeting with my defender.

Heading for my office, I wound through stacks of small clay pots and the newer lightweight containers. A smile tugged at my lips over the fierce independence Hazel demonstrated. Nearing sixty, she was blossoming like a third-year perennial. I strolled past the french doors leading to display gardens. In minibeds, I'd planted every plant I sold, so my customers could see them in a real garden setting. Today, azaleas and rhododendrons swarmed with riotous color, and the perennials peeked their first greenery above the heavily composted soil from a winter sleep.

In the back of the first service bay used for teaching Saturday gardening classes, I'd set up a small café with wrought iron seating. My customers could relax, browse through catalogs and magazines, and sip the finest of coffee. Wrapped up in my own problems, I reached the coffee counter before I spotted Lisa sitting at one of the tables.

"Hey," I said and pumped coffee into a mug. "Hazel didn't tell me you were here."

"She's too worried about you to think straight. I don't know what you did to earn her loyalty, but I'll never cross you again for fear you'll sic her on me."

"She's my new secret weapon." Cup in hand, I crossed the room to join her. "I think I might have just sicced her on Mitch."

She closed the *Fine Gardening* magazine and peered at me with tired eyes. "Speaking of Mitch, anything new since last night?"

I sat across from her. "No. Our meeting is still scheduled for ten thirty. If all goes well, I'll be back here to give Hazel her lunch break."

She raised her eyebrows. "Really? You think Mitch'll be finished grilling you by lunchtime?"

I gawked at her. My best friend thought I was going to jail. She might be dressed like a debutante at a garden party, in her cute linen capris and sleeveless top, but she sure knew how to speak plainly when she wanted to. Her blunt assessment of the situation revived my stubborn thoughts of doom along with the beginning of tears. "I don't know when I'll get back. I better get Teri to relieve Hazel in case I end up in jail."

"Oh, wait. . .what jail? No, I didn't mean *that*. Perry says it'll probably take until Friday before they finish with the forensics. Mitch can't do anything official until then. I just meant that Mitch probably won't let you go quickly today." She pulled a tissue from the large navy mom tote that accompanied her most places and handed it to me.

Whew, that was better—her explanation *and* not wiping my nose like she might with the twins. But what did she know? Did she really understand what was at stake? Unfortunately, I did. The tears really kicked in.

I sniffled and wiped. "Do you realize what we're talking about? My freedom. I could go to jail for something I didn't do, just because I can't prove where I was."

"Hey, stop or you're gonna make me cry. Besides, you'll get through this."

I peered at the tin-covered ceiling and kept my head up until the tears stopped. Or maybe the force of gravity pushed them back in. "I don't know, Lisa," I said in a blubbery voice. "I don't think I'm strong enough."

"That's what I thought when Ben died. But I made it, didn't I? God got me through it."

"Yeah, well, your faith has always been stronger than mine."

"Not always. Not until Ben died. That's when I figured out nothing in life was in my control. *Nothing*. I was in the same place you're at right now. No way you can handle this alone. Don't waste any energy trying. Let God take you through it."

"Says you," I snapped. She'd pushed my button. Control. I could control this. Adam was coming, and together we'd succeed. After a final swipe with the tissue, I pushed back my chair and stood. "I have the best attorney and a few ideas to follow up on. When I get back from the meeting, I'm going to investigate and find out who did this."

Lisa rose, empty cup in hand. "Good for you. You need to think positively and move forward. All I'm saying is remember who's in charge along the way."

I peered at Lisa, her face open and vulnerable. She meant well, meant to help, but the last thing I could do now was sit back and let God take the wheel. I had to act.

"Paige," Adam called from around the corner.

"What's he doing here so early?" Lisa stifled a yawn.

I shrugged. "He was supposed to meet me at the studio after the show."

She shoved me toward the back. "Well, go clean up. You don't want him to see you with mascara running down your face."

I laughed at her decorum. "He's a criminal lawyer, Lisa. I'm sure he's seen far worse."

"Yeah, but as you so clearly pointed out last night, he's an available man. And you're still very much single, in case you forgot."

I groaned. What was with this sudden attempt at match-making? No matter. I planned on cleaning up. Not to impress Adam. No, I needed to present a strong front when I walked down the street and met with Mitch later.

In the tiny bathroom, I called Teri to relieve Hazel then repaired my makeup and straightened my plain white blouse.

Straightening out my life? That was something else altogether. I could survive the unfounded accusations and figure out who killed Bud, I just needed a break. One that Adam was most likely to aid me with.

When I returned to the fragrant bay and spotted him, he was huddled with Lisa at the table so deep in conversation they didn't notice me cross the room. Today Adam wore khaki pants, polished loafers, and an olive green dress shirt under a corduroy vest. One corner of his collar sat on top of the vest, the other was tucked under. My fingers itched to adjust one of them, but that was too forward, even for me. So I waited and stared at the pair until he looked up and grinned.

"Something wrong with me?" He sat up and preened like a showy hibiscus blossom.

He asked for it. I came forward, a playful grin in place, and slipped the hidden collar point free. "Not anymore."

Lisa scowled. "Please, Paige, don't start with this again today."

I gave her a quizzical look. "Weren't you the one who just reminded me that we're both single?"

"Paige." Lisa's hand flew up. "Don't you ever know when to keep what I tell you to yourself?"

"If I did, how long would it be before I found another opportunity to ask Adam if he was in a relationship?" Lisa freaked. Adam and I laughed. "Besides, when I came out here, you two couldn't look any guiltier than if I actually caught you with your hands in the cookie jar."

"We were just talking about the meeting with Mitch." Lisa's tone was all defensive.

"And your expressions say I'm sunk." I took the chair to Lisa's left.

Adam locked gazes with me. "I'm not, by the way. In a relationship, that is."

"Good to know." I smiled. "I'm surprised to see you this early."

"I thought we could talk before your show. Maybe set a plan so when we meet with the chief we're both on the same page."

"I like the sound of both of us on the same page." I grinned at him, and he returned it with a high-wattage smile of his own.

"Focus, you two." Lisa tapped her watch. "Show time. Twenty minutes."

Adam turned fully toward me. "Now that I've had a chance to think about this, it seems as if our only course of defense is to produce evidence of someone else's guilt."

Could he get more lawyerly than that? Actually, I found it kind of cute and had a hard time not reverting to our previous topic. "I'm all for coming up with another suspect for Mitch to pick on."

"Have you thought of anyone who might have killed Picklemann?" Adam asked.

"No, but I have two thoughts to follow up on." I cringed as I realized I'd admitted to having only two thoughts. "The first one is to check out who was wearing white yesterday." I looked at Lisa. "Remember I saw something white in the park from my apartment?"

"Yeah, but, Paige, you can't check with everyone in town to see who wore something white yesterday. And if the killer really did dress that way, do you think they'd admit it?"

I shrugged. "Probably not. Charlie had on his white pharmacy coat. He also argued with Bud and threatened him, so we need to at least put him on our follow-up list."

Adam nodded. "Makes sense. You said two thoughts?"

"Right. The obvious suspect in many murders is the spouse.

I saw Rachel Picklemann near the park around eleven o'clock yesterday, so we should look at her."

"I can't imagine that," Lisa said. "Bud treated her like a princess. Gave her everything she wanted. Most importantly, he put up with her selfishness. Why would she want to kill him?"

"Spousal murder is often committed in a fit of rage over something personal," Adam said. "Often doesn't make sense to the outside world."

"My point exactly." I slapped a high five with Adam.

Lisa waved us off. "I don't think you should waste any time on Rachel unless something else points in her direction."

Sadly, I kind of agreed with her, but I didn't want to give in so easily. "I have to start looking somewhere. Unless I find a better suspect, I'll go after her."

"I—" Adam quickly glanced at Lisa, who nudged his elbow. "*We* think you should leave the investigation to a professional— hire a private investigator."

What else had they had time to discuss while I was primping? I sat back and studied their faces. It looked as if they really thought I was in deep water. I wasn't nearly that desperate. There was no deep water anywhere around me. A puddle maybe, or a wading pool. I was still breathing, and the water hadn't even neared my knees. True, I'd just shed a few tears, but that was a weak moment brought on by Lisa's overly emotional mothering.

I looked at Lisa then back at Adam with a purposeful stare. He came here to make sure we were on the same page. After the P.I. suggestion, it was obvious that we weren't even in the same book. "I think we should check around ourselves. I can spend all my free time looking into this."

"You don't have any experience," Lisa whined.

"I don't know." I shrugged. "I followed the trail of a pretty killer mint plant until I found the source and eradicated it. How much harder could this be?"

"Paige, we're serious." Lisa crossed her arms.

"An investigator would be able to make faster progress," Adam added.

"They cost money. Money that I don't have right now. So no to the investigator."

"Told you she'd say no right off the bat." Lisa's tone was an exact imitation of her twins when they lost custody of one of their toys. "How are you gonna investigate this when Mitch locks you up?"

"*If* Mitch locks me up, I'll think about hiring someone." Wanting to end this discussion, I reached out and tapped her watch. "Time to go." I stood and glared at my defecting friend. "Let's get the show on the road so I can meet with Mitch."

Lisa stood, came around the table with a solemn expression, and wrapped her arms around me. "I only want what's best for you, you know?"

I pushed back and looked into her eyes. "I know, but next time, talk to me about it, not Adam."

"Okay, but next time, you consider what I say and don't dismiss it right away." Lisa headed for the door before I could respond.

I wouldn't dwell on it. My mind had returned to the upcoming meeting at the city hall. The very meeting that could determine my future.

CHAPTER SEVEN

"This is Tim Needlemeyer, asking all the wonderful citizens of Serendipity to consider filling in for Greg Watson, aka Briny, who has suffered a most unfortunate accident resulting in a broken leg. Briny will be unable to attend Pickle Fest unless we find a substitute, and we only have a few days to fill his pickle shoes. So please, stop by the HR department at Pacific Pickles to apply. We now return to our locally acclaimed show, Through the Garden Gate, *with Paige Turner."*

Seated in the soft chair with a headset on, I tried to focus on the show that dragged along. The end of my hour loomed large. Depending on the upcoming caller's chattiness, this might be our last call of the morning. Then the fun would begin. The really big fun. My meeting with Mitch. The sooner I met with him and cleared my name the better my mood would be.

Head down, ear to the phone, Lisa positioned her fingers in our caller-on-the-line signal. She was supposed to find out the reason for the call and give me a heads-up, but once again, I was flying solo.

I put a smile in my voice and punched the blinking button. "This is Paige Turner. Go ahead, caller, you're on *Through the Garden Gate.*"

"Hi, Paige, I just wanted to give you an update on things."

Wait, I know that voice. "Weed Whacker, is that you?"

"Ah, yeah, it's me."

I glanced at Lisa. Only the top of her head was visible. I guessed she let Weed Whacker through because she was a frequent flier on our program. "Welcome to the show again, Weed Whacker. For those listeners tuning in for the first time, Weed Whacker is one of our regulars."

"That's right, listeners. I wouldn't miss this show for anything. Paige gives the best advice." She sounded like a used car salesman. "That's one of the reasons I'm calling. I wanted to thank you for helping me yesterday. I feel much better."

"Well, that's certainly good to hear. Does this mean you worked things out with your husband?"

"Sort of, but we still have a few problems. I could really use your help again."

I silently groaned. "Okay, Weed Whacker, what *gardening* question can I help you with?"

"I need to buy a shovel and was wondering if you would tell me how to choose one?"

"Oh, good question." My tone was filled with relief—relief that she had moved back to needing real gardening advice I could easily provide. "When purchasing a shovel, make sure it has a solid blade, a comfortable handle, and a flat edge at the top of the blade for your foot. Most importantly—are you listening Weed Whacker?" I asked to make sure there were no future problems with giving her advice.

"Yeah, I'm here."

"Most importantly you need to match the tool to the task you have in mind. A wide variety of shovels are sold today—ones for transplanting, sawtooth shovels for heavy or rocky soils, straight blades, curved blades, and on and on. What are you planning to do with the shovel you buy?"

"I have to dig a hole. A big one. About three by six and nearly six feet deep."

Odd job. "For a huge project like that I'd recommend renting a backhoe, not buying a—wait, why such a big hole? Weed Whacker did you use the herbicide even after I told you not to? Put your husband on the phone." Silence, deadly and long. "Weed Whacker? Weed Whacker? I need to speak to your husband."

Bzz. . .

"Well, listeners, Weed Whacker must have had a pressing engagement, as she's hung up. Don't worry, though. She'll surely call back tomorrow." I tried to telegraph concern with my eyes to Lisa. She held up a dry-erase board with POLLY IN PORTLAND written in blue marker. After that last call, I would have liked her to give me a subject as well. But, since Weed Whacker hung up so unexpectedly, Lisa must have had to push ahead.

I dug to the depths of my reserve left untouched by nutty callers and dredged up a cheerful tone. "Hello, Polly, this is Paige Turner on *Through the Garden Gate.* How can I help you?"

"Is it true, Paige?" Her tone was mixed with excitement and disbelief. "I heard on the local news that you killed a man with a shovel and buried him in some mulch."

Not caring that I was on the air, I groaned and gave Lisa an evil glare. "No, Polly, I had nothing to do with killing him. I was simply the one who found him."

"That's not what your chief of police said in the interview. He said you were a person of interest in this case."

"Again, not a suspect, Polly." I looked at Lisa who held up the board. This time it said, 25 SECONDS. WING IT. I wanted to wing her all right, with a shotgun, but sat up straight and considered how to explain this situation to my listeners before Polly convinced them I was a murderer.

"I don't know, Paige. That seems like a lame defense. Cops use the phrase 'person of interest' at first, and that person usually winds up being the killer."

"Since you brought this up, I would like all my listeners to know I did not, nor would I ever kill anyone. I was—"

"Excuse me, but I think your listeners need to know you threatened the deceased not long before he ended up buried in the mulch." Her voice had turned sharp and brassy. "You may not have gotten his head on a platter as you threatened. From what I heard, the police found it on your shovel."

I rolled my eyes and spotted Lisa giving me the wrap-it-up signal.

"Please believe me when I say, I had nothing to do with Bud Picklemann's death. Unfortunately, we're out of time for an explanation." I signed off and slammed my headset onto the counter. "Why did you let her through?" I shouted so loud Lisa must have heard me through the window.

She stood and opened the door between us. "Polly said she wanted to talk about gardening events in the news. How did I know she meant your gardening events in the news?"

The phone rang, and Lisa shot her hand out to answer. She was probably glad to do anything to avoid my wrath. My anger dissipated at her soft tone. As much as I wanted to keep screaming at her, she wasn't to blame for my situation. She had done her job. The misguided caller was the only one who deserved my frustration.

Lisa put her hand over the receiver. "You're not gonna believe this, but Weed Whacker's on the phone. She says it's urgent. I think you should talk to her."

I took the phone, cupped my hand over the receiver, and gave Lisa a conciliatory smile. "I'm sorry I yelled at you. It wasn't your fault."

She smiled back. "I'll cut you some slack because of this whole murder thing, but don't make it a habit."

I had the feeling she might be cutting me more slack than she ever imagined over the next few days. I sighed and turned my attention to the coming conversation. "Weed Whacker, what's wrong?"

"Oh, Paige, thank goodness you answered. I needed to make sure you were okay." Her words gushed out like a frantic mother who'd found a lost child.

I glanced at Lisa to see if she was listening. She stared into the distance with a faraway look on her face. "Why wouldn't I be okay?"

"I'm worried about the last caller. She seemed a little deranged."

Seriously? Look who claimed someone was deranged. "I don't think she meant any real harm."

"Well, I do. You need to be careful. She could have stirred up all kinds of nuts out there."

I laughed off the chief nut job's concern. "I appreciate your concern, Weed Whacker. I promise to be careful."

"I mean it, Paige. Don't just promise. Do it."

I was getting uncomfortable with her passion. Time to change the subject. "Don't worry. Suppose you tell me why you're digging that big hole."

"Uh. . .no. . .sorry. I've gotta go. Earl's calling me."

The line went dead, and I handed the phone back. "She's going to drive me crazy. At least it sounded like Earl was okay."

Lisa hung up the handset. "That why she called?"

"No. You're not gonna believe this. She thinks I'm in danger from Polly."

"I didn't get that vibe at all."

"Me neither. If I needed to worry about anyone it would be Weed Whacker." I laughed and glanced at the cute watering can-shaped clock on the wall. "Can you close up without me? Adam's waiting."

Lisa's eyes crinkled, and she sent a warm smile my way. "Good luck, sweetie." She yawned then wrapped her short arms as far around my shoulders as she could. "Everything is going to be okay. Wait and see. Remember to trust God to get you through this."

As I headed down the hallway, I kept Lisa's words in mind, actually deriving comfort from them. I could do that. It was simple. Just trust God to get me through this. No need to worry or fret. Everything was going to be okay.

"Paige. A minute." The sharp tone of the station manager punched out of his office and broke through my peace.

I turned back and went through the open doorway. Roger Freund, one of the many city folks who had relocated to Serendipity, sat behind a slick glass and chrome desk with a warm smile planted on his square face. He wore his usual designer suit and crisp white shirt. Old enough to be my father, he looked about my age except for a few wrinkles by his eyes. Could be due to the moisturizer I caught him applying one morning, or because he was rarely seen outdoors.

"Paige," he said, his smile disappearing, "I'm not sure what to do about your show."

What did he mean? My show was great. I clasped the back

of a black leather chair I'd seen in a furniture catalog. "I don't understand, Roger. Is there something wrong with my show?"

He snapped forward in his high-backed chair. "Not until today. You've posted the best ratings of our local programs. Listeners love those crazy callers you and Lisa make up."

"Ah, Roger, we don't make them up. They're real."

"Really? Imagine, people being that ignorant."

"Yeah, imagine."

He shook his head. "Anyway, after the last caller announced your involvement in Picklemann's murder, I'm wondering if we should give you a brief hiatus. Might be time to run some 'best of' shows until this is cleared up." He rested his chin on pointed index fingers. "Of course, if this goes on long enough, we might lose our audience and need to pull the show all together."

I let out a gush of air. "How about we play it by ear, Roger? Let's try a live broadcast tomorrow. If it turns ugly again, we can reconsider."

He looked at me, his ice-blue eyes serious and appraising. "Fine, one more day. If there's even a hint of trouble tomorrow, I'm going to play reruns of the show for a few days to see if it blows over. If it doesn't, I'll pull the plug. Permanently. And consider your live show from the Pickle Fest cancelled. No way I'll take the chance of someone from the crowd going nuts. Harly'll be glad to have another hour added to his program."

Dismissed and deflated, I sauntered into the hall. It was getting harder to keep up my spirits. Not only might I lose my radio gig, which gave me needed business, ultimately I could lose my shop, the main source of my income. Not to mention incarceration.

I stepped into the parking lot to join Adam for a meeting that was certain to be tense. I scoffed at Lisa's advice. Trust God? No way. Look at what had just happened.

CHAPTER EIGHT

"And now, enjoy the best of Through the Garden Gate *with your beloved host, Paige Turner."*

"Hi, Paige, this is Disappointed. I wanted to clarify one of your earlier hints."

"Okay, Disappointed, what can I clear up?"

"Well, you mentioned the stunning flowers you can get from bulbs, and it sounded like an easy way to garden."

"That's right. Especially if you live in a part of the country like ours where the winters are mild and bulbs don't have to be dug up to prevent freezing. Once you plant them at their optimum depth, pretty much the only work they require for beautiful flowers year after year is a little fertilizer and dividing them when they get large."

"I wish I had the problem of them getting too big. I bought every kind of bulb I could think of and so far, no flowers at all."

"Really, I'm surprised. What type of bulbs have you tried?"

"Forty watt all the way up to one hundred

twenty. Even tried the new compact fluorescents,
with no success."

True to Mitch's offensive behavior so far, he kept Adam and me waiting in the lobby past our scheduled appointment time. On our walk to city hall, Adam told me he'd used his time wisely during my radio show. He talked with Ernie, who admitted to overhearing my entire argument with Bud. Not good news, but I was working hard to convince myself I needn't worry about it unless I was arrested in the upcoming meeting. Still, the thought dampened our mood, and as we entered the building, we fell silent and sat in chairs facing one another. I tried not to be concerned. I failed. As the minutes ticked by, my hands grew moist.

Adam, on the other hand, leaned back, crossed perfectly pressed khaki-clad legs, and moved into a meditative trance. Worried or not, I didn't miss the chance to look him over in the daylight. As we'd walked here, the women we passed gave him a second look—a deserving look from what I could see. The sunlight filtering through the clouds and glinting off the window brought out hints of red in his dusty-brown hair. He'd gelled it up again, giving himself a GQ appearance with which I could find little fault.

In fact, when the receptionist told us we could go in, I was reluctant to take my eyes off him and make the move. He stood first, brushing imaginary fuzz from his vest and shouldering his case. With a warm hand, he helped me to my feet. His fingers pressed on my back, gently guiding me down the hall.

"Remember," he whispered in my ear as we walked into the conference room, "watch me. I'll tell you which questions you should respond to. And keep your answers to the point. Don't ramble. Don't explain. It's up to the chief to prove your guilt. Don't give him the ammunition he needs."

Much like Adam had done when he stood, I pulled back my shoulders and marched into the room. I'd expected the TV version of a small airless cell with hot lights, two-way mirrors, and table with chair. Instead, Mitch waited for us in a small conference room with rich walnut furniture, a pitcher of water and glasses in the center of a long table, and ten plush chairs. A window filled the far wall, letting in plenty of sunlight for the ficus sitting in the corner. The poor little baby was dropping leaves much the same way Mitch would be dropping this case if I had my way. I made a mental note to check on the neglected darling if the meeting ended amicably.

"Sit," Mitch commanded. The room might be nice, but Mitch was the same old grump.

I chose a chair and took a good look at my adversary. The gray in his hair was more obvious in this lighting as were the crinkle lines that had formed around his eyes. He must have gotten those from laughing. So where were the jokes when he was with me?

I'd barely sat when Mitch reached across the table and slid a microphone in front of me. "We'll be recording this. Speak clearly. Okay, let's get started." He leaned forward and rattled off my name, the date, and other statistics then glared at me. "Yesterday, you told me you went to The Garden Gate after your fight with Picklemann."

"Alleged fight," Adam said.

"Fine, alleged fight. Walk me through your morning, step-by-step."

I looked at Adam for permission to speak, and he gave me a clipped nod. I slowly and purposefully revealed the details of my morning so Mitch wouldn't have to ask any additional questions.

Except I couldn't get out the part about changing clothes.

Mitch leaned forward, his eyes never leaving my face. "Is it usual for you to go home in the middle of the day?"

Great. He didn't miss a thing. "Sometimes. For lunch."

"And is that why you went home yesterday?"

I cut my gaze to Adam, who gave me a nod of encouragement. "I did get lunch there, but mostly I went home because I got a stain on my shirt from picking up those soggy scrapbook papers. My work shirts are expensive, and I didn't want the stain to set in."

"Are you saying you went home to wash your shirt?"

I nodded.

"So you lied to me yesterday." His eyes drilled into me. "Or are you lying today?"

Adam held his hand in front of me and said to Mitch, "Care to rephrase that last question, or should I take my client and go?"

Mitch glared at Adam then locked gazes with me again. "Fine. You omitted this piece of information yesterday. How do you explain that?"

"I didn't even think about how washing my shirt would look."

His mouth dropped open. "You expect me to believe you didn't think I'd need to know about this? Even after I asked for your clothes?"

"Honestly, Mitch, I was so in shock over finding Bud that until Adam brought it up late last night, I didn't think about it."

Adam leaned forward. "She's being straight with you, Lawson. If you could've seen her reaction last night, you would know she hadn't made the connection."

"Spoken like a true lawyer." Mitch scowled and sat back.

And so it went. Mitch pelted out questions like hail on a

garden, trampling everything under his fury. He met each of my answers with skepticism or downright disbelief, even when I told him about seeing something white moving in the park and seeing Rachel there, too. Now, after nearly an hour of questioning, Mitch transitioned to the same ground for a third time.

Adam pushed his notes away in frustration. "All due respect, Chief, but you seem to have something against my client. She has been forthright with you. You've tried to trip her up by asking the same question multiple times. She continues to give you the same answer because she's telling the truth. It's time you cut her some slack."

Mitch sneered. "No one cut Bud Picklemann any slack."

"Then maybe you should focus your effort on finding the real killer." Adam shot to his feet and packed his things into his briefcase. "Paige had no motive to kill Picklemann. Sure, he presented her with a problem, but she solved it, and with no detriment to her company. If you'd stop and look at the case with an open mind you'd see the details don't add up. *If* Paige killed Picklemann, why would she find the body and call 911? Why would she hide the body on her work site? And for that matter, why hide him at all if she was just going to turn around and find him? Then there's the murder weapon. Supposing the forensics report does state that her shovel was used to kill Picklemann. Why leave it in the park with her fingerprints all over it?"

"I don't think—" Mitch said.

"Maybe you should start thinking." Adam turned and urged me to my feet. "Unless you have any charges to bring, we'll be going."

Mitch's furious gaze locked on my face. "You're free to go for now, but you can be sure once the forensic team is finished and the autopsy is completed, we'll be revisiting all of this. So don't leave town."

I gave the ficus one last look before Adam escorted me out of the room, down the hall, and into the lobby. Jubilant over the outcome of the meeting, I turned and threw my arms around his neck. He was tall, and I stood on tiptoes to reach around his broad shoulders. He smelled of minty soap and a light musk aftershave. Like a lawyer should, I suppose. He also felt solid, firm, muscular, as if he worked out. Very unlawyerly.

Umm, nice. I was merely thanking him, but now. Now, what? What was I doing as I clung to him? The boyfriend sweater from last night popped into my mind. A strong urge to snuggle followed.

Adam awkwardly fumbled with his briefcase and finally clasped my arms to set me away. His eyes were far from excited over my unbridled display of affection.

"Sorry." I reluctantly moved a step back and looked into his eyes. I'd felt a connection, strong and solid. Not like a lightning bolt, nothing earthshaking or stomach turning, just a solid sense of his goodness. He cleared his throat, and I leaned back. "I guess a client shouldn't fawn over her attorney like that."

He smiled, and from where I stood, I could see a tiny scar on his chin that winked when his lips turned up. "Don't get me wrong, Paige, I'm not at all opposed to the hugging. I just don't want you to get so excited over this little victory. We have a long way to go until you're in the clear."

"Don't worry. I know I'm still the prime suspect without an alibi." Smiling over my connection with Adam, I slipped my hand through his arm and tugged him toward the exit. "It just felt so good to see the thunderous look on Mitch's face, I wanted to celebrate for a minute."

He pulled open the door and waited for me to step outside. "Okay, as long as you realize we still have a lot of work to do."

"Umm, yes, work. Lots of work." My thoughts still on the hug, my voice sounded more dreamy than businesslike. "How about we tackle some of it over lunch?"

He glanced at the tall clock tower on the corner. "It's a little early for lunch."

Eleven thirty, early? Maybe in the civilized world. In the boonies people often ate at this time of day. "Well, maybe it's a tad early." I batted my eyelashes. "So how about you hang around until it's time to eat?" Flirting. Not very well, but flirting? My future freedom was in jeopardy, and I was flirting. I had to stop. This was crazy. I needed to remember why he was here. "I'm not asking you on a date or anything. We have to plan a strategy, and we both have to eat." Trying to control my behavior, I kept my wayward lashes still and peered at him.

"Aww, really, no date?" His eyes turned mischievous, giving him a little boy look that was extremely enticing.

I was in trouble. "Nope, strictly business."

"A business lunch would be good." His eyes said he knew what I was up to. His voice was all professional and controlled. "Give me a computer and phone to use for the next hour to get a little work done, and I'm all yours."

"Deal," I said before he changed his mind.

Relieved to have that settled, I kept my arm from darting out and linking with his again and resumed our stroll toward The Garden Gate. Before I blurted out some other stupid comment, I focused on the success of the meeting and my lifted spirits.

We strolled side by side down Main and across Oak. I not only enjoyed my small victory but the spectacular May morning as well. Still in the sixties, it was cool enough to warrant the sweater I'd brought along. By the time we sat down to lunch, we should have a perfect shirtsleeve day.

I raised my face to the warmth of the sun. "I love it when summer finally gets here. I never get enough sun."

He snorted. "Tell me about it. I moved here in the summer during the dry season. If someone told me most every day for the rest of the year I'd be ducking raindrops, I might not have made the move."

I laughed at his dismay over our gloomy winters. "Guess that means you're not a native Oregonian."

He shook his head. "Nope. Californian born and raised."

"That's right, you and Perry went to law school at Stanford," I said then turned and nodded at Mrs. Beneford, who was sweeping the sidewalk across the street in front of the movie theater. She nodded back and stared with the same kind of interest I had in finding out about Adam's past. "So how did a big shot lawyer like you end up in McMinnville?"

He laughed. "Not sure the big shot fits, but I did work in a large law firm in San Francisco. A couple who worked with me there came up here on a winery tour one weekend and never went back to California. Literally, never. They liked Oregon so much, they bought a business on the coast and had their things packed and shipped. I took care of selling their house. As a thank you, they invited me up for a week. I guess I caught the bug and here I am." He grinned, the little boy back in charge. "So how about you?"

"Lived with all of this through high school." I spread my arms to encompass the final steps of Poplar Street before we arrived at The Garden Gate. "Then I moved to Portland. Got a degree in landscape design and went to work for Ten Trees Landscaping. About a year ago, I'd finally saved enough money to move here and start my own business."

"So you're one of the natives then?"

"Uh-huh, and proud of it."

The impish glint in his eyes intensified. "Then you won't mind if I ask you to clear something up for me."

"Sure, why not."

At the end of the alley, he tugged me to a stop. "I've been told—mind you it might just be a rumor—that native Oregonians are born with webbed toes so they can survive all the rain."

I'd heard this silly Oregon joke lots of times, but I played along, mocking offense by crossing my arms. "Now, Adam Hayes, I don't think you know me well enough to ask to see my toes."

"Guess we'll have to fix that then, won't we?" He smiled, wide and dazzling. "I'm dying to know the truth."

"Paige, there you are," Velma Meyers yelled from the back stoop of her Scrapbook Emporium. "I really need to talk to you." She shot a fawning smile at Adam. "If you're not too busy."

Before Velma asked for an introduction, I nudged Adam toward the door, where I entered my code into the automatic lock. "My office is the second door on the left. Make yourself at home while I talk to Velma."

I pushed him through the door. "I'll be there in a few."

Velma had hobbled halfway across the alley by the time I got to her. Her right hand, gnarled from arthritis, peeked from a berry-flowered cuff and grasped a cane made from driftwood she'd picked up at the coast.

"Is it true, Paige?" she asked, her usually warm eyes filled with worry. "Do they really think you killed Bud?"

"For now. But it'll be okay. They'll find the real killer." In thanks for her concern, I patted her slumped shoulder. "So how about you? Any idea who might have wanted to kill him?"

Before she could answer, Gus Reinke drove his battered truck down the alley, forcing us to move to the other side. She looked around furtively, as if checking to see if anyone might overhear us. "Pretty much everyone in town had a reason to do Bud in."

Everyone? I knew about Bud's reputation as a brutal city manager, and I'd experienced his tyrannical behavior firsthand, but *everyone* wanting to do him in? Seemed a bit of an exaggeration. "Could you narrow that down, Velma? Maybe think of someone Bud was extra mean to?"

She tilted her head to the left. A slip of white hair dangled from her tight bun and swung like a silver lace vine in a strong breeze. While I waited for her to run the possible suspects through her mind, I looked at my garden beds sprinkled with the dying greens from stately yellow and white daffodils and the smaller, more delicate grape hyacinths.

Still waiting, I silently hummed the final *Jeopardy* melody.

Halfway through the song a second time, she straightened as much as her curved spine would allow, and her eyes lit up. "I've got it. There was a group of homeowners that Bud really did wrong a few years back. Know the pickle factory?"

I nodded. Anyone who drove into town could figure out there was a pickle factory in Serendipity. If the pickle trash cans dotting the park and a Pickle Fest banner strung over Main Street weren't enough clues, there were the cucumber-filled semis that frequented the streets. Still, I wondered how a pickle factory had anything to do with the death of a Picklemann other than in the name.

"Go on," I said.

"Bud got the entire city to change zoning laws so that factory could locate on the outskirts of town. He said it would be good for our economy. That kids would stay here after graduation because they had jobs. People who lived by the site fought hard to keep the factory out, but Bud lied to get us to vote for the change. He said the company would make sure the factory didn't affect the quality of life for local homeowners. The factory owners never did what Bud promised. The noise and activity dropped the value of the homes to next to nothing. Even though their property was worthless and they couldn't sell the houses, most folks near the factory moved away."

Yes! Finally, suspects. Real suspects. Even though I was elated, I forced the excitement out of my tone. Velma would mistake my happiness and think I didn't care about others' misfortune. "How many people were there, and did you know any of them?"

"Just a handful. Didn't know most of them. One of the ladies, Ida Carlson, used to visit the shop. She stopped coming in a long time ago. Now that I think about it, I don't know what happened to her."

"Any idea how I could find more information about this?"

"I would imagine you could get it from the library. City council minutes are published every month. The *Times* should have the details."

I thanked Velma and raced back to the shop to tell Adam about my good news—maybe to gloat a little over the fact that I, without the aid of a private investigator, had my first clue in very little time. With this kind of result, I'd know the identity of the killer by nightfall.

CHAPTER NINE

"And now, enjoy the best of Through the Garden
Gate *with your beloved host, Paige Turner."*

*"Hi, Paige, this is Banned in Sisters. About six
months ago you did a show about researching plant
properties."*

*"Right you are, Banned. When planning a
garden, research, research, research. To be successful
you must discover, at a minimum, a plant's water
and sunlight needs and the heat and cold extremes it
can survive. I believe I suggested a trip to the library
to consult the American Horticultural Society's* A-Z
Encyclopedia of Garden Plants.*"*

*"Yes, you did, and that's where our problem
started. Our librarian has banned us from the
library."*

"Now why would she do something so drastic?"

"She said we were destroying the book."

*"I don't understand. Was she worried that you
were using it too often?"*

*"Not exactly. We might have gotten a little bit of
dirt on the pages."*

"Dirt?"

*"Yeah, we needed to identify a few of our plants
so we dug them up and laid them by the pictures in
the book. We tried to clean it up. Honest."*

Outside my office door, I stopped and peered into the small
space. Adam was seated behind my monster of a desk, and
his long tapered fingers clicked away on my keyboard while he
talked into the phone wedged between his ear and shoulder. He
glanced at me and smiled. My face warmed over the memory
of our earlier hug. How nice it would be to snuggle in that spot
again.

As much as I wanted to talk to him, he had to finish up
before we could go to lunch and discuss this new development.
Reluctantly, oh so reluctantly, I pushed off the doorjamb and
went in search of Hazel.

Lisa, eyes drooping and chin resting on her fist, delayed my
search. Her index finger rested on the same magazine as earlier.

"You're back," I said approaching the table.

She raised her head as if it weighed hundreds of pounds.
Please, say it isn't so. My daisy was wilting as her morning caffeine
wore off. A tired Lisa meant a contentious Lisa. She needed
eight hours of sleep or she was craaaaanky. Until her twins slept
through the night, she'd been almost unbearable.

"Don't make such a big deal about me being here, Paige. I
just wanted to find out what happened with Mitch." She cut her
gaze toward the office. "Adam already filled me in."

Warily, I chose a chair as far from the crank as possible and
slipped onto the padded seat. "That's not all the good news I have."
I replayed my conversation with Velma. "Do you remember all of
this happening?"

Lisa pondered my question then nodded slowly. "Sure, yeah, I remember. I don't know all the details, but it was a big mess. People were mad as can be. Bud really pulled a fast one."

"I don't get it. If everyone around here hated Bud for that, how'd he keep his job?"

"Business, pure and simple. He's been good for the town. Bringing in tourism, even the factory. The place employs two hundred people. Kids are staying around after graduation now because they can find jobs."

I shook my head. "Still, doesn't seem right to me. One of the reasons I left city life was to get away from big businesses that care only about money and nothing about people. I never expected to find that kind of attitude alive and well here."

Lisa's eyes widened, and she motioned toward the back hallway. "Don't look now, but *your* big business is on his way from the office."

I turned and made eye contact with the advancing Adam. We locked gazes. I returned his sweet and comforting smile with what I hoped was a bold flirtatious look.

Lisa twisted the flesh on my forearm, and I swiveled so fast the room spun. "Why'd you do that?"

"Thanks for sharing all the juicy details of what happened to put that kind of look on your face," she whispered.

I sat back and waited for a forked tongue to whip out and stick me. "We'll talk about him and your wayward fingers later."

Oblivious to our little spat, Adam stopped behind my chair and placed his hand on my shoulder before squatting and peering into my eyes. "I need to send a fax. It's long distance, and I wanted to be sure it was okay."

Umm, brown. No, cocoa. His eyes are cocoa. They go well with the milk chocolate tufts of his hair. He was just plain yummy.

I was going to have to get a grip or find a new lawyer.

Lisa kicked me under the table, and I willed my mind from the intensity of his eyes. "What? A fax? Oh, sure. Yeah. It's okay."

"Great." As if he knew the effect he had on me, likely from past experience at charming women, he stood and grinned, setting that little scar to winking again. "I still have a few things to do. Can you hold out for another hour until lunch?"

Another hour? My happy bubble melted. Then again, maybe this was a good thing. I could use the time to go to the library. When we did have lunch, I'd have concrete facts instead of a local gossip's theory to present to him.

"Fine," I said while rising. "There's something I need to take care of anyway. I'll meet you at the Bakery in an hour. Remember where that is?"

His lovely eyes clouded over. "Hard to forget, since it's across the street from the park. See you in an hour." He retreated to the office.

I grabbed Lisa's elbow. "Come on. Two can work faster than one." I jerked her to her feet.

"Where are we going?"

"Library. To look at old newspapers. I need details about the people Bud hurt when he brought in the factory." I dragged her through the shop, toward Hazel.

"I called Teri," I yelled as we rushed past Hazel, who looked at us as if we had escaped a loony bin. "She'll come in to give you your lunch break. I'll be back as soon as I can."

Mr. T, asleep in his cage, woke up. Arching his back, he swung his beak from side to side and ruffled his feathers. "'Quit your jibba jabba.'"

I shut out his echoing Mr. T'ism by closing the door.

"Would you please let go of me?" Lisa pulled her arm free.

"Sorry, it's just that we have to hurry. I don't want to be late for lunch." I didn't wait to see if she would follow. I was sure she would be dying to talk about my budding feelings for Adam. I was so baffled by them myself that I didn't want to discuss it. Not until I had a better handle on my motives. I mean, he was cute, and I could fall for his charms, but that did not a real relationship make.

The dressier shoes I'd paired with my khakis for the interview clicked on the sidewalk like a woodpecker tapping on a tree. Lisa caught up. Surprisingly, she didn't mention my tête-à-tête with Adam and pulled out her cell instead. She gabbed with her mom about picking up the twins, and I marveled at how much Serendipity had changed since I left after high school. In the sixteen years I'd been gone, wineries had sprouted up in the Willamette Valley, bringing plenty of weekend tourists to town and making my plan for a small nursery and landscape business viable.

To cater to the weekenders, the locals had spruced up store-fronts, painting them bright colors. After a facelift, the old Cameo Theater sparkled in its former glory, and the brick courthouse had been nipped and tucked as well. Along the sidewalks filled with planters, antique wrought iron lamps lit the evening shopping experience on most of the main streets. Even as I turned left on Oak, I passed the renovated elementary school, now a hotel-brew pub that anchored a string of thriving antique shops.

The library was located on the back side of the fire station. I'd always wondered who came up with the idea to pair a quiet library with a noisy firehouse. If it hadn't been this way since I could remember, I'd blame it on Bud's mismanagement.

Waiting for Lisa to finish her phone call, I shoved open the glass door and looked into the simple one-room building. Our library, filled to the brim with reading materials that were an essential part of the residents' daily activities, resembled most libraries in Oregon. Book circulation in this state, likely due to the continuous rain, hit record highs. Facts were facts. We were all big readers.

Lisa clamped her phone closed and trudged past me, her face fixed and determined. Though testy and irritable, her body language screamed a perfectly put together, albeit tired Stepford Wife.

"Do you know the librarian?" I asked as she passed me. "What's her name? Stacey?"

"Yeah, she's a real sweetie. Loves the twins when I bring them in."

I closed the door silently. "Are we talking about the same person here? She's always been cranky to me."

Lisa pointed at the counter. "Just look at how nice she's being to old Frank."

I followed the line of her finger. Stacey slid out cards from the back of books as she conversed with irritable Frank Becker. Slender, on the fashion side of thin actually, Stacey wore a knit dress. Although her lower half was hidden behind the counter, I was positive her skirt was cut short to draw attention to her Barbie-doll legs. Her shoulder-length bottle-blond hair, alive with ringlet curls, accentuated a heart-shaped face boasting full lips lacquered in a berry frost.

If she were in my garden, I'd want to plant her front and center to show off every inch of her beauty, but she was too tall for the front. Still, even in the back of a garden bed, all eyes would go straight to her. The only flowering plant I'd ever seen with that type of power was *Crocosmia,* the 'Lucifer' cultivar, to be specific. This plant produces scarlet red flowers borne along the upper portions of arching stems that rise up to four feet above sword-shaped leaves. A true beauty that no gardener should forgo.

That's where Stacey differed. I could do without her, even though she was pleasantly entertaining Frank as if he were a neighborly man instead of a curmudgeon.

"You feeling better today?" Frank asked her.

Her head popped up, and she peered at him. "Fine, why?"

He jerked his head at the door. "Came by here yesterday around eleven. Found a closed sign on the door."

Stacey's mouth dropped open. Frank had obviously hit on something she didn't want to talk about. What could she have been up to yesterday morning?

"I had a little problem to deal with." She schooled her features then resumed checking out his books. "Couldn't seem to stay out of the bathroom. By noon, I was fine. You know how that goes."

Frank snickered. "Don't I ever. Wait till you get old. I ain't had a regular—"

"That's fine then, Mr. Becker." She shoved a stack of books into his hands, preempting additional description of his irregular habits.

Maybe she was embarrassed. I didn't buy her explanation about her supposed health problem and made a mental note to put her on my follow-up list. I turned back to Lisa. "I guess you're right. Stacey is being nice to Frank. I still think it'd be better if you asked for the newspapers. Make sure she gives us the—"

"I know what we need," Lisa interrupted and set off, mumbling, "I could tell by your tone that you said I was right just to make me happy. I don't know why I do these things for you when you're not up front with me."

Shaking her head, my drooping daisy approached the counter. Frank greeted her with a grumbled hello. I hoped his demeanor wouldn't force her to wilt further before we could retrieve the information we needed and get her home for a nap.

Frank spotted me and growled like a rabid dog. Turning to Stacey and Lisa, I did my best to ignore him. Lisa's usual gentleness overcame the funk she'd embraced for the last hour and as they chatted, Stacey warmly responded. Maybe I was the problem here. Maybe. . .but I didn't want to think about that right now.

I leaned on the juvenile mysteries shelf. The bold titles on colorful spines piqued my interest. I looked down the aisle at *The Secret of the Old Clock*, the first Nancy Drew I'd read, right in this room. I'd spent countless hours nestled in a monster beanbag chair under the window, with the tall pine tree outside shading my eyes. I devoured Nancy Drew novels until my mom closed up and dragged me out the door.

I went over to the books and longed for the days when my mom used to make everything okay. I was sure she could even handle murder accusations. If she were still alive, what would she do? Actually, I didn't really need to wonder. She would tell me to speak my mind, not run and hide. To quietly find the killer and clear my name. Exactly what I was doing, albeit not quietly.

"She's getting the papers," Lisa said as she approached, banishing my thoughts to the recesses of my mind where they belonged. "See how easy that was?"

"Point taken." Still longing for the feeling of peace I used to find in this room, I ran a finger over the spine of *The Hidden Staircase*.

"You weren't even watching, were you?" She tapped my finger. "Nancy Drew makes an appearance and you veg out. Nothing changes."

"Thanks for the idea." I pulled the first four titles off the shelf. "If I read these at bedtime, maybe I'll forget all about Adam and my problem and get some sleep."

"Argh," she grumbled.

Books in hand, I went to the circulation desk and waited for Stacey to return. Lisa moseyed behind, stopping at the kids' section. She loved to read to the twins. I fished my library card out of my wallet and tapped it against the aged laminated counter, working up a good rhythm as I scanned the room.

Hold up. A white sweater hung on a chair behind Stacey's desk. I tamped down my eagerness and strolled over to look. As I reached out to check for stains, Stacey lumbered from the back room, the muscles in her fit arms bulging from the weight of two file boxes.

I let my hand fall and followed her to the checkout station.

She dropped the boxes on the counter and looked at me. "Can I help you?"

Care to tell me if you killed Bud while wearing that white sweater? Better not to say anything until I came up with a motive. I slid the books and my card across the counter then reached for the boxes.

"What are you doing?" she snapped. "Those are for another customer."

"I know. Lisa Winkle. We're together. Thank you for getting them for us."

"I didn't get them for *you*. I got them for Lisa." Her voice skated higher with each word.

"Hey, Lisa," I turned and called out in a library whisper-shout, "can you come over here a minute?"

"Shhh, you're disturbing our patrons." Stacey's tone reminded me of my eighth-grade math teacher. I piped down like I did in math class, where I fought to comprehend why letters were ever introduced into a subject where numbers should rule.

Stacey busied herself checking out my Nancy Drews, and I thumped my fingers on the counter to keep from speaking. I was thankful when Lisa slipped a tall picture book onto the shelf then joined me at the counter. I rolled my eyes over the two-faced librarian and nudged Lisa toward the desk.

She furrowed her brow at me then smiled at Stacey and tugged the boxes off the counter. "Stacey, thanks for getting these so fast. I can always count on you to be helpful."

Stacey sent a starlet smile back at Lisa. I'd never seen this side of the woman—a side that would melt most men's hearts on the spot. Not at all librarianish, if you asked me.

"You're welcome," she said with genuine warmth coloring her voice. "I can't wait to see those precious girls again." She handed the books to me and her smile faded. "Please be sure you keep the newspapers in order. I don't have the time or the workforce to clean up after you."

Lisa wound through displays of gardening and canning books and the reference section until she reached the back corner. I followed close behind, stopping to admire one of my favorite gardening books.

"You see?" I said when I caught up to her. "That woman is out to get me."

Lisa shrugged. "She was kind of mean to you. You must have done something to her."

I chose not to argue. I would never win with Lisa in this mood. She set the boxes on a table in front of the rack of current newspapers and magazines.

"Did you see what was on her chair?" I asked.

"No. Should I have?"

"A white sweater."

Lisa shook her head. "You are so far off base. Why on earth

would Stacey want to kill Bud?"

"I don't know yet, but he was her boss."

"Oooh, that's a reason for murder if I ever heard one." She grabbed the top box and moved to a table by the magazines.

I wanted to point out that Stacey had closed the library around the time Bud was killed, but I didn't think I'd get very far. I kept quiet and took the other box. "Let me know if you find anything." I sat with my back to her to keep from making faces over her comments.

As we worked, the room remained quiet. Library quiet. If I hadn't heard the occasional pages of the newspaper rustling, I might have peeked at Lisa to see if she kept her eyes open. Knowing the sooner I finished this task the sooner I could go to lunch with Adam, and as a bonus find the killer, I plowed through the papers. I found council minutes, lots of them, but nothing in the reports raised a red flag. I neared the bottom of my box and the bottom of my hope in locating a clue. Lisa came over and slapped the current week's edition of the *Serendipity Times* in front of me.

Disappointed, I sighed and looked up. "Seriously, Lisa. Why can't you help me here? I thought you were going to look in the old files, not read today's paper."

"I did both. I didn't find anything in the box, but you're going to want to read this." She stabbed her finger at the headline on page one.

IDA CARLSON DIES, SUICIDE OR ACCIDENT?

I picked up the paper. "Ida Carlson. Why do I know that name? Ida Carlson? Wait, oh yeah! Velma told me she was one of the people involved in this mess."

"Good job, Sherlock." Lisa rolled her eyes and sat next to me. "She owned a house by the factory. I remember her fighting for some sort of reprieve from the factory's noise. They refused, and she seemed to give up. No one ever really saw her much after that."

I scanned the story. Six months ago, Ida's daughter, Nancy Kimble, had her mother declared insane and moved her from Serendipity to Hillsboro, where Nancy could care for her. Last week, Nancy found her mother on the floor of her bedroom with empty pill bottles scattered across the room. No one could prove it wasn't an accidental overdose, but Nancy believed her mother killed herself. She went on to say, if her mother's death was intentional, Bud Picklemann's decision to bring the factory to town was the driving force behind her insanity and the desire to end her life.

I finished the story and looked up at Lisa, satisfaction swelling my chest. "Finally, a concrete motive. Nancy Kimble had every reason to want Bud dead. Now all I need to do is prove it."

CHAPTER TEN

"And now, enjoy the best of Through the Garden Gate *with your beloved host, Paige Turner."*

"Hi, Paige, this is Chirpy in Salem. My wife and I love to listen to birds singing outside our windows and found your advice about attracting humming-birds very interesting."

"Oh, yes, Chirpy, I bet you've added red flowers to your garden, and you've planted all sorts of nectar rich flowers, since it is really the sweet nectar that brings the hummingbirds into the garden."

"Right, we did all of that, and we even put out fresh drinking and bathing water every day."

"Well, it certainly sounds like you're doing everything right. So what is your problem? No hummingbirds yet?"

"You nailed it. We're so disappointed. After your show, we couldn't wait for those birds to sit in our trees and hum away in harmony to our singing friends. But we're spending all of our time chasing away stupid little birds that just flutter around, taking up the place where the birds that hum would

be. What can we do?"

Seated across a small two-person table from Adam, I nearly salivated as the Bakery owner, Donna Davis, set a steaming bowl of vegetable soup with homemade biscuits in front of me. She stepped to the other side of the table and watched Adam move his legal pad out of her way. While our food was being prepared, Adam and I had talked about my discoveries, and he jotted down ideas for follow-up.

Donna placed a large oval plate with a Reuben sandwich and seasoned french fries where the pad had been. "Nice meeting you, Adam. Hope we'll still see you around town once Paige's name is cleared." She winked at me then giggled like a schoolgirl and strolled away.

Argh! People around here never minded their own business. We'd been here for twenty minutes, and Donna had found a reason to make four trips to the table already, each time grilling Adam about his background. While Adam and I brainstormed, I'd moved closer to him to keep our conversation private. Or maybe, if I really thought about it, which I didn't want to do, I'd scooted closer so that as his head moved under the fluorescent light, I could better see the shifting change in the color of his eyes.

Like they changed now from cocoa to cinnamon as he chewed the first bite of his sandwich. He swallowed and then groaned with delight. "You were right. This is the best Reuben I've ever had."

I gave up my perusal of his eyes and watched him bite off an extra large chunk. "Donna's sandwiches have been written up in the *Oregonian* a couple of times. On the weekends, tourists stand in line for them."

"I can see why." He took another gigantic chomp and looked

around the restaurant as he chewed. With each movement of his head, his jaw tightened and his brows furrowed. "Is it always like this in here? People staring at you?"

I grimaced and swallowed a bite of buttery biscuit. "It's not usually this bad. People are just curious since I found Bud."

"Paige! Paige, oh. . .my. . .gosh!" Both our heads swiveled in the direction of the shrill female voice.

From the doorway, Uma Heffner waved sparkly orange fingernails then tottered toward our table on three-inch metallic slides. Her beehive looked skyscraper high from my angle. She wore a formfitting knit top in bright chartreuse and even more fitted neon orange capris. Our fellow diners' gazes followed her *clip-clop* path across the room.

"This must be just devastating to you." She slid out a chair and slowly lowered herself, making eye contact with Adam by batting her obviously false lashes. Just when I expected her to latch onto him permanently, she swiveled and clasped my hand.

Fearing her talons, I pulled back. "Uma," I said, "why don't you sit down?"

"What? I am sitting." Her face crinkled. "Oh, you." She swatted those nails at me again. "I get it, you're making a joke. I'm glad you can still joke with all this hanging over your head. Despite what everyone in town is saying, I so know you didn't kill Bud." She peered around the room. "Did you hear about Rachel?"

I shot a quick glance at Adam. He was listening, albeit happily chewing at the same time. I shook my head. "What about her?"

Uma slid closer. "She didn't cry or even get upset when Mitch told her Bud had been killed."

"I didn't hear about that."

Uma laid a hand on her ample chest. "Not surprising. You know how people are afraid of her. No one is gonna risk getting caught gossiping about her."

Not me. "I saw Rachel fighting with Charlie. She caught him in the park yesterday right after you let him have it. Think they were arguing about the same thing as you and Charlie?"

"That? Oh no, Rachel isn't involved in that." She looked away as if bored.

I couldn't let her get off without telling me about their argument. "I caught Charlie disagreeing with a lot of people yesterday."

"Really? It was the other way around with us. I probably shouldn't tell you this." This sentence came out of her mouth hundreds of times a day when she gossiped to her customers as she snipped their hair. She scooted her chair so close I could smell the minty gum she chewed. "You know the company that turned the old school into a hotel?"

Renovations on the school were complete before I moved back, and I'd heard nothing odd about the company that bought the building. Based on her whispering, I was about to. "I'm not real familiar with them."

She snapped her gum. "Leever is their name. Anyway, just this month, Bud arranged for them to buy up all the land bordering the highway. You know that stretch out by the River Road where a bunch of us live?"

Bud again?

Adam's cell chimed, interrupting my fixed attention on Uma.

He jerked it from his belt clip and looked at the caller ID. "I have to take this call. Excuse me for a minute." He rose from the table.

I let my gaze follow his long strides away from us, feeling a sense of loss as he went. *Focus, Paige. He'll be right back, and you have a viable clue just waiting to be unearthed.* I turned my gaze back to Uma. "I don't get it. Why would you want to sell your house? Where would you live?"

"That was the beauty of the deal. This company wanted the land, not our houses, for an investment. They would buy us out, and we could stay there rent-free as long as we lived. They would even pay for any upkeep on the houses. Stupid old Charlie was taking his time in deciding. The rest of us were already on board. We'd have our houses, and we didn't have to pay a stitch of rent as long as we lived there." She crossed her arms and slumped back in her chair.

This sounded way too good to be true, and like my parents drilled into my head, when it sounded too good to be true, it usually was. I opened my mouth to tell her that, but she continued.

"Without Bud around to help them out, I don't know what that Leever company will do." As if she were merely dismissing a bad hair day, she glanced around the room. "Look at that darling outfit Stacey is wearing."

I followed her gaze. Stacey stood near the counter with an order ticket in her hand. "You know her very well?"

Uma shook her head. "I do her hair, but she's a quiet one. Keeps to herself."

"Did she know Bud?"

Uma nodded. "Sure, he hired her."

"Ever hear anything about them fighting or arguing?"

"Just the opposite. She worshipped the ground he walked on." Uma studied my face. "What do you know that you're not telling me, Paige Turner?"

I laughed. "Nothing. I'm just covering all my bases, trying to figure out who did Bud in."

She jerked her head at Stacey. "Well, that's one person you don't need to look at."

"You haven't said who you think killed him."

"Lots of people were mad enough to do it. I've been thinking about it, but I can't come up with anyone I think is capable of murder. You know what I mean?" Her gaze drifted off again then locked on Adam winding through the crowded tables.

I forgot all about my questioning of Uma. His stride and squared shoulders spoke of his self-assurance, upping my heart rate. He reached our table, and we shared a smile that sent the room packed with clanging silverware and chattering patrons to the background.

Uma clamped her hand on my arm, jerking me out of la-la land.

Adam sat, and her gaze zeroed in. "You must tell me who this delicious young man is."

Feeling protective, I said, "My attorney, Adam Hayes."

Surprise flashed on her face. "So this isn't a date?"

I blurted out, "No."

"Yes," Adam said at the same time.

"Well, which is it, yes or no?" Uma let her gaze slide back and forth between us as if willing us to answer.

Adam shifted closer to me and laid his hand over mine. "It's a date, all right. Paige is just a little shy, that's all."

Uma's face turned incredulous. I didn't blame her. No one had ever accused me of being the least bit timid.

"Well then," she said, "Paige isn't getting any younger, so I better get out of your way." She stood, smiled wide at Adam, and twirled her finger in a circular motion. "If this little thing between you two doesn't work out, you can find me at the Crazy Curl down the street."

When she was out of earshot, I pulled back my hand and groaned. "Why'd you tell her we were on a date? She'll blab it all over town."

"Didn't you see the way she looked at me? I've never seen a barracuda close up like that." He gave an exaggerated shiver. "I need you to protect me."

That gave me warm fuzzies. "Fine, but when Lisa hears about this and grills me, I'll send her to you."

"No problem. Lisa will be a lot easier to handle than that woman." He shoved his empty plate aside. "She have anything of importance to say?"

I explained about Leever. "Does that sound suspicious to you?"

He shook his head. "Land is a good investment. Maybe this company has plans to build in the future and doesn't want to wait with the way land prices are skyrocketing in the valley. Anyway, doesn't sound like it's related to Picklemann's murder."

"What Uma said about Rachel's reaction to Bud's murder could be."

He nodded. "Sounds odd, but she could very well have been in shock. Wouldn't be the first person who reacted to bad news that way."

"I'm not gonna let it drop that easily."

"You might have to. As a possible suspect in her husband's murder, it's not like you can go talk to her."

"I'll figure something out."

The man next to me scraped his chair back, slamming it into my leg. He stood then strode away without apologizing. I would have to follow a similar technique with Rachel if I got to talk to her. I'd hit her with a quick question and run if she reacted negatively.

Adam pulled his legal pad closer. "I need to hit the road. Before I do, I'd like to go through our list and set a timetable for completion. What are you planning to do first?"

Cry because you're leaving me? "The best suspect is Nancy

Kimble. I'll go to Hillsboro this afternoon and see what she knows."

He peered at me, concern tainting those marvelous eyes. "I really wish you would wait and let me do that. If Nancy did have something to do with Picklemann's death, you might be in danger."

"I wish I could wait, too." Trying to blow off my unease at confronting a potential murderer, I laughed. "But you can't fit it in your schedule for two days, and she's our best lead right now. Besides, Lisa agreed to go with me. We'll be fine."

"Did she tell Perry she was going?"

To avoid answering, I stuffed my mouth with the last piece of biscuit.

"I'll take that as a no." He tapped his pen on the paper and slid his chair back. "If I talk to Perry, I'll have to tell him."

"Fine," I said. "I'm still going."

"At least promise me you'll be careful."

That's what I like. A lawyer who cares. Even better, a cute lawyer who cares. "I will. So what else is on your list?"

He checked his pad. "Guess we can cross Uma off the list." He made a forceful slash across the page. "Next is talking to Charlie. When do you think you can do that?"

"If I have time when I get back from Hillsboro, I'll do it then. If not, it'll have to wait until morning."

"That leaves Stacey. Although I think you're grasping at straws with the whole sweater thing."

"You might be right, but I'm taking no chances. I'll visit Charlie first, and if I strike out, then I'll move on to Stacey and Rachel."

"As your attorney, I recommend you think twice about talking to Rachel. Seems like all it'll do is backfire on you."

I shrugged. He had a point, but I was desperate.

He took a long drink of his iced tea. "Okay, should we get going?" He wiped his mouth, a mouth comprised of full, kissable lips, and dropped the napkin on the table.

"Fine," I said, still watching his lips and imagining what it would be like to be on a real date with him.

He cleared his throat. His eyes were clearly assessing something. He sat back as if he wanted me to say something. I couldn't. I mean, did I confess to liking the way his eyes changed colors or the way his scar winked? Did I tell him that I imagined us on a real date, not sitting in a crowded restaurant discussing my part in a murder? Or would that scare him away? Send him running back to McMinnville? Was I even interested in him, or was I merely looking for a diversion to the stress of the situation?

"Look," he said and ran a hand around the back of his neck as if suddenly stressed. "You hired me to represent your best interests. I'm not so sure I can do that when you look at me that way." Before I said something I'd regret, I sucked in a deep breath.

He quickly sat forward and held up his hands. "Don't misunderstand, Paige. I want to get to know you as a person, not a client. I just think we need to wait until after all of this is over before we pursue any of that."

"Just for the record, so I won't do it again." I paused and smiled. "How exactly was I looking at you?"

He pointed to one of the tables. "The same way that lady is looking at her cake."

Well of course, she was nearly drooling. The cake mounded high on her plate was a deep chocolate with a glossy frosting like Adam's eyes. The yummy rich frosting oozed down the sides of the huge hunk of cake and dripped over the edge of the plate.

I settled back on my chair. I had no idea how this lawyer/client thing was going to work. I could no more hide my interest in Adam than I could in a mouth-watering dessert. It wasn't my fault. God gave Adam the chocolate eyes. I simply admired them.

CHAPTER ✂✂ ELEVEN

"And now, enjoy the best of Through the Garden Gate *with your beloved host, Paige Turner."*

"A very economical way to expand your garden is to receive plants from another gardener. Walk around your neighborhood, and if you see perennials that you simply are dying to include in your garden, don't hesitate to ring the doorbell. Usually a moderate amount of hinting will encourage the gardener to offer you a start of the plant."

"Hi, Paige, this is Bruised calling. I know you mean well when you give that advice, but I've tried it, and I have to say, it didn't work out so well."

"I'm sorry, Bruised. Could you elaborate?"

"Well, my neighbor said she needed to divide her asters and if I would do the work I could have half of them. Wanting to be very careful and not take more of her plant than I should, I brought my ruler and cut exactly eighteen inches off the tops, took my part home, and planted them. Nothing has come up yet, and my neighbor is furious. She's acting like I mutilated her garden."

Lisa shifted in the passenger seat of my dusty truck. She'd napped while I lunched with Adam, and her mood had transitioned from grumpy to bearable. Still, she squirmed on the seat like her twins and couldn't settle down. She sighed, unearthed a tissue from her mom bag, then wiped the dashboard. "Are you sure this is a good idea?"

"One tissue probably won't do the trick, but go ahead, my truck could use some cleaning." I laughed and made a left turn off highly traveled Baseline onto quiet and residential Seventh Avenue.

She wadded up the tissue and tossed it at me. "You know what I mean. Maybe we should have waited until Perry or Adam could come with us."

"Relax, we'll be fine. I called Nancy before I picked you up to see if she'd meet with me. She sounded more than willing to help me out."

Lisa retrieved the tissue that had ricocheted from my shoulder and landed on her muddy floor mat. "What if she tries something? She might be the killer."

"That's why I brought you. Think about it, Lisa. Bud's murder was clearly a crime of passion. No one could predict he'd be at the park or that my shovels would be there. So if Nancy killed Bud, she didn't have a plan for doing it, and she won't have a plan for doing the same thing to us." At Lisa's open-mouthed stare, I tipped my head toward Tuality Hospital. "Relax. We're next to the hospital. If she did hurt us, it wouldn't take long for an ambulance to arrive."

"That's your logic? I'm telling you, if Nancy killed once, she'll kill again." Lisa crossed her arms and slumped toward the window muttering, "I don't know why I let you get me into these things."

My little daisy wasn't as cranky as she had been before, but she still pouted like a professional. I glanced at her body, rigid and snugged to the door. Years of our friendship told me this body language meant only one thing. Leave her alone. She was sulking. Not that she often sulked. When she was worried, this attitude came out. So once again, I forgave her odd behavior and concentrated on navigating down the narrow road.

Nancy lived near the quaint downtown area of Hillsboro, a western suburb of Portland. The sides of the street were dotted with trees that had recently dropped a carpet of pink, fuchsia, and red blossoms onto the healthy grass in the median. Behind the trees, one-story houses of an older vintage huddled close together. Some had been remodeled and were home to local businesses. Many remained as dwellings. Like my target address coming up on the right. The pristine white bungalow with the red SUV sitting in the driveway had been lovingly restored and maintained.

I parked behind the car and pulled out my keys. Lisa kept her statuelike pose. I poked her to see if she was sleeping. "Please don't make me go in alone."

She clutched the handle and shoved her shoulder against the door. "Fine, I'll go with you, but if she doesn't kill you, I might."

I exited and marched, Lisa trudged, up a short sidewalk lined with perennials at about the same stage as my gardens. These beds were well planned and carefully tended. Either Nancy had a fantastic gardener or a green thumb. I opened my mouth to mention this to Lisa but clamped down on my lip instead. The logical conclusion from this observation was that Nancy knew how to handle a shovel, and I didn't want to scare Lisa more. I knocked on the leaded glass door. Lisa shifted back and forth as if she might make a run for it.

"You need to settle down, or you're gonna spook Nancy," I said and bent my head to protect my face from the light drizzle now falling.

The door creaked open. A women I pegged at fifty stared down on us with harsh eyes. Long ebony hair streaked with gray hung over her shoulder. Her round face was devoid of makeup as was common in the Northwest, and her mouth, as she studied us, puckered into a scowl.

I assumed this was our subject, Nancy Kimble. Nervously, I rushed ahead. "Hi, Nancy. I'm Paige Turner, and this is my friend Lisa Winkle. Thanks for seeing us on such short notice."

She didn't move. Was she going to refuse to let us in? Not if I could help it. Searching for an icebreaker, I looked at her gardens. That's it. Compliment her. No gardener could resist praise for their hard work.

I poked my index finger toward the nearest bed. "Man, you have one talented gardener. Looks like that bed'll be a stunner once the weather warms up."

Nancy's brow arched ever so slightly. "I'm the only gardener around here."

As she took the bait and seemed to savor it, I smiled. "No gardener, huh? I'm a professional landscaper and take it from me, you garden like a pro."

Nancy's face cracked in a minuscule smile that widened ever so slowly. "So how can I help you?"

"Like I mentioned on the phone, Bud Picklemann was killed, and I found his body. The police think I did it. I have to clear my name and hoped you'd be able to help me."

"Not sure what I can do," she stepped back, "but come on in. No sense us all standing out here in the rain." She pushed the door closed and gave us another smile. "Thought we were gonna have a nice day so I was putting out my dahlias. You'd think I would've lived here long enough to know it's still too early in the year for the rain to quit."

Pleased at her sudden chatty behavior, I followed her through a short hallway that led to a large family room with coved ceilings and french doors overlooking a backyard. Lisa clomped behind, halting at the camelback sofa while I went straight to the doors to admire the garden.

Nancy's small lot was typical of the area and backed up to another home. Garden tools rested neatly against a shed under an overhang to keep them dry. As soon as the rain abated, if she was like any other gardening buff, she'd return to her dahlias. I was sorely tempted to talk with her about her choice and layout of bulbs, but my questions held priority.

I strolled toward Nancy standing in front of the sofa and gazing down on Lisa like she was a slug in her garden. At the sound of my footfalls, she pivoted and watched me cross the room. "Can I get you anything to drink?" she asked in a pleasant enough tone but with a scowling face that said please don't ask.

"Not for me," I said and sat on the red velvet sofa next to Lisa.

"Nothing for me." Lisa's gaze darted around as she answered, then she clasped her hands so tightly they turned white.

Nancy chose a flowered chair in the corner and lowered her body onto the seat. She sat back as if at ease but returned her focus on Lisa's fidgeting and began tapping her fingertips on the rolled arm of the chair. If I didn't draw her attention away from Lisa, Nancy would know we suspected her of killing Bud and clam up.

I donned a superficially pleasant tone and said, "Thank you for your kind hospitality, but we don't want to take up too much of your time."

"So you're interested in hearing about that awful Bud Picklemann." She lurched forward as if even saying Bud's name was painful. "Can't say as I'm sorry he was killed. I'm only sorry I didn't have the courage to do it myself."

Lisa gasped and leaned back as if trying to get away from Nancy. I was thankful I sat between Lisa and the door so she couldn't make a run for it. I slid forward and concentrated on making my muscles relax and my face and body open and sympathetic. "Would you tell us what Bud did to make you feel that way?"

Nancy calmed a bit and settled against the overstuffed cushions. "A few years ago our son got involved with a gang in LA. To get him away from their influence we moved here. Mother didn't want to live near a big city, so we hunted for a town that might make her feel at home, but still be close enough for visits. One weekend we found Serendipity. Mother bought a cute house on the edge of town. Very private. A few neighbors to her right, but miles of empty fields behind. We settled in here, she settled in there. Life was good until Picklemann got greedy and brought in that factory."

She planted her hands on the arms of the chair and clutched the edges. She took several deep breaths, letting the air hiss out through puckered lips. Her gaze wandered the room as if searching for a way out. Was it too painful for her to tell her story? Was she going to change her mind? Throw Lisa and me out?

I had to keep her going. "I can see how hard this is for you. I would really appreciate it if you could go on."

She stood and went to the french doors. Her back to us, she continued, "Picklemann said the factory execs promised to erect a sound wall behind the houses and place the compressors and parking areas on the north side of the lot, away from the homeowners." She spun around, her eyes ablaze with hatred. "They lied. All of them. They put several large compressors that hummed nonstop right outside Mother's bedroom window. If that wasn't enough, the factory was lit up like a Christmas tree all night every night, keeping Mother's house lit as well. She couldn't sleep, couldn't concentrate. Wasn't long before she started to lose it. We begged her to come live with us, but she was stubborn. Said she wouldn't let that man run her out of her own home." Breathing hard, Nancy returned to her chair and dropped onto it as if too weary to go on.

I waited for her breathing to even out before I said, "You don't strike me as the kind of person who would sit back and accept this kind of treatment."

"You're right, I didn't. I kept after it. That's when I found out." Her lips turned up in a sneer. "It was Picklemann's land, you know."

"What was his land?" I asked.

"Where the factory sits. That's why the factory was built in that location, even though there were far more suitable places."

"I didn't know that," Lisa said. "No one in town did. I'm sure of it. We would have done something about it if we had known."

I smiled at Lisa in thanks for her courage to speak up when she was scared then turned back to Nancy. "If you knew this, why didn't you try to stop the construction?"

"I was too late. No one, including me, found out what Picklemann was doing until after the factory was built. It took me that long to discover that Picklemann hid his ownership in a corporation named Fulcrum."

Fulcrum? I knew that name from somewhere. Was it today at the library? The newspapers? Maybe this was Bud's secret that

Charlie threatened to reveal in the park. "Okay, so the factory was built, but you could still have told about Bud's role in all of this."

"Believe you me, I did." She bounced her knee, and her foot slapped against the wood floor in a rapid beat. "By the time I got the city council to listen to me, the factory was open and folks were happy about the new jobs in town. The only people really hurt by it had moved away. Still, I brought it up at a council meeting. The chairman took me aside and said if I went public with this information, I'd regret it. The man was so convincing, I figured he'd follow through on the threat."

This was getting very interesting. "Do you remember the chairman's name and when this meeting took place?"

"Remember, hah! How could I forget? His name was Gus Reinke and the meeting was in December of 2000. Worst Christmas we ever had."

I made a mental note to check the council minutes again, this time to confirm the chairman's name and to see if there was any mention of this meeting. "Any idea how much Bud made on the deal?"

"About a quarter million. That jerk sold out my mother for a quarter million bucks." Disgust at a level I'd never known poured from her. Disgust that said she could have easily killed Bud.

Lisa reached out and clutched my leg. I didn't want to stop the interrogation to comfort her, so I ignored the fingers bruising my flesh and went on. "I'd want to go after him, if it was me."

"Hah! You have no idea. Picklemann as good as killed my mother." She took deep breaths and fixed her gaze on me for a disquieting moment. "S'pose that was some sort of code to ask if I killed him." She shrugged, as if Bud losing his life was of no consequence to her. "Like I said, I didn't, but I'd be happy to shake the hand of the person who did."

I wanted to believe her, but this was too important to give in so easily. I needed to keep pushing. "You have to admit it's an awfully big coincidence that he was killed right after your mother died."

"Yes, and that's all it is. You're barking up the wrong tree if you think it was me. I was at work the day he died. My boss can confirm that."

Even though she had great motive and anger, her offer of an alibi did sway me toward believing in her innocence. Still, we were talking about murder here. I had to be sure. "So you wouldn't mind writing down your boss's name and phone number for me, then?"

"You've got some nerve, you know that?" She stared at me for a few seconds. "I agree to help you out, then you accuse me of doing him in."

Oops, pushed too hard. "I'm sorry. Really, I am. I'm just desperate to clear my name." I tried to telegraph my desperation in my gaze.

She sighed and grabbed a notepad and pen off the table. "I don't like your tactics, but I can understand your position." She scribbled on the pad then ripped off the page. "You're wasting your time, but here's his name and number."

"Thank you. You don't know how much I appreciate this." I took the paper and tried to relax and regain her trust. "Do you think Bud's murder had something to do with the money from the factory deal?"

"Possible, I suppose." She glanced past us, then her eyes cleared as if coming to some resolution. "That's all I have to say to you ladies." She tipped her head toward the french doors and stood. "As you can see, the sun is out. I need to get back to my garden."

The sun had indeed peeked out, sending a warm ray dancing

across the patterned area rug. A ray that seemed to force the bitter Nancy out of the room with its cheery glow. I wanted to keep pumping her for information, but the set of her face before she stood confirmed the futility of such a plan.

Lisa and I rose then followed Nancy down the hall. Lisa stayed close to me like a fearful child. I stuffed the paper in my pocket and dug my business card from the other.

Nancy yanked open the door. "Good day, ladies."

I handed her my card. "You might know something else that is important in solving this murder. If you think of anything, will you call me?"

Eyes cold again, she stepped aside so we could exit. "I'm done thinking about this. As far as I'm concerned, the killer did us all a favor and deserves to be free." She flicked the card my way and slammed the door.

I turned to Lisa. "That went pretty well."

"At least we're alive." She sighed then gave a nervous giggle. "Do you believe her?"

"Enough to look through the papers again." I clicked the remote lock for my truck. "I'm sure I saw Fulcrum listed in the meeting minutes, but I don't remember reading anything about Nancy coming to a meeting. Which means a trip back to the library." I checked my watch. "If we hurry we can still get there before they close."

"There's no 'we' here, Kemo Sabe," Lisa said as she trotted to keep up with my longer strides. "I need to go home to my kids. You'll have to settle for being the Lone Ranger."

Hmm, the Lone Ranger. Not a bad thing to be, I guess. The Lone Ranger righted every wrong he set out to fix. He had a fabulous horse, and with my dark coloring, I did look good in white.

I climbed into my truck and fired up the engine.

Yes, Tonto by my side or not, I'd keep going. *"Hi-ho, Silver, and away."*

CHAPTER ▮▮ ▮▮▮ TWELVE

"And now, enjoy the best of Through the Garden Gate *with your beloved host, Paige Turner."*

"Paige, this is Fit To Be Tied. Could you explain again about espaliering trees?"

"Thanks for calling, Fit To Be Tied. This is a perfect topic to touch on again for those city dwellers out there with ugly fences to hide. Now before you turn off the radio over a strange term like espalier, in the garden, it simply means to train a tree to grow flat on a trellis or structure that you provide."

"Yeah, Paige I got all that part. I want to know how to do the actual training. I've tried everything I can think of. And before you think I'm a novice at this, I'm not. I train dogs for a living, but my tree just doesn't seem to listen like the dogs do."

After dropping Lisa at her mother's to pick up the twins, I drove into town. The library had closed by the time I arrived, so I headed to The Garden Gate. I'd taken advantage of Hazel's kindness and loyalty, and the least I could do was close up shop. I pulled the truck under the front portico that covered the old fueling area. I'd left the antique red and yellow pumps out front and hung huge baskets of annuals from the posts above. My plan was purely decorative. Turned out, I sold more hanging baskets from this spot than anywhere else in the shop.

Through the windows, I could see Hazel talking to sweet old Emma Gherkin. Emma was dressed in a floral shirtwaist, with thick stockings, white gloves, and old-fashioned shoes that laced up the front. I'd dubbed her a hollyhock—an old-fashioned cottage garden staple that had an unsurpassed nostalgic charm. Mrs. Gherkin always dressed from a bygone era and was as crinkly as a hollyhock flower. Still, she was fun loving and had a gentle spirit that drew people to her. Since I'd moved back to Serendipity she'd tried to convince me to call her Emma, but I couldn't.

"Who's Paige Turner?" Mr. T announced my entrance in his favored *Jeopardy* format.

"Oh, Paige, sweetie." Mrs. Gherkin threw open her arms. "I am so sorry to hear you found Bud Picklemann that way. If he'd only come to our meeting, he might still be alive today."

"Meeting?" I stepped into her embrace for a quick hug. "What meeting?"

Hazel's face was alight with excitement. "Go ahead, Emma. Tell Paige what you told me."

Mrs. Gherkin released me from her gardenia-scented embrace and rested a gloved hand on my arm. "When I heard about Ida— you know she and I used to crochet together until her faculties got confused—I called her daughter, Nancy. Do you know Nancy?"

I nodded and climbed onto a stool next to Hazel. "Just came from her house as a matter of fact."

"Then most likely she told you about the underhanded way Bud hurt poor Ida. The nerve of him hiding his company like that just so he could make a few dollars."

I snorted at the mention of a few dollars. "Nancy didn't say she talked to you about it."

"That's my fault, dear. I asked her not to mention our conversation to anyone. I wanted to work on Bud Picklemann's conscience—if the man had one—and get him to do the right thing by Ida's family."

"This is where it starts getting good," Hazel said, saliva fairly dripping from her mouth.

Emma opened her mouth to speak, but her face was less excited and more weary than Hazel's, as if she'd been tormented by this problem. "On Monday morning, I was going to Bud's office to demand he compensate Ida's family. If he didn't, I would make sure he lost his job. Before I reached his office, I ran into him on Main Street." Usually soft spoken, Mrs. Gherkin's voice blazed like a fire-and-brimstone preacher. "He said I must have misunderstood what happened. He wanted a chance to explain, but he had something to take care of at the moment. So he asked me to meet him at his office later in the morning."

"Bet he was on his way to find you in the park," Hazel blurted out.

Mrs. Gherkin gave a serious nod of her silvery-purple hair. "From what I've heard, I think so, too."

I sat up. "So what happened?"

"I went to the Bakery and had one of Donna's lovely fritters then walked to city hall. Bud never arrived. He might have been dead already." She took a pressed linen hankie from her sleeve and dabbed her eyes. "And there I was, sitting in the vestibule, waiting to take him down a notch."

I patted her bony shoulder. "That's okay, Mrs. Gherkin. You couldn't have known."

She sniffled. "Well, I'm not going to let my compassion for his wife and family sidetrack me from my mission." She dabbed her eyes again. "Are you familiar with Gus Reinke's wife, Winnie?"

I nodded, and Hazel smirked as if she couldn't wait for Mrs. Gherkin to get her story out.

"About ten years ago, Gus gave Winnie five hundred dollars in cash. Out of the blue. He came home for lunch, plopped it on the table, and told her to spend it on anything she wanted. Can you imagine?" She clutched her chest.

I nodded again, though I couldn't imagine a frugal man like Gus giving his wife a quarter much less five hundred dollars. Even if she did work full-time in their hardware store.

"I've never talked to anyone about this as I hate to spread gossip, but Winnie was so shocked, she told anyone who would listen, so I guess it's okay if we discuss it." Mrs. Gherkin paused as if seeking confirmation that she could share the news without gossiping.

I squeezed her arm.

"Well, as if getting that money once wasn't enough to make a body shake with surprise, he's been doing the same thing on the third Monday of every month since then. Every month!"

"That's an interesting story, Mrs. Gherkin, but I can't see how it's related to Bud."

"Go on, Emma. Tell her. Tell her." Hazel hopped from her stool and danced like a child that's waited too long to go to the bathroom, sending Mr. T into a circling tizzy.

"Gus has given Winnie five hundred dollars every third Monday for ten years, but. . .he didn't give her anything this past Monday."

Hazel clasped my arms. "Isn't this great?"

"'Whatchoo talkin' 'bout, Willis?'" Mr. T squawked then flapped his wings and danced a frantic jig.

"And?" I was as confused as Mr. T.

Hazel slapped her palms on the counter. "Bud was killed the Monday Winnie's money dried up. What if Bud was paying Gus to keep quiet about the factory? He could even have been on the way to give Gus his monthly payment."

I bolted upright. "Blackmail. You think Gus took the information Nancy gave him about Fulcrum and was blackmailing Bud over it." I pondered the idea and grew to like it mighty fast. "Oh yeah. This makes sense for sure. Bud knew how the grapevine works around here. If Gus didn't start a rumor, it couldn't spread."

Mrs. Gherkin returned her hand to my arm. "Now we have to figure out how to prove it."

Yes, blackmail, a perfect conclusion, but. . . "There could be a logical explanation. Maybe Gus was sharing the store profits with Winnie. He could've had a bad month so there wasn't any extra cash."

Mrs. Gherkin shook her head. "I highly doubt it. Winnie has been suspicious from the first day Gus gave her the money."

"Then why didn't she ask him about it?"

"My dear, one doesn't ever question one's husband about finances." Mrs. Gherkin clamped her overly embellished lips together and pointed at the door.

The bell chimed, and I spun around. Drat! The town's gossipy hairdresser.

"Uma, what brings you here?" I asked as she swung through the opening with large black sunglasses covering her eyes.

"'Danger, Will Robinson,'" Mr. T screeched.

Uma whipped off the shades, gave Mr. T a quick glare, then tottered toward me. "I had an unfortunate incident at the shop. You know that big plant you sold me last month?"

"Sure, the dracaena," I said with trepidation. "I hope it's working out."

She rolled her eyes and shook her head. "It was, until I accidentally poured hair stripper in the pot instead of water. Now I need a new one."

I wasn't going to ask her how she made such a horrific mistake, and I surely didn't want to sell her another one of my babies so she could strip its very life away. "Maybe you should consider silk plants."

"No, they look fake." She flicked her fingers.

Seriously? Everything about her screamed artificial, but she wouldn't own silk plants? I turned back to Mrs. Gherkin and Hazel. "If you two will excuse me, I need to help Uma find the perfect replacement."

"That's okay." Mrs. Gherkin gave a wave of her wrinkled hand. "I need to stop by the repair shop to pick up my good shoes for Saturday night. I sure hope I can stay awake until the crowning ceremony is over."

I smiled. "Congratulations, by the way. I can't think of a better Pickle Princess than you." I tipped my head toward the first service bay where we kept all the indoor plants. "C'mon, Uma, lets see if we can find something you like."

We rounded the corner together, and Uma halted abruptly in front of a huge dieffenbachia. "Don't you think it's kind of crazy naming that old lady as Pickle Princess just because of her name?"

I didn't want to get into the subject with someone who couldn't understand how much being an honorary princess meant to Mrs. Gherkin. I stood to the side of the plant and gnawed on my lip.

Uma looked up. "Oh, by the way, I heard something this afternoon that might interest you."

"Really, what?" I didn't bother hiding my enthusiasm.

Uma smirked. "I won't name names, but *someone* told me they saw Charlie fighting with Bud in the parking lot after church last Sunday."

"Do you know what they fought about?"

"Bet—I mean, my source said she couldn't hear them. She did say if Rachel and the kids hadn't gone over there, she thought Bud and Charlie might kill each other." Uma stroked a thick waxy leaf. "I think I'll take this one."

My mind wanted to ponder the news about Charlie, but I wouldn't sell an accident-prone woman like Uma a highly poisonous plant. I tugged her gently by the arm and directed her to another display. I spent the next thirty minutes talking to her about the care and feeding of plants and found training Uma far more challenging than training an espaliered plant. In the end, she decided to take another dracaena and try using only water.

Passing an eye-rolling Hazel who had Mr. T on her shoulder, I accompanied Uma to the door. Since it was closing time, Hazel was escorting the nutty bird to his cage in my office, where he slept in the dark and quiet. With Uma finally on her way and the front door locked, I went in search of Hazel. I found her sitting at one of the round tables.

She looked up from a notepad covered with dark scribbles. "I didn't know how long it would take you with the blabbermouth, so I wrote you a note about the day."

I pulled out the chair across from her. This woman was priceless, greater than any amount of money could buy, just like those credit card commercials. She kept the shop going even when I didn't give it a moment's thought. "You know, despite what you said this morning, *I'm* the lucky one in this relationship. You're a real asset to the business, and I'm sorry I haven't been here today."

Hazel blushed and shoved the paper across the table. "Here're the orders I placed. Oh, and the delivery of those containers that were supposed to come today is delayed until tomorrow. Kurt's truck broke down. He said if things work out he should be here by eleven."

"If they get here in the morning, we'll still have enough time to prepare the pots for Pickle Fest." I reviewed the items ordered, penned in big swirly letters. "Our favorite gardening gloves are really catching on, aren't they?"

Hazel snorted. "Could be because we both wear 'em and tell everyone how great they are."

"Point taken. Okay, well, this looks good." I set the note on the table and glanced at a shiny dieffenbachia. "I hope Uma didn't cut Mrs. Gherkin off before she was finished telling her story."

Hazel shook her head. "She got it all out. We just need to figure out what to do with her info. I think I'll confront Gus tomorrow. See what he has to say."

I flashed up my hand. "Wait, no. Not yet. I'm all for moving along in solving this, but Emma's story is hardly enough to accuse Gus of anything."

"I suppose you're right. There has to be a way to find concrete proof." She sat back and tapped her chin with her index finger. "What if Bud had the money to pay Gus when he was killed? The cops would've found it in his pocket. Any way we can ask?"

Perry's source. "I'm pretty sure I can find out."

Her eyes were as sad as a little girl who didn't get any presents on her birthday. "I guess it's a good idea to wait, but man, Paige, I was ready to let him have it."

I laughed at her vehemence. "Tell you what. If I find out Bud had a load of cash on him, I'll let you go after Gus." I stood and stuck out my hand. "Deal?"

"Deal." As we shook, both sets of hands calloused from hard work moved abrasively against the other.

I smiled. "You've had a long day. Why don't you go on home? I'll cash out the register and close up."

"I'll go, but not home. I have to meet with the chief first."

I shivered at the reminder of her visit to Mitch. "I wish I could spare you that."

"I don't mind. I'm glad to do every little bit I can to help." She slung her bag onto her shoulder. "I'll tell you all about it tomorrow."

Thinking maybe Hazel was my silver bullet sent to replace Tonto who abandoned me, I walked her to the front door. I waited until she climbed into her beat-up Jeep, then I turned the lock. Smiling, I went to the register. This day had provided me with a plethora of clues. Now all I had to do was connect the dots, and I'd soon know the killer's identity.

CHAPTER ♦♦♦ THIRTEEN

*"And now, enjoy the best of Through the Garden
Gate with your beloved host, Paige Turner."*

*"Hi, Paige, I got so excited after your show about
the challenge of designing garden beds that I put the
plans for three beds on paper that very day."*

*"Congratulations on completing three of them in
one day. Because of all the things one must consider
to create a successful garden bed, things like water,
sunlight, harmony of color, and texture of the foliage,
I often struggle for days to come up with plans for a
simple renovation. Never have I completed three new
beds in one day."*

*"Honestly, Paige, I don't want to sound cocky
here, but there really isn't as much to it as you said.
I even installed the beds the same day. My only
challenge has been hauling the mattresses inside
when it rains so they don't get wet."*

After making a call to Perry to ask him to check into Bud's
cash situation, it didn't take long to close out the register and
deposit the money in my office safe. Since Mr. T needed his rest, I

grabbed a legal pad and my laptop and returned to the classroom area. My stomach rumbled in hunger, but before getting dinner, I wanted to jot down my suspicions about each of my suspects while everything was fresh in my mind.

I slashed two bright red lines down the page. I labeled the left side, NAME, the middle, CLUES, and the right side, MOTIVE. Happy with my start, I sat back to think.

Let's see. Who should I list first? On TV, the wife was always guilty, so I'd start there.

Under NAME, I jotted, Rachel Picklemann. Under CLUES, I wrote "didn't get upset when told about Bud's death," and "was in the park on the morning of Bud's death." Now, motive. I had nothing that pointed to a motive except that she was Bud's wife. I'd never been married, so how should I know if that was a good enough motive or not?

Yes, this is a good start. Who next?

Stacey Darling's clues were her white sweater, closing the library at the time of death. And motive, hmm, she worked for Bud and that was motive enough for anyone.

Gus Reinke—giving money to Winnie every month. Clear motive, blackmail. Or was it? I needed to confirm cash in Bud's pocket to make sure this one was viable.

Nancy Kimble—No real clues but plenty of motive in blaming Bud for her mother's death. Call her boss to confirm alibi.

Charlie Sweeny—white lab coat. SECRET. Caught fighting with Bud, TWICE!

I ran my finger down the list. Lots of possibilities. Nancy had the strongest motive, and yet, I didn't think she did it. I did have a strong feeling she was right about the murder being connected to Fulcrum in some way. I needed to know more about Fulcrum to be sure.

I flipped up the top of my computer and clicked open an Internet page. With such a common name, the search engine returned over five million hits. I added the city and state to my search criteria, and my list barely topped five hundred. As I worked down the links, I fought to keep my eyes open. I'd slept little the night before and the excitement and tension of the day was taking a toll.

My cell rang, and I nearly bolted from the chair.

"Hello," I said, so flustered I didn't check caller ID.

"Did I wake you?" Adam's low voice hummed through the phone and brought me the last few steps to awake and alert. On the way back from Hillsboro, I'd left a message about Nancy, and he was likely calling to talk about that.

"Hi. . .no. . .I was just doing some research on the Internet. Looking for Bud's supposed company, Fulcrum. I didn't sleep much last night." As if on cue, I yawned. "I think the computer screen was hypnotizing me."

"Hypnotized, huh? In case that makes you open to suggestions . . .have dinner with Adam, have dinner with Adam, have dinner with Adam."

His imitation of a hypnotic voice could use some work. Still, I nearly succumbed to the temptation of seeing him. Seeing him? Maybe he was hinting at a date. He didn't mention wanting to have dinner to talk about Nancy. The thought of spending time with him again was almost too much to bear, but I had to work on this murder, and I was beat.

Wanting to pinch myself for my stupidity, I said, "That sounds really good, but honestly, I'm too tired to drive all that way."

"No problem. I brought dinner to you."

"Say what?"

He laughed. "Come outside. I'm here with my favorite Chinese spread."

Laughing, I headed up front and spotted him through the glass door. He jiggled a large plastic bag with one hand and snuggled his leather binder under the other arm. I hung up and stowed my cell. My first reaction was to race to the back and clean up, but then he'd know I primped for him, and that wouldn't do for our *business only* relationship.

I let him in and stepped back as the tangy scent of Chinese food overtook me. "How'd you know I'd be here?"

"Your message."

"But you didn't know I hadn't eaten."

He laughed and pushed past me. "No, but I was hungry. I figured I might as well bring enough for you."

Great, this wasn't a dinner date. It wasn't really even dinner. The man was hungry and thought he could multitask. Still, the savory aroma set my mouth to watering. I tamped down my petulance and retrieved disposable plates and forks from the wall cabinet as he set the bag on a table and pulled out container after container.

I laughed. "You must think I eat like a horse or something."

He grinned. "Didn't know what you liked, so I brought a variety."

I had to admit he was kind and considerate, even if this was all in the name of work. "So what do you think about Nancy's news?"

He peered at me. "You might be on to something. I can't be sure until we dig a little deeper." He took a plate and handed it to me. "That's one of the reasons I came over. It might be time to rethink hiring a private investigator."

I scooped out a chicken and mushroom dish with spices that tingled my eyes. "We've been all over that. I can't afford more expenses right now."

"What if I didn't charge you?"

I looked into his earnest eyes. "I can't let you do that. You're already spending a lot of time on this, and you deserve to be paid."

"I know. . ." As if afraid to say what he was thinking, he alternated looking at me and scooping food onto his plate. When the plate was mounded with colorful dishes, he set it down, fixed his hands on the back of a chair, and looked at them. "I know we agreed this is supposed to be a job, but I have to admit that I've never driven an hour to deliver food to my other clients." He slowly raised his head and studied my reaction.

I liked that he hinted at a personal relationship, and hoping he'd continue along those lines, I gave him a reassuring smile before I finished filling my own plate.

He cleared his throat and continued, "We're sure to talk about the case during dinner. I can't charge you for that time. If our short history repeats itself, we'll get sidetracked. . .often. I won't know when to cut off my billable hours. If I do this for free, I don't have to waste any time calculating what part of our sessions are work related."

"I'm going to pay you." I took my now laden plate and sat where I could keep my eyes fixed on him. "It's either that or I find another lawyer."

He stared back.

My eyes said, "Don't look at me that way."

His said, "Don't be so touchy."

Touchy? Touchy? I was not touchy. Well, maybe just a little.

He finally shook his head and took the chair next to me. "This is all about losing control, isn't it? You think if you pay me, you're in charge and can dictate the outcome. Honestly, Paige, whether you pay me or not, you have little to no control over what's happening here."

His words were as right as his eyes, convicting me. But no way would I admit it. "So, you want me to find another lawyer? Because I'm paying you. End of story."

I wanted to take away the sadness, or maybe disappointment, that crept onto his face, but I sat mute and watched.

He shook it off and stabbed a fork into his lo mein. "We'll talk about it later. Right now I want to eat before my food gets cold."

I let the subject drop, and we moved on to a superficial "get to know you" conversation that floated through the air like the pungent spices of our meal. We had more in common than I imagined, pointing to a possible future. *If* I lightened up. *If* I gave up some control. *If* I stopped obsessing about everything. He was certainly worth the effort.

I mean, look at him—his eyes turning to dark chocolate as he discussed how he felt closer to God in his practice than he ever did in the big corporate firm. The conviction of purpose flowing through his tone. His face handsome and alive. He had it all. The question was, would I ever be part of that all?

"Don't worry, Paige. Everything is going to work out." He slipped his hand over mine. He must have interpreted my angst about a relationship with him as worry over the murder charge.

No matter. I let his hand lie there, feeling his warmth. With his long fingers completely dwarfing mine, I could almost imagine that he was right, and we would find the killer in time to keep me from going to jail. Almost. Every passing moment ticked closer to my incarceration. Perry said I'd likely have until Friday, three more days, to clear my name. I'd used this one up without any real success. How many more would it take before I found the killer?

"Are you okay?" Adam asked.

"Not really. I have to admit I'm worried about not finding out who killed Bud."

"So take my advice. Hire an investigator."

I shot him a testy glare. "No, and mentioning it again doesn't help my mood."

He stood and picked up the plates. "Fine, let's talk about something we can agree on."

We cleaned up the dinner mess while chatting about the list I'd just completed. My mood improved, and Adam's kindness never abated. When the table was clear and the leftovers neatly packed into a bag for him to take back to McMinnville, he insisted on seeing me home. I left my truck at the shop and rode in his sleek black BMW to the alley behind my apartment. I chose to take the back stairway. It was less prone to busybody interference and right now, I didn't want to share Adam with anyone.

On the landing outside my door, I twisted the key and turned to face him. He'd jumped up another notch on my list when he insisted on being a gentleman and walking me to my apartment. "You really didn't have to come up here with me. I'm a big girl, you know."

He grinned and stepped closer. "My mom taught me to walk a girl right to her door. No dropping her off in the street when I brought her home or sitting outside honking when I picked her up for a date." He slipped strands of hair over my shoulder and leaned close. "She didn't teach me this, though." His head dipped lower, his lips ready to settle over mine. I closed my eyes, waiting . . .waiting. . .huh?

I opened my eyes.

He was peering at me with a mixture of longing and horror. Quickly and surely, he pushed me away. "You're a client. I can't do this. I have to go. Talk to you tomorrow." He scrambled down the steps as if I were a blazing fire chasing after him, mumbling repeatedly, "She's a client, she's a client."

I rushed inside nearly as fast as he'd traveled away. Leaning against the door with my arms wrapped around my middle, I preened over the almost-kiss. If only I weren't his client. I'd have a real kiss to ponder as I hugged my arms like a lovesick teenager. Even when the ringing phone ripped through the quiet, I stayed put, smiling like a fool.

On the fifth ring, the answering machine picked up. "Paige, this is Gus Reinke. Wanted to let you know that the council has decided to cancel your contract. We'll pay the cancellation fee, of course. Give me a call and let me know where you want the maintenance man to store your temporary fence when he cleans up the park."

"Great, they fired me." I let my arms and my dreams fall and trudged toward my bedroom, intent on sinking into my comfy bed and forgetting about my problems with a Nancy Drew book. I had no choice. I had to escape into a book to forget about this situation. I couldn't constantly live with the roller-coaster emotions of the last two days.

I had had enough of that life when I turned ten and my dad died unexpectedly. After an unsettling year of ups and downs, I sat myself down and resolved to keep things under control from that day forward. For the most part, I had.

The craziest thing I'd done since then was to open The Garden Gate. Look where that had gotten me—out on a ledge, ready to plunge into the abyss. No way I'd listen to Adam and let someone else be in charge of this investigation. Controlling my life kept me safe. Let me sleep at night. If that meant Adam moved on after this was all over, so be it. I would, as usual, be in charge of my life, and everything would be fine.

CHAPTER FOURTEEN

"This is Tim Needlemeyer, host of Success Serendipity Style, *inviting you to attend Pickle Fest right here in Serendipity this weekend. You won't want to miss the exciting events we have planned, starting on Friday at eight with our kickoff, an accordion concert by our own Serendipity Squeezers. Be sure to squeeeeeze this event into your schedule. Get it, squeeze? Ah, c'mon, it was funny. Okay, well, be sure to bring the kids on Saturday as we have found a wonderful replacement for Greg. Briny, the world's one and only pickle mascot, will be there to join in all the fun and games."*

"Now we return to the locally acclaimed show, Through the Garden Gate *with host Paige Turner."*

Today was a new day, and I'd adopted a new attitude. I pummeled myself with positive thinking as I dressed this morning and all the way to the radio show, which had for once gone smoothly. No thanks to Lisa, I might add. She was distracted and living in another world.

"We're back in five." Her gloomy tone droned through my

headset. "Only enough time left for this caller. Make it short."

What was going on with her? She sat back and picked at her fingernails, the same distressed expression on her face that she'd worn the entire morning. She didn't appear to be tired, so what was fueling this attitude?

In a break, I'd tried to get her to spill the details of what was bothering her. Instead, she snapped at me, went into her booth, and shut the door with a leave-me-alone thump. Her girls were gaga over Briny, and one would think Tim's announcement that Briny would definitely appear at Pickle Fest would brighten her day. Instead, without bothering to look at me, she signaled the caller was on the line.

Fine. Maybe the caller would be more enthusiastic. "Go ahead, you're on the air."

"Is this that *Through the Garden Gate* show?" The deep and angry male voice boomed into my headset.

"Yes it is, caller, and you're talking live with Paige Turner, the host."

"Well, Miss Paige Turner, I've got a bone to pick with you."

What now? I held my hands palms up and quickly cut my eyes toward Lisa, hoping she might hold up the board explaining the caller. She looked so distracted it was amazing the caller even got on the air.

I had to make do without her. "Caller, would you please identify yourself?"

"This is Earl. My wife, I think she goes by the crazy name of Weed Whacker, said you wanted to talk to me."

He was alive. "Oh yes, great, thank you for calling, Earl."

"I don't know what you could want with me. I hate gardening."

"I just wanted to find out if everything is okay at your house.

You know, between the two of you."

A long moment of silence filled the line. "What's it to you?"

Excuse me for wanting to make sure you're alive. "I don't mean to pry, Earl. I like to take a personal interest in my callers, that's all."

"Guess I shouldn't have yelled at you like that, but I'm gettin' sick and tired of my wife yammering on about how wonderful you are. Don't know what you've done to her. Since she discovered your show, all she wants to do is dig in the dirt."

His praise, though roundabout, brought out a big ole smile on my face. "I'm sure you're exaggerating."

"Hah! Shows what you know. If you were in a sinking boat with me and her, she'd probably save you first."

Sounded like I had my first groupie in Weed Whacker. I cut my eyes to Lisa, who was sticking her finger in her mouth and fake gagging. She reminded me of the herbicide threat.

I turned back to the mic. "Thank you for the compliments, Earl. By the way, I was wondering if there were any signs of excess herbicide being sprayed around your place?"

"Herbicide? Nah, my wife said she was gonna start trying that organic way of gardening she heard about on one of your shows. Only thing I smell around here is the new cologne she gave me. If I didn't love the woman so much I wouldn't spray it on every morning when she asks me to. It smells as bad as some of those garden chemicals she used to use."

Cologne that smells like herbicide? Was Weed Whacker really poisoning him?

Lisa knocked on the glass and gave me a double slash across the throat, which meant wrap things up and do so in less than fifteen seconds.

"That's all the time we have for today, folks. Earl, please stay on the line, and for the rest of our listeners, keep your radio on for the *Farm to Market Report* and *Success Serendipity Style*. Until tomorrow, this is Paige Turner, signing off."

I flipped on the *Farm to Market Report* and picked up the phone. "Thanks for waiting, Earl. I'm curious about the brand of your new cologne."

"Don't know. Doesn't have a label. The wife musta gotten it at one o' them outlet stores she's always goin' to. They don't label everything." A short beep traveled over the line. "That's my call waiting. I gotta go."

"Wait, Earl," I said.

Silence.

"Earl, are you still there?"

More silence.

Oh, well. I didn't really think Weed Whacker was poisoning him. I hung up the phone and went straight to Lisa's booth to see if I could uncover the reason behind her mood. "What's up with you? You've been distracted all morning. And don't say nothing, 'cause I know you're worried about something."

Lisa looked up, her eyes vacant. "Have you ever bought anything from the boutique section of Uma's shop?"

All this funk was over clothes? And Uma's clothes no less? This was Lisa, the prim and proper mother, asking about purchasing provocative clothes and thinking I might have already done so. She was so far off base. I rarely bought anything feminine, let alone something from flashy Uma.

I opened my mouth to offer a smart reply, but Lisa's vulnerable expression stopped me cold. She was serious about this. Why, I didn't know, but I had to tread lightly. "Uma's things aren't really my style. Why do you ask?"

She looked at her nails and picked the pinkie with only a spot of pink polish left on it. "No reason, really. I just wondered what you thought of her stuff."

"C'mon, Lisa, you'd never ask something like that without a reason."

"Well, I did, okay?" She jumped to her feet and grabbed her handbag. "No need to grill me about it."

Fearing she might gore me like a bull, I stepped out of her way. "Okay, okay. I just thought with the way you've been acting today, there was something you wanted to talk about."

"Well, there isn't." She headed for the door.

If I couldn't find out what was ailing her, maybe I could distract her. I followed her into the hall and changed the subject. "Wasn't that weird what Earl was saying about Weed Whacker saving me over him? He seems awful paranoid."

Lisa shrugged. "Either that or she has a weird stalker kind of thing for you. You know, like big-time celebrities sometimes get."

My eyes flashed open. "Seriously, you think it's that bad?"

She laughed for the first time that morning. "She does call into the show all the time. Then there was that direct call yesterday."

I grabbed Lisa's arm and turned her to face me. "Do you really think she's a stalker?"

Lisa shook her head. "Nah, it's probably nothing to worry about." Her words said no, but her eyes said maybe.

"Are you sure?" I asked.

"As sure as I can be." She turned and headed for the exit.

I traipsed behind with an unease settling over me. A stalker was all I needed right now. What if Weed Whacker did something dumb and jeopardized my show? A show that was already on thin ice with Roger. Wait, Roger. I should check in with him.

I jerked my thumb toward the open doorway on my right. "I'm gonna stop at Roger's office to see if he listened to the show.

I want to make sure he heard there wasn't even a hint of the word murder this morning."

Once again, in whatever world Lisa had been living in since she'd arrived, she waved a hand. "Fine, I'll see you later."

I paused outside Roger's door and waited until Lisa stepped outside, letting the sun drift into the hallway as she exited. Maybe the sun's bright rays would wash out her mood. I wished I could figure her out, but whatever was going on with her would remain as elusive as Bud's killer for now.

I peeked into Roger's office. Drat. It was empty. I wanted to talk with him, but I really needed to get to the shop to create dazzling containers to sell at the Pickle Fest on Friday. That is, if the shipment that went AWOL yesterday arrived. Even with Hazel's help, that project would take the remainder of the day.

Resolved to put the mystery behind for now and head to the shop, I jumped in my truck. Outside the drugstore, I spotted Charlie entering the building, and my resolve vanished as quickly as it had arrived. I glanced at my watch. Ten fifty-five. I could make a quick detour to see Charlie. Even if Kurt was on time, he had to unload the containers.

I swung into an angled parking space in front of the drugstore and jumped from my truck with renewed vigor. This interrogation would end with important information revealed. It just had to. Inside, I found Charlie rounding the pharmacy counter, ready to disappear into the back room.

"Charlie, hey, Charlie," I called and rushed forward. "You got a minute?"

He turned and gave me an impatient stare. "A minute. That's all I've got. What do you need?"

I decided to be as blunt as he usually was and hope for the best. "Remember in the park on Monday when you threatened to reveal Bud's secret? What kind of secret did Bud have?"

Charlie's eyes narrowed. "That's personal information."

Blunt did not work. Time for the sneaky underhanded approach. "Okay," I said and nodded as if I planned to follow his wishes. "I understand you might want to keep that quiet out of respect for Bud, but you were so mad at him. Were you ever able to talk to him again?"

"If you're hinting that I found Picklemann in the park later and killed him, you're sadly mistaken." His eyes bored into me.

I wanted to squirm but forced my shoulders back. "So you didn't get to resolve your problem, then? That's too bad. Maybe if you tell me what you were so angry about I could help."

"Young lady, didn't anyone teach you any manners?"

"What? Did I say something wrong?"

"This is none of your business."

I held up my hands. "Okay, okay, don't get so mad. I'm just trying to help. I suppose you have been able to talk with Rachel since then. I mean the two of you were going at it that day, too. Was it about the same thing?"

He answered me with crossed arms and a glare.

"No, huh? That's too bad. Must be hard carrying that secret around. Stressful, if you ask me. Especially when you're already upset over that Leever company putting pressure on you to sell your land."

"We're done here." The muscles in his jaw worked overtime as he took a step away.

"But Charlie, I'm only trying to help find out who killed Bud."

Charlie spun around, his rubber-soled shoes squeaking on the floor. "I don't think you honestly care about who killed Picklemann. You just want to clear your name. I've already told Chief Lawson everything I think he needs to know. If he decides it's relevant, he'll deal with it."

So much for trying to be Mister Nice Guy, er, Girl. I crossed my arms. "You're just like the rest of the people around here. You think I killed him, don't you?"

"You are the most likely person. New to town, with a big grudge against Picklemann."

I stomped my foot. "I am not new to town. I grew up here. Remember? And I didn't have a grudge against Bud." I stared at Charlie, his closed stance, his hard eyes. "Oh, what's the use? I can't change your mind. You're going to believe whatever you want to believe anyway. Since nobody is willing to entertain the idea that I didn't kill Bud, you all better hope that no one else gets hurt."

His eyebrow jerked up as if trying to reach his receding hairline. "Is that a threat? Are you saying you're going to kill someone else?"

Argh. "What I meant was, if you would help find the real killer, then none of us would be in danger. If you keep focusing on me, the real killer is going to go free, perhaps to kill again."

"That's why we have a police force. Lawson will figure it out. Good day, Paige." Charlie marched into the back room.

Frustrated beyond measure, I spun around and stormed down the pain reliever aisle. If I took every drug I passed, it still wouldn't be enough medicine to eliminate the pain I just talked to. I shot out the front door and headed for The Garden Gate. That did not go well. Not at all. Charlie knew something of value, I was sure of it, and I had no idea how to get it out of him. I wouldn't give up. No siree. I would keep after him like a tick on a dog, irritating him until I got what I wanted.

Just as I'd hoped the sun would improve Lisa's mood, I now wished it would help me. I looked into the clear sky, white clouds inching their way across the vast horizon. The rays warmed my face but did nothing for my attitude. I reached the shop, and the glare simply reminded me to clean the glass in the shop's doors and windows, which were as smudged as my mood. I had to find a real clue. Something that moved me in the right direction.

I yanked open the door and stormed inside.

"You look upset," Hazel said from a stool placed next to Mr. T's cage.

"I am." Wishing the only problem facing me was which ladder to climb on, I stopped to watch Mr. T move around the top of his cage for his daily exercise. As much as Hazel pretended not to like the goofy bird, she doted on him and made sure he was well taken care of.

"'Sunday, Monday, Happy Days,'" he sang out and hopped from his exercise area to the counter.

I stroked his soft head. "You couldn't be more wrong, old buddy."

Hazel stood. "So what's up?"

I described my swing and miss with Charlie. "There's got to be a way to get him to talk."

"That old coot won't have a decent conversation with anybody. He's probably a lost cause." Hazel held her arm out for Mr. T to hop onto. "Any word on whether Bud had any money on him?"

I shook my head. "It's about time we get some good news, though. I'll go check on my source. See if he found out anything." I took a few steps and turned back. "Did you hear from Kurt?"

Hazel shook her head. "Not yet. If he doesn't get here pretty soon, I'll give him a call."

She lifted Mr. T to the cage door. "Okay, fella. I've got work to do. It's back to the big house for you."

Normally I would smile at her jailhouse reference, but being so close to incarceration myself, I could only imagine the rest of my days in a cell.

Blessedly alone in my office and able to sulk over Charlie, I pondered my next move. Who did I know that could talk to Charlie? Had to be someone he respected, had never argued with him, and someone with a reason to pursue the matter. Did such a person exist?

Maybe when I called Perry, he'd recommend someone. I selected his number on my cell, but had to leave a message—a pathetically desperate plea to call me back ASAP.

Great, strike number two, and we hadn't even reached noon. I glanced at my desk and spotted my suspect list. All it would take to follow up on Nancy's alibi was a simple phone call. Since Kurt hadn't arrived, I punched the number for Nancy's boss into my phone and tapped my foot.

"Hello, you have reached Terrance Paulson. I can't come to the phone right now so please leave a message at the tone."

Argh. I detailed my question then slammed down the phone. I plopped onto my chair, air gushing out the sides. Well, that was strike three. I was out. Or was I? I looked at my hastily scribbled writing. Mrs. Gherkin might have come up with some way to get Gus to talk.

I looked up her number in the phone book and dialed. Another voice mail, another message. Seriously, even Mrs. Gherkin had voice mail? Didn't anyone in this country answer the phone anymore? As if on cue, the shop's phone rang. Well, I wouldn't let my caller have to deal with a recording.

I snatched up the handset on the third ring. "Thank you for calling The Garden Gate," I answered with extra jubilance, as if to prove answering a phone was the proper and polite thing to do.

"Paige, oh, good. I'm glad you answered."

"Weed Whacker?" I glanced around. Had my worlds somehow collided? Radio world and Garden Gate world merging? Was this the end of the universe?

She cleared her throat. "I just wanted to check in and see how things were going. You haven't had any nutsos bother you since I last checked, have you?"

None, other than you. "Really, Weed Whacker, I think you're overreacting."

"Overreacting? We're talking about murder here." Her tone shot high. "People do odd things when they think someone is a killer."

"Well, I appreciate your concern, but you needn't bother." *Translated, stop bugging me.*

"No bother at all, Paige. It's the least I can do for all the advice you've given me. I'll check back later. Just to make sure everything is all right."

She disconnected and I sizzled. At least I'd discovered an answer to one of my questions. This was precisely why no one answered the phone.

CHAPTER FIFTEEN

*"And now, enjoy the best of Through the Garden
Gate with your beloved host, Paige Turner."*

*"Hi, Paige, this is Hank Wilkins from El Paso,
Texas. I'm visitin' my daughter here in Oreeeegon
and caught your show. Really enjoyed it, but I'm
confused about one thang."*

*"Well, thank you for calling, Hank. Gardening in
different regions of the country can lead to confusion."*

*"Right. Well, my problem is about those slugs you
kept mentionin'. You said that you had to bait for
slugs on a regular basis up here in Oreeeegon. When
we go huntin' in Texas, we don't have to bait for our
slugs. We just go down to the hardware store and buy
us a box of whatever size fits the gun we're using. If
it's such a big deal to get slugs up here, I could send
you a box ever' now and then."*

Once my fog of frustration cleared, I remembered that I
hadn't asked Hazel about her visit with Mitch. By the time
I returned to the front, Mr. T was happily playing with a rope toy
strung from the top of his cage, and Hazel had already begun the

dirty process of filling a decorative container. Three others sat at her feet, but these were from our regular stock, not the delivery.

I approached, and the earthy smell of the potting mixture riled up my desire to garden. "You call Kurt?"

Hazel continued to scoop rich soil into the bronzed urn. "Now he says he'll be here by noon."

I smiled at her efficiency. "Then it's a good thing Teri's coming in this afternoon. We'll need every available hand to finish on time."

Hazel turned the container, punching down the soil as she moved it. "Teri's a good worker. You planning to switch her to full-time when your landscaping business takes off?"

"*If* my business takes off, yes, Teri is my first choice. Of course, we'll have to bump you up to manager status and hike up your pay."

Hazel's head shot up. "Honestly, manager?"

I looked at her and laughed. "Well, sure. You didn't think I could handle all of this by myself, did you?"

"No. But I figured you might look for someone with that kind of experience."

"You already have the experience. You've basically been running the place this week while I've been tracking down Bud's killer."

She slowly stood upright, stretching as she moved. "Do you really think we can figure out who killed Bud?"

I wanted to tell her the truth—that I'd about given up on clearing my name then boohoo on her shoulder, but she'd already seen me dejected. I didn't want to take her down with me. "Don't worry about that. Of course we will. Maybe if you tell me about your appointment with Mitch, it'll trigger something that will help."

She waved a hand. "Not much to tell. He kept badgering me about where you were on Monday morning. Asked the same question over and over again. Guess he was trying to trip me up or something." She shook her head. "Sure glad I live in the country and don't pay his salary with my taxes. S'pose he might be good at what he does, but I don't like it much when it's aimed at my friend."

"Well, thanks for sticking up for me. I need—" The door chimed, and my name was screamed at a pitch so high only a dog should hear it.

"Paige." Lacy Winkle and her twin, Lori, launched their little bodies in my direction.

I braced my legs and waited. Three, two, one, impact. I staggered back at their combined force. They left me tottering for a moment until I regained my footing. Two sets of miniature arms clamped around my waist and squeezed like they never intended to let go.

Mr. T broke into an anxious dance and then climbed to the top of his cage. "'Quit your jibba, jabba, quit your jibba, jabba.'" The poor bird didn't much like children since an unfortunate incident involving his tail when he was young. I had no such incident, but my comfort level had been breached.

Lisa meandered behind the girls. Unlike her deliriously excited daughters, her face held the same tight and troubled look from earlier. Normally after this length of time, she would have instructed the girls to let me go, but she leaned against the counter and watched as if having an out-of-body experience.

I needed an out-of-body experience, too. Out of the clutches of these little bodies. I squirmed free and stepped behind a tall plant in a defensive move. The girls grabbed hands and circled like wagons in the old west.

"So," I said to the twins, "to what do I owe this unexpected visit?"

Lori stopped and looked up at me. Her usual plate-sized eyes were narrowed below her yellow bangs. "Huh?"

"Right." I laughed. "Three-year-old speak. Why are you guys here?"

"We need new flowers." She took on a grown-up and very self-important look. "Mommy's disappeared."

I tapped my chin. "Hmmm, disappearing flowers. That's quite a mystery."

"Mommy planted them. Now they're gone." Lacy lifted her tiny hands in the air, and her face screwed up.

I looked at Lisa. "Are we talking about the primroses you bought last week?"

Lisa, eyes sheepish, nodded. She held out a nail and picked at the polish.

I crossed over to her and put my face in her path. "Let me guess. You planted the flowers and forgot to take care of the slugs like I told you?"

She jerked back and crossed her arms. "I didn't think it was *that* important."

"Didn't I mention that slugs like primroses as much as these girls like cheesy macs?"

"We love cheesy macs," Lacy said, nodding and sending her delicate curls bouncing.

"That's our favoritest food in the whole world," Lori ended with a serious nod of her own.

I looked at the pair that I thought of as *Stachys byzantina*, the plant that was nicknamed lamb's ears for the fuzzy soft leaves that felt a lot like the girls' soft curls. "Slugs like to eat primrose leaves just as much as you like cheesy macs."

"Ewwww," Lacy said, and Lori chimed in, adding a silly dance to the mix. Within moments, they were whooping and hollering at top volume.

"Now, girls," Lisa said in a soft tone and without any real effort to still her twins.

Enough. If Lisa didn't even expend the energy to try to make the girls behave, something was terribly wrong. Time to get her to willingly spill, or I'd force it out of her.

"Hazel," I shouted above the clamor, "could you take the girls outside to find half a dozen primroses while I talk to Lisa?"

Hazel laughed and brushed the dirt from her hands. "C'mon, girls. We'll get the flowers, and then I'll make you some hot chocolate."

"Yay," they screamed and trailed after Hazel.

Cali shot through Hazel's feet, as the furry feline often did when someone opened the door first thing in the morning. She rushed past the girls' outstretched hands and ran under a plant display.

I turned back to Lisa. "Let's go to the office."

She gave an absent nod and trudged beside me.

Cali bolted from her hiding space and trotted just in front of my feet, pausing every so often to be sure I followed. This sneaky little one wanted to get into my office. One of her favorite spots to sleep was on my expensive desk chair. After a few punctures of the buttery soft leather when she was in the room with Mr. T, she was now only allowed in the office when I was present and Mr. T was up front. That didn't stop her from trying to sneak in.

I took my chair, and Cali hopped onto my lap. She exposed her belly and immediately rumbled into a purr.

With a tsk, Lisa cleaned the mound of gardening brochures off the side chair and sat. "Why didn't you tell me about your date last night?"

"First of all, you were so distracted this morning you wouldn't have heard me even if I did tell you. And secondly, it wasn't a date. Just a working dinner." I grabbed an envelope in hopes of sorting through piles of mail on the desk while we talked.

She shrugged. "Same dif. Especially when Adam told Perry he wanted it to be a date."

He *did* want to date me. Score!

Not wanting to burst out in joy when Lisa was so troubled, I stifled a smile and tossed a junk flyer for pest control into the trash. Hmmm, pest control. Maybe I should reconsider and use the service on pest Lisa.

For now I'd settle for outing her part in this supposed admission from Adam. "Guys do not talk to each other like that. Are you sure you didn't get in on the conversation?"

"Maybe just the tail end." Her eyes turned impish, and she giggled.

I couldn't help but smile over how much her face had brightened from when she'd arrived. Leave it to Lisa to giggle when she'd done something underhanded like talk to Adam behind my back. Normally I'd call her on it, but I didn't want to risk returning her to her crabby state.

She leaned closer. "Did you have a good time, too?"

I mocked offense at her interference with a pout. "I'm not going to tell you. This is just like grade school. You'll go running back to Adam with whatever I say."

"Oh, puh-lease. Admit it. You're interested in him."

I looked up and thought about it. Was I really interested in Adam? Was this the kind of guy I could build a relationship and future with? He seemed like a good candidate from what I had seen so far, but that's the way most relationships started. Then the guy wanted to step in and take over. Wrestle away control.

"Earth to Paige," Lisa said.

"Sorry, I was just thinking. Honestly I'm not sure about Adam. He's not really my type."

Lisa snorted. "That's a good thing. You usually pick the bad boys."

I chucked two bills onto the "to be paid" pile already threatening a landslide. "I'll admit it. I do go for the troubled sort. Perhaps I'm only interested in Adam because I'm projecting my troubles onto him. Maybe once this is all resolved, I won't find him attractive at all. We'll just have to wait and see."

She sighed. "Fine, I'll be patient. As long as you admit that Adam is a keeper like Perry."

Perfect opportunity to change the subject. "Speaking of Perry, he owes me a call." I told her about Mrs. Gherkin's news, the blackmail theory, and how I'd asked him to follow up on the cash.

"I can ask him about it. We're having lunch."

"Ooh-la-la. A date with the hubby."

Lisa's face returned to her angst-filled scowl, and she sat back in silence.

What'd I do now? Everything was going along fine until we got onto the subject of Perry. The severity of this look was foreign to Lisa, at least since she'd gotten over Ben's death. Alarm bells clanged in my head.

I sat forward. "Lisa, what's wrong?"

She said nothing for a few uncomfortable seconds then blurted out, "Have you noticed that Perry's been kind of unhappy lately?"

I dropped the rest of the mail onto the desk. If Lisa and Perry were having troubles, I needed to give her my full attention. "Unhappy? Not that I noticed. Why?"

"I don't know." More silence. "He's been acting odd for a while. Like he's bored with his job, or me and the girls."

I never felt more out of my league than now. I had nothing to base any advice on, and I really didn't know what to say. "Are you sure you're not imagining this?"

"I thought so, for a while. Then Perry reconnected with Adam. It seems to have gotten worse. Like Perry wishes he was doing criminal law. Or maybe he wants to be single like Adam."

I wanted to blurt out that I'd go ahead and marry Adam if that would solve my best friend's issue, but I knew better than to be flip when she was pouring out her heart. "Have you talked to him about it?"

"Nah, I can't seem to bring it up. What if I do and he says, 'yeah, sorry babe. I want my freedom. See you later.'" Her pain distorted her voice, sending a fresh wave of worry over me.

She was way off base on this, though. Perry wasn't that kind of a guy. At least, I hoped he wasn't. "You know Perry would never do that. You just said he was a keeper, and he is. Talk to him. Find out what's going on."

She sighed again, this one long and drawn out like a leaking tire. A commotion in the background drew my attention, but barely fazed her.

"Lori, it's not a good idea to dump that on the floor," Hazel shouted.

A crash split the silence, followed by the sound of breaking pottery, jolting Lisa out of her stupor.

She slowly pushed to her feet. "I better go before the girls tear your store apart."

Unable to come up with a way to relieve her concern, I let her go and sat back. Cali, who'd curled into a tight ball in my lap and purred even through all my mail-sorting maneuvers, shifted. I scratched her head and stared at the door. Lisa's news was almost as bad as being accused of murder. She could be overreacting and maybe nothing was wrong, but I couldn't help worrying about her and Perry. And I had no idea how to help her resolve things. The same feelings of helplessness surged through me like they had when Ben died.

Cali meowed and looked up at me. I rubbed my thumb down her nose. "Life is much easier with you than a real family, isn't it?"

Maybe I didn't ever want to get married. Maybe life with a cat and a bird was just fine.

CHAPTER ⚏ SIXTEEN

"And now, enjoy the best of Through the Garden Gate *with your beloved host, Paige Turner."*

"Hi, this is Perplexed. I wanted to add a caution to your advice about hedge trimmers."

"Hello, Perplexed, I'm so glad you caught the show when I suggested to our listeners who find themselves surrounded by hedges to invest in a hedge trimmer. They're inexpensive, do the work in no time at all, and they're right there in your shed or garage whenever you need them so you don't have to run out and rent one."

"I agree with you on your first two points. It's the last one I want to caution others on, or they might just lose their hedge trimmer like I did."

"Oh, goodness, this sounds serious."

"Well, it is. My hedges were perfect until I heard your show and asked my hedge trimmer if he minded living in my garage so he'd be available whenever I needed him. Hector gave me a crazy look and stormed off the job. I haven't seen him since."

166 NIPPED IN THE BUD

Lisa, Lacy, and Lori had departed, and since the containers hadn't arrived yet, I decided to go to the library. With a promise to Hazel to return shortly, I left the shop and schlepped into the now overcast day. Springtime weather in the Willamette Valley was unpredictable. Once we hit the Fourth of July, the sun shone almost every day, and little rain fell until October, when it consistently drizzled until May. Then we had a mixed bag of sun and rain, rarely experiencing thunder and lightning. At least not outside my head.

The musty aromas permeating the old library brought back my past and helped me force a warm approach. Stacey doused it with another cool reception. While she retrieved the newspapers, I looked around her personal space for any clue as to why she might have something against Bud or me. What I found were hints to her personality. A designer purse like Lisa's peeked out the top drawer of her desk, the latest smartphone sat on the desk, and today a quality leather jacket hung over the white sweater. Common items you might find in a work space. Nothing that would tell me if she killed Bud, or why she didn't like me.

Unless, of course, she had something against all women who wore little makeup, dressed practically, and often had dirt on their clothes and under their nails. Still, it took a lot of money to support the trendy items I'd found, and a librarian in Serendipity was not likely well paid. I made a mental note to add this piece of news to my suspect list and pulled back my shoulders as the subject of my thoughts approached.

"I could only carry two boxes. You can start on these." She dropped the boxes on the counter. "When I'm free I'll get the last one."

Free? Free? I was the only one in the place. Not a silent person by nature, I literally had to clamp down on my tongue. No way

I'd alienate the woman who stood between me and the last box of papers I needed to review. I took my boxes and went back to the same corner as yesterday.

I flipped through older papers and worked my way forward through the month Nancy claimed she spoke to the council. After several stacks, one thing became clear. The name Fulcrum came up often, but not in relationship to Bud. And conspicuously absent was Nancy's attendance at any meeting. I did confirm that Gus Reinke was the council chairman at that time, and I made a note of the other council members' names. Still, I plodded on, occasionally glancing at the "About Town" column and shaking my head when I spotted personal snippets that described dinner or lunch guests and the menu served.

Finished with the boxes, I sat back and let my mind wander to the copy that would appear in "About Town" if anyone reported my dinner with Adam. It would be especially embarrassing if someone followed me home and saw the incredible male specimen run from the idea of kissing me.

Before letting my mind drift too far away, I stacked the papers in proper order and exchanged them for the final box that Stacey had left on the counter. Thankfully, there was no sign of Stacey, and I avoided another scolding.

On the way back to my little corner, my cell vibrated. I pulled the phone from the holder, and upon seeing Adam's name, tamped down my excitement and greeted him with an even tone.

"Hi there." I purred into my phone much the way Cali had purred on my lap.

"Hi to you, too. I just called. . ." he stopped for a dramatic pause.

"To say, 'I love you'." I internally finished the first line of Stevie Wonder's song.

"To say I'm sorry." He rushed the words out as if apologizing was tough for him.

Oops, wrong song. Hold up, sorry? Why did he have to apologize? What did he do? Did the forensics come in? Did he fail to keep me out of jail?

"Sorry? For what?" I asked tentatively.

"I shouldn't have tried to kiss you last night. We agreed to a professional relationship until you're cleared, and I didn't abide by that decision."

I exhaled the breath I didn't realize I'd been holding. "You don't have to apologize for that."

"Yes, I do. I wasn't much of a gentleman."

"You are more of a gentleman than any other man I've dated." I didn't think it necessary to mention that the list of men I'd had relationships with in the past was about as long as the guest list at a party on *Gilligan's Island*. "The only thing you need to apologize for is not following through on the kiss."

"Aw, Paige, c'mon. You're killin' me here. Don't distract me like that."

"I thought I only did that when I looked at you."

He groaned. "I think it's in both our interests to handle your case by phone and e-mail from now on. No personal contact except when required by an outside party."

"That doesn't sound like much fun."

"No, but neither does jail. I'll do a better job for you if my head is fully in the game. So, can we try?"

"Fine, but you know what they say. Absence makes the heart grow fonder. Don't blame me if that happens."

He laughed, deep and breathy, and altogether pleasant to listen to. "So tell me what you've been up to today."

I gave him precise details of my conversation with Charlie

and my multitude of phone messages. "I'm still waiting for Perry to check into the cash. I've pretty much struck out with the papers on finding any information about Fulcrum. I did find the name of the reporter who wrote up all the council meetings. He disappeared about the same time Nancy Kimble said she confronted the council. I'd like to talk to him, so I'll make a trip to the newspaper office to see if Jack can give me the reporter's contact info."

"Might be a good time for us to sit down with the police chief and fill him in on what's happening."

"Mitch?" I shrieked then held my breath in wait for a Stacey reprimand. I scanned the room and didn't see her. She must still be in the back room but I lowered my voice anyway. "Are you kidding? He'd just laugh in my face. No, I can't go to Mitch until I've solved the whole thing."

Silence, long and uncomfortable, filled the phone. "Be careful, Paige. You should tell as few people as possible about what you've discovered. If this Gus fellow was taking payoffs from Picklemann, even if he didn't kill him, he might make trouble for you. And if he did kill Picklemann. . .well, he might strike again."

I laughed. "You're overreacting. I don't think there's a cold-blooded killer running around here. I'm sure Bud was killed in the heat of the moment."

"Doesn't mean they won't strike again. Listen to me, Paige. I've seen it many times in my career. Someone kills out of passion then figures they have to keep killing to cover their tracks. So, like I said. Be careful. And keep me informed of your whereabouts. Just because we can't see each other doesn't mean we can't talk."

We offered pleasant good-byes, and I settled back to work. Just hearing from Adam gave me the incentive I needed to plow through the final box. I picked up a paper and began flipping through the pages.

Wait, what's that?

I flipped the page back.

Well, I'll be.

The résumé of one Stacey Darling, my librarian nemesis, was posted right below the council minutes in the month she was hired. Boy, she had a lot of experience as a librarian, and a master's degree to boot. Stacey might just wear her age well, but I was certain she wasn't old enough to have obtained her master's degree *and* have worked all of the jobs on her résumé. The fact that she had been ugly to me made me feel a little less guilty for the intense scrutiny of her past that I planned to engage in.

After finishing the stack, I photocopied the résumé and then returned the box to the counter. Stacey rose from her desk, cold eyes appraising me as she glided my way.

"Thanks for your help," I said, all cheerful and polite. I should have stopped right there, but her attitude needed adjustment, and as usual, I thought I had to be the one to do it. "These papers have been most helpful. Found lots of interesting things." I made a big production out of setting the copy of her résumé on the counter. "I'm curious. With all your great experience, why would you choose to work in this little town?"

Eyes wary, posture less assured, she shrugged. "I wanted to work where people are warm and grateful for my help. Serendipity seemed like that kind of place." She jerked the box off the counter. "If this is all you need, I have work to do."

Her tone resembled Charlie's, and I would get nothing more out of her now. It was clear that I was on the right track. She was hiding something. I simply needed to find out what it was. "Once I have time to make sense of everything I found, I'll be back."

I snatched up the résumé and let my words hang in the air like the warning I intended. Forcing out a smile, I spun and slowly walked to the door. I let a big grin consume my face and kept it there all the way to the shop.

The morning had all but disappeared, and I expected to find Hazel literally up to her elbows in potting soil.

"Sorry, Paige," she said. "Kurt still hasn't been here. We might have a late night."

I checked my watch. "Teri's already on her way in. When she gets here, how about I treat you to lunch at the Bakery? Maybe I'll get a call about Bud having cash. If I do before we're finished with lunch, we'll both go confront Gus. What do you say?"

"Lunch followed by a nice dessert of confrontation? I'm in." She grinned with excitement.

I thought about actually discovering something of importance when we questioned Gus and resisted the urge to rub my hands together like an evil villain. There would be plenty of time for that once I knew the killer's name.

CHAPTER ⛩ SEVENTEEN

"And now, enjoy the best of Through the Garden Gate *with your beloved host, Paige Turner."*

"Hi, Paige, this is Daniel in Clackamas. I'm like your biggest fan, but I have a problem with something you mentioned about dinner plate dahlias."

"Oh, Daniel, I'm so glad you brought up dahlias. They're one of my favorite plants and the hybrid 'Mystery Day' with its big skyrocket purple and white blooms really make a big impact in your garden. I can't get enough of them. They produce flowers seven inches across and have really earned the nickname 'dinner plate.' So, what's your problem, Daniel? Did they not grow large enough for you? If not, you probably need to give them more water."

"No, that's not it. My wife and I are just really disappointed in how poorly they hold our food. Dinnertime at our house is getting really messy."

Hazel and I tucked into our fresh yummy sandwiches as if we hadn't been fed in months. When Nancy's boss called on the way over to the restaurant, confirming Nancy's alibi and wiping out a suspect in one fell swoop, I thought I might not have an appetite. Even more so when we arrived to find the Bakery jammed with lunchtime customers who kept glancing at us and whispering behind their hands. But then Donna set the food before me, and suddenly I was ravenous. Who knows, maybe I was getting used to being fodder for the town's gossip.

"I hope this whispering ends soon," I said to Hazel and snagged a chip. "I wonder what or who they'll move on to next."

Hazel set down her sandwich and leaned across the table. "Used to be me. Now that I've been working for you, most of the folks have gotten a little more accepting."

"It's not right. Why do we have to judge people all the time?"

"Guess it makes some people feel better about themselves."

"Well, you're a perfect example of being judged one way and then proving them all wrong."

She gave me a forced smile. "You'll do the same once we figure out who killed Bud."

We ate in silence, relishing every bite of our lunches. Having watched Adam eat a Reuben yesterday, I'd ordered one dripping with sauce, cheese, and sauerkraut. Hazel chose a burger, rare and juicy and topped with a thick slab of Swiss cheese and mounds of mushrooms.

She'd nearly devoured the whole burger when she looked toward the door and stopped chewing. "Hey, look, there's Lisa's husband. I hope Lisa and the girls aren't coming, too. They wore me out."

Chewing and feeling Hazel's pain, I pivoted in my chair. As Perry scanned the restaurant, probably for Lisa, I caught his attention, and he wound his way through the curious diners.

He stopped in front of our table. "Hi, ladies. I was just looking for Lisa. We're having lunch today."

"She told me," I said and stuffed the last bite of Reuben into my mouth.

He looked around again as if searching the crowd would make Lisa materialize. "I wonder where she is. We were supposed to meet here fifteen minutes ago. I thought I'd be in trouble for being late."

I finished chewing. "Maybe she had a hard time getting the girls to settle in at her mom's."

He nodded. "Yeah, that's probably it. Say, listen, as long as you're here, I have some information for you." He pulled out a chair, and as he sat, he glanced at Hazel. "It's kind of private."

"Is it about Bud?"

He nodded.

"Then you can tell me. Hazel's been helping me find Bud's killer." I smiled at Hazel, whose eyebrows rose. "In fact, she's the one who found out about Winnie."

Perry's forehead creased as he studied my eyes. Then as quickly as the crease came, it left, and he shrugged. "Well, okay, if you're sure. I've got good news and bad news. Which do you want first?"

I groaned, not only from having to make the decision but from an overly full stomach. I shouldn't have eaten the whole sandwich and definitely not so fast. "Don't make me choose. You pick."

He leaned forward. "Okay, here goes. My source says the police are expecting a report on forensic evidence by the end of the day. He said Mitch is eagerly waiting for the proof that your shovel killed Picklemann."

A forensic report arriving in Mitch's eager little—er—big

hands, tying my shovel to the murder, meant Mitch was proceeding with his quest to jail me. I glanced at Hazel and hoped my face didn't hold the same tight, fearful response as hers did. "I'll assume that's the bad news. And the good?"

"Picklemann had three thousand dollars in cash on him."

Hazel shot a fist into the air. "That is good news. Bet with that much dough in his pocket he was paying off the whole council."

"Not so fast, Hazel," Perry said. "A sum that large might mean it's totally unrelated to Gus." Perry faced me. "I asked my friend if they'd done any digging into Picklemann's finances. He said they had, but they hadn't found anything yet. I'll keep after him, though."

I didn't know what to make of this development. As Perry said, it might mean something totally different. Perry moved to stand. I snagged his wrist and pulled him back down. "Speaking of digging, do you remember Zac Young, a reporter for the *Times*?"

Perry snatched a chip from my plate and thoughtfully chewed. "Yeah, sure. If I remember right, he got tired of small town life and left for the big city."

Did I detect a wistful tone in his words? I sat forward and peered into his eyes. Was Lisa right about his unhappiness? I needed to pursue this and see if I could learn anything that might help calm Lisa's worries. "Take it from me, the big city isn't all it's cracked up to be."

His eyes clouded over as he picked up another chip. "No, I guess not. Especially once you're married and have kids. Zac was young, just out of college. I think he was dying here."

And *I* was thinking Lisa was right. Perry did look a bit unhappy. "You lived in a big city when you went to college. Is that something—"

A commotion by the door caught Hazel and Perry's attention. I followed their gazes only to wish I hadn't. At the counter, standing proud and as tall as her five-foot-three body could manage, was Lisa. She wore the most atrocious sparkly halter-top, form-fitting black pants, and shoes that shone as bright as the top. She'd been shopping at Uma's boutique.

The room buzzed with conversation. A few titters broke the hum, and Lisa's eyes turned wary. Perry shot to his feet and rushed to her side. He protectively wrapped his arm around his wife and whispered something into her ear. She lurched back, nearly stumbling from the sudden move in three-inch heels.

"I'm *so* sorry I'm an embarrassment to you," she shouted at Perry. "I was just trying to spice things up so you wouldn't leave us."

"Leave you?" Perry's words came out in a high squeal. "What are you talking about?"

"Don't pretend you don't know." Lisa spun on her heels and marched out the door. Perry made a quick sweep of the room with his baffled gaze then ran after her, letting the door slam and the bells tinkle.

I cringed and huddled in my seat. My little Shasta daisy had tried to be a bright showy dinner plate dahlia and failed in what was the most desperate attempt to keep a man I'd ever witnessed. And it was perpetrated by my best friend, who I would have to convince at some point today, that her public debacle wasn't as bad as it appeared. That she wouldn't be the laughingstock of the town or that people wouldn't gossip about her. She thrived on propriety, and it could take a long time for her to recover.

"Think she's okay?" Hazel asked.

I turned back to Hazel, noting that others were staring at me again. "Let's get out of here."

I tossed some bills onto the table and slowly wound through

the chattering customers to the outside, where it had begun to mist and was now severely overcast, very much like my mood. I couldn't bear to see my best friend's suffering, and it made me feel helpless.

Hazel patted me on the back. "They'll be okay. It'll just take some time."

"This has put me in the mood for grilling Gus. How about you? Ready to talk to him?"

She grinned. "Try to stop me."

We hurried through the drizzle to Gus's hardware store a few doors down. Hazel rushed ahead like a storm trooper ready to invade a foreign country.

I grabbed her arm. "Hold up. We need to approach him calmly, or he might clam up. Follow my lead."

We found Gus dumping a carton of pipe fittings into a dingy plastic bin. "Hey, Gus," I called out and strolled down the aisle. "Got a minute?"

His head raised, his eyes friendly. He stood to his full height, planting a hand on the small of his back as he grimaced in pain halfway up. "If the two of you need some help fixing something, I'm your guy."

"Actually, we do need your help fixing something." I quickly glanced at Hazel and gave her one last warning look to stay calm. "Do you remember a company named Fulcrum?"

A flash of surprise coupled with caution took over his face then rapidly faded. "Fulcrum, Fulcrum, let me see. It does sound familiar." He put his finger by his mouth and looked up. "You know, I think that might be the name of the company that Pacific Pickles bought their land from."

"Oh quit putting on such a big show," Hazel blurted out. "You know very well who Fulcrum is."

So much for calm. "So, Gus, do you remember a Nancy Kimble by any chance? Ida Carlson's daughter?"

"No, can't say that name sounds familiar to me."

Hazel snorted. "Hah! Think you'd remember the name of the person who made it possible for you to collect monthly blackmail payments."

Under Gus's intense scrutiny, Hazel's shoulders rose and her back straightened. I could almost see his thoughts running from one side of his brain to the other. I decided to wait until he spoke before saying anything else.

"I think it's time you minded your own business," he said, with hard eyes aimed at Hazel. He swung his gaze to me. "And that goes for you, too."

Well, then. This was going well. "Now, Gus, Hazel jumped the gun there. We were just wondering if it was a coincidence that in the same month the council learned Bud owned Fulcrum, that you started giving Winnie a nice allowance to spend as she wanted."

He had managed to gain control of his expressions, and this accusation didn't faze him at all. He held up a hand. "Like I said, you better mind your own business if you know what's good for you. In fact," he tipped his head at the door, "I suggest you leave before I get mad."

"Gus," I said, letting my frustration drip off his name, "you might as well tell us the truth. You know I'm going to get to the bottom of Bud's murder, and that means this will all come out."

Gus stared at me, fire flaming from his eyes. He perched one hand on a hip covered with a dirty work apron and pointed at the door with the other.

I backed up a step. "Okay, okay. We'll go, but our next stop is to see the other council members. One of the five of you is bound to confess to blackmail."

"Fine, have at 'em. We have nothing to hide."

Not the response I'd hoped for. Or was it? He said, *we* have nothing to hide. "Let's go, Hazel. Looks like Gus is going to keep his secret to the bitter end." I gave him a quick skewering with my gaze. "And make no mistake about it, Gus, the end will be bitter."

We shuffled out of the store and stood under the overhang to stay dry. I let out a deep breath and was surprised at how badly my hands were shaking.

"I'm not cut out for this," I said to Hazel, whose eyes were alight with excitement.

She clamped her arms closed. "I'm just plain mad. That man is lying to us and you know it."

I looked around and considered our next option. "If you were Gus, what would you do next?"

"If I was guilty like we think he is, and if the other men were involved, I'd call them up and get together to form a pact not to talk. And the sooner the better."

"That's what I'd do, too," I said, barely able to contain my enthusiasm over an idea that popped into my head. I grabbed her arm and dragged her to the alley behind the store. "Let's hang out here for a while. See if Gus goes somewhere or if the other men come here."

We slipped into an alcove next to the entrance and waited. As if assisting with our hiding, thick gray clouds covered the sun, dimming our space.

"Let's try not to talk much," I whispered to Hazel. "Gus might be meeting the guys somewhere else, and he'll hear us if he leaves."

She nodded and slid her fingers across her lips like a zipper.

To pass the time, I named in my head all the plants I could think of in alphabetical order. I'd reached hydrangea, the *oakleaf* species, one of my favorite semi-shrub perennials, when the first councilman and my radio show boss, Roger Freund, arrived. Oops. I'd forgotten the man who held my radio career in his hands was also a member of the council. He plowed across the street with a deep scowl on his face, the same scowl that often rested on his face at work when things went wrong.

Waiting for him to pass so I could talk, I mocked choking myself in a mime of what could happen with my career, and it was nearly our undoing. Hazel, a boisterous laugher, had to clamp her hand over her mouth to keep quiet until Roger slipped inside.

"Now what?" Hazel whispered.

"Let's wait to see if others arrive. Then we can go back in and listen," I whispered back, causing Hazel to clutch my arm and do a small jig.

I resumed my plant naming, reaching *Lamium,* a wonderful little ground cover, at the same time as Walt Cunkle turned the corner. He yawned and stretched, making his way toward us. Owner of the bowling alley, he often worked nights. His day was probably just beginning.

Hazel and I shared an aha-we-were-right look and went back to watching the road.

Not one to keep my enthusiasm hidden, I returned to the plant thing to distract me from the excitement of seeing the council members arrive. At periwinkle, a vine-type ground cover that I loathed for its aggressive spreading habit but loved for its tiny violet flowers, Tim Needlemeyer arrived, with his usual cheery smile. I'd never seen Tim without a goofy grin. Fitting for a man who spent his days in sales. As a used implement dealer, he had to be nice if he wanted to eat.

Finally, reaching zinnia, Ollie Grayson rushed down the street, eyes darting about. He acted as nervous as my stomach felt. The long lean farmer wore striped bibs with mud encrusted knees, as if the call had ripped him out of the fields.

Once he disappeared inside, I grabbed Hazel's hand and crept out of the nook.

I peeked inside the back door. The coast was clear. The men had moved in far enough for us to spy on them without being seen. I cupped my hand around my mouth. "If we get caught, I'll disavow all knowledge of our mission."

After all, actually carrying this thing off bordered on a "mission impossible", didn't it?

CHAPTER ⛩ EIGHTEEN

"And now, enjoy the best of Through the Garden
Gate *with your beloved host, Paige Turner."*

"This is Stumped in Eugene."

*"Tell me, Stumped, are you one of the many
people in Eugene affiliated with the University of
Oregon?"*

"No. I don't want nothing to do with that place."

"Oh, okay. How can I help you?"

*"I'm calling about the show where you told us
how to do a soil test."*

*"A soil test, yes, that's a must to determine what
type of soil you have so you can add the appropriate
amendments. Especially in the northwest where we
have such heavy clay soil."*

*"Well, I missed most of the show and don't
want to have to go thinking up things on my own. I
wondered if you could repeat the list of questions you
ask when you give your soil a test."*

We crept into the back room and halted by the door. The
men were grouped near the entrance to the retail space,

far enough away to miss seeing us enter. Gus, with animated gesturing, brought the men up to date on our little visit. I wedged myself between stacks of boxes. From this spot, all five of the men were in my view, but I was hidden well enough that I was free to observe their interaction without any threat of discovery. Hazel scooted herself into a spot to my right, close enough to communicate nonverbally. I only wished we knew sign language.

Ollie leaned against the jamb of the doorway. Tim perched on an old wooden barrel and shook his legs as if he was jittery. Gus lurked in a shadow, so I could barely make out his face, probably a good thing, as I was still mad at how he treated us. I might be tempted to let him have it if I could see him clearly.

Roger and Walt stood in the middle of the group, neither of them choosing to lean against or sit on anything. Maybe this was my first clue. They were strong enough to withstand the pressure without support. Maybe they were the most likely to commit a crime. I was grasping for straws here, but I was so thirsty for clues that I had to find something.

"Well," Gus said and peered at his fellow council members. "Now that you heard the problem, what do you think we should do?"

Ollie pulled back his shoulders and a devious grin crossed his face. "Other than to tell those nosy broads to mind their own business, you mean?"

The men snickered, my fist curled, and I shared a just-wait look with Hazel.

Walt, the only nonsnickerer of the men, loudly cleared his throat and held it long enough to silence the others. When they had quieted, he said, "I say it's time to fess up and let the good people of this town know what we did."

"Hah," Roger shouted. "Don't be such a sissy, Cunkle. I'm not giving up without a fight."

"Hold it." Gus waved his hands. "We don't need a fight at all and especially not between us. We made the decision as a group to keep Picklemann's ownership of the land quiet. We'll decide as a group what to do next."

At his admission of their cover-up, I grabbed Hazel's hand and squeezed. She punched her other fist up, hitting a precariously placed box that teetered. She uncurled her fingers and stilled the box while I exhaled quietly.

"We sure can't tell people Picklemann was paying us to keep quiet." Ollie made eye contact with each man. "No one around here would talk to us again. Especially my wife."

"Not to mention what this could do to our careers," Roger added.

"It doesn't matter what happens to us." Walt puffed out his chest. "I think it's in the best interest for folks around here to know the truth. Especially if it leads to finding Picklemann's killer."

The group erupted in violent voices and waving of arms and hands. Shouts of, "it would only point the finger at us," "we didn't have nothing to do with the murder," "if you say one word," shot through the air. Then the men began to threaten each other.

Gus smacked his bear-sized paws together until the other men came to order.

"The one thing I'm hearing from everyone but Walt is that we keep quiet," Gus said, and the men nodded. "So we're agreed. We won't admit a thing."

"I'll do what the group decides for now," Walt said. "If Paige is arrested for Picklemann's murder, I'll come forward. We all know she didn't kill him."

"Then who did?" Ollie's arms hung at his sides, his hands fisted in balls.

"Now, men." Gus held up his hand. "We aren't here to figure out who killed Picklemann. We have more pressing matters. What to do about Paige and her snoopy employee."

"What are you suggesting, Gus?" Roger's face lost color at the implication hanging in the air.

I stared at Hazel. What were they planning? Would they do us in? Maybe they weren't murderers now, but would they become killers?

Gus ran his hand over his bushy white hair. "I don't have a clue. I think it's best if we sleep on it and get back together tomorrow morning to discuss the options. Agreed?"

Grumbling approval traveled around the group, and Tim pushed off his stool as if ready to leave.

Time for us to skedaddle. I gained Hazel's attention and tipped my head at the door. She confirmed my plan with a quick nod, and we both made our way quietly to the exit. When she pushed open the door, the sun's rays now beaming from the sky caught me by surprise, and I released a huge sun sneeze.

"What was that?" I heard Gus ask.

I clutched Hazel's arm and ran, half dragging the older woman with me. We scurried down the alley to the pharmacy and ducked into the back entrance, surprising Charlie, who was counting round white pills into a small tray.

"What're you doing back here?" he asked in a sleepy tone.

"Sorry, Charlie," I said and winced when I realized I'd inadvertently mimed the tuna commercial's tone of voice. "We need to use the bathroom, quick. Hazel feels like she might throw up."

I nudged her, and she quickly caught on, making a few retching sounds.

Charlie's face blanched. "So what are you waiting for? Get in there, then." He shook his head.

I held in my laughter and pushed Hazel into the ladies' room. With the door closed, neither of us could keep from breaking up. I hadn't had this much fun since I was a kid.

"How long do you think we need to stay in here?" I leaned against the door as the automatic freshener sprayed the air with a tangy orange scent.

Hazel followed my lead and wedged her bottom onto the stained porcelain sink. It groaned from her weight, and she stood upright. "Doesn't take long to barf. We could go out anytime, and Charlie would believe us. Do you think the other guys saw us and followed us here?"

"I don't know. I can't imagine they would. We should probably wait a few minutes to be sure."

"At least we heard the truth. Bud was paying them to keep quiet." In a burst of excitement, Hazel grabbed my arms, pulling me from the door and dancing us around the tiny space.

I let her lead until she tired and sagged against a wall. "I guess that's good news. Still, it doesn't prove one of them killed Bud."

Hazel's eyes narrowed. "I say we check out their alibis for the time Bud was killed. The question is, how do we search out their alibis without tipping them off to the fact that we know what they did?"

I thought about the men and saw them marching off to their jobs the morning of the murder. There were only five of them, not the full contingent of seven dwarfs, but still a picture of the dwarfs singing, *"Hi ho, hi ho, it's off to work we go,"* marched through my brain.

I shook out the vision. "Their alibis might be hard to come by since Roger is the only one who works a regular nine-to-five job. Maybe we should just come right out and tell them what we know and ask where they were when Bud was killed."

"Might spook them, and we'll never find out what we need to know."

I ran the men through my mind again. Dopey, Grumpy, Sleepy, wait Sleepy. "Maybe we should start with Walt, the one man who didn't want to go along with the group."

Her eyes tightened, and she raised a skeptical brow.

"Look, Hazel," I said, letting a burst of passion heat up my words. "I know it's a long shot, but I can't wait around and play it safe. I have to find out who killed Bud before Mitch makes good on his threat to arrest me." I checked my watch. "Let's go back to the shop and work on the containers. That'll give Walt time to go over to the bowling alley and get settled for the day. Then I'll go over there. I'll say I was walking by and needed one of their pizzas. While I wait for it to cook, I'll feel him out."

"Okay. Be careful. We might not get a second chance." Hazel flushed the toilet and grinned. "In case Charlie can hear it."

I watched the water swirl around and disappear down the drain. Walt had to have information about the killer. He just had to or my life might be flushed away, too.

After our close encounter of the dwarf kind, we went to The Garden Gate to work on the containers. They hadn't arrived, so I sent Teri home. Hazel set up for the weekend traffic, making space for some of the containers up front. When we did get them planted, we could slip the pots into the display area we created. I went to the office to follow up on other leads.

I searched through my bag and located Stacey's résumé. The Beaverton Library was her last place of employment. I located the library's phone number online and dialed. The receptionist transferred me to the city of Beaverton human resources, who handled all employment verifications.

"Hi, I'm calling to confirm employment," I said in my professional tone. "Could you verify Stacey Darling's employment at the Beaverton Library?"

"I'm sorry. We don't give out that kind of information without a release from the person in question." She might as well have been a recording for all the inflection she failed to put in her voice.

"Oh, please. I just want to confirm she worked there from 1996 through 2000."

Sigh. "I wish I could help but that's confidential." Her tone was growing irritated.

"Can you tell me if she worked there at all?"

"Who did you say this was?"

Busted. "I didn't. Thank you for your time." I hung up and moved down the list of employers, who I discovered were equally familiar with employment laws. In our lawsuit-happy culture, few businesses today would risk giving out information without written consent.

Striking out on the job front, I located the college Web page where Stacey supposedly received her master of library science. I first confirmed that such a degree was conferred at this university and then located alumni services. No point in contacting the school. They wouldn't give info over the phone. I found an online community where I posted a notice asking if anyone knew Stacey during the years she attended school there. I would check back in the next few days to see if anyone recognized her name.

Frustrated by more dead ends, I went to help Hazel until it was time to question Walt. In a way, the work was therapeutic. It gave me time to brainstorm ideas on what to do next in my Stacey quest and think through my strategy for confronting Walt.

Now, as I opened the outer door of the Serendipity Bowl, prepared to do battle, I reminded myself that Walt was a gentleman, usually levelheaded and not a conniving money grabber, but, and this was a big but, my plan was to out a blackmailer. Levelheaded or not, our confrontation might not end well. Resolved to dig up as much dirt as possible, I pulled open the inner door.

Phew, man! This place reeks.

The stench of stale cigarettes and beer snaked up my nose and threatened to permeate my skin. I momentarily regretted my decision to choose the bowling kingpin as my first interrogation victim. Still, I could bathe and eradicate any smell that clung to me. I couldn't bathe and eradicate a prison sentence.

Walt, a silo of a man, stood behind the shoe rental counter, another spot that rated high on my "ick" factor. Who wanted to put their feet into shoes worn over and over again by virtual strangers? Even if they were disinfected. In one shovel-sized hand, Walt held an aerosol can, in the other, a large two-toned shoe. He gave quick spurts of the spray into the shoe.

The door slammed behind me. He looked up and arched a brow ever so slightly. "Well, Paige. Can't say I'm surprised to see you."

"I just had to have a pizza, Walt," I said, trying to sound as if I was really starving.

He set the shoe and can on the counter. "I know you like our pizzas, but let's cut to the chase, Paige. We saw you and Hazel running down the alley, so I reckon you're really here to find out what I know about Fulcrum."

My mouth dropped into a big fly-catching cavern.

He chuckled. "Right. How about we go to the break room? I just made a fresh pot of coffee."

He didn't wait for a response, but flipped up the hinged section of the counter and lumbered toward the far end of the long room. I picked my chin up from the floor and followed, sidestepping another employee who rolled a dolly with cases of beverages toward the bar area. The sound of balls rushing down the alley and crashing into pins was absent. Wednesday night was league night, and the sessions didn't start for another forty-five minutes.

The ten-by-ten space of the break room was just large enough to hold a counter with a sink and a round table surrounded by chairs that had more duct tape holding the seats together than vinyl. The laminated-plastic-topped table, a bright yellow with sparkly flecks, had obviously been through many years of bowling wars. It held cigarette burns as testament to its years of service. Fortunately, the tiny room smelled only of the rich aroma of fine coffee.

"Go ahead, sit," Walt said, his tone friendly. He washed his hands, thank goodness, and grabbed a full coffeepot. "You take cream or sugar?"

"Black is good," I answered as I selected the least cracked vinyl chair and sat.

He brought over two white mugs. "I'm not sure how much of this story you know, but I'm tired of keeping it quiet. I'm going to let it all out once and for all. That okay with you?"

Feeling a little guilty at not having to pry out the details—or maybe I was disappointed at the lack of challenge—I accepted the mug and nodded.

He dropped his heavy weight onto a cushion that wheezed out a steady stream of air until he'd shifted around and finally settled. "First let me say that Bud Picklemann, no matter his underhanded methods, has been good for this town. Don't let anyone tell you differently. He brought more jobs and commerce to Serendipity than anyone in our history, and *I* think he's the reason the town is still viable. Now, that said, he was a rascal."

Walt shook his head sorrowfully. "What you want to know about is the day Ida Carlson's daughter came to our council meeting. She was mad. Boy, was she mad. Told Picklemann off like a pro, she did. Also told all of us that Picklemann owned the land through his company, Fulcrum. She even brought papers to prove it." Walt stopped and sipped his coffee. "Well, I tell you, that was like dropping a bomb. Gus took over like he always does and talked to the woman. Don't know what he said to her, but she left."

"He threatened her and her mother," I blurted out. "Nancy Kimble told me that."

He shook his head again. "I'm real sorry to hear that. All these years I thought Picklemann was paying her off like he was paying us off. I'd hoped Ida was being compensated that way." He stopped and stared into the open doorway.

I watched for a while, growing antsy. "What happened after she left?"

"Chaos broke out. Now, I'm not usually a leader, but I felt real strongly that if this news got out, people might boycott working at the factory. We needed that place. It was time we provided jobs for our kids so they didn't have to go elsewhere." His tone bordered on televangelist zeal.

"You sound like you really believe that."

"I do. My oldest son, Billy, works with me, but I didn't have enough business to keep the other two employed. They're both in Portland. Don't see them or their kids as much as I'd like." Another long drag on his cup until a faraway look cleared from his eyes. "So anyway, as I tried to convince the men to let the ownership thing go, forget all about it, Picklemann pops up and promises to pay each of us five hundred dollars a month not to tell. Well, I tell you, I didn't have to say another word to the men. That was the end of the discussion, and Picklemann came through with cash every month."

I leaned forward, careful not to touch the germ-laden table. "You said at the hardware store that if this came out in the open it might help solve the murder. What did you mean by that?"

Walt lowered his coffee and slowly twirled the liquid. "I didn't mean anything in particular. I just thought that maybe this was all tied together somehow. If we told Chief Lawson the truth, we might expose the killer."

"So if you had to choose, which one of the council members do you think might have done Bud in?"

"Now, Paige. I think you're misunderstanding me. I've had the pleasure of serving on the council for years with these men. They all took money for the wrong reason, but I would bet my own life that none of them had a thing to do with Picklemann's death. And if their reputations don't convince you, think about it. Why would any of us kill the source of a monthly payment? Picklemann paid every month, right on time, and never hinted that he might stop."

"What if one of the men got greedy? Or had problems with his finances and asked for more money?"

Walt shook his head. "In a town this small, I'd a heard if one of the guys was hurting. And why after ten years of a good deal would someone want to make a change? No, I think Picklemann was killed because of something more current."

Unfortunately for me, Walt made complete sense. "Any ideas?"

He sat back and pondered my question. "I watch those *CSI* shows all the time. Seems like money is the number one reason people are killed. I know Picklemann was struggling with Charlie Sweeny over something. I don't mean to imply Charlie's capable of murder, simply that he's been different since his son died."

"What were they struggling over?" I tried to keep the excitement out of my voice, but there it was, thick and heavy in my words. The hope that this might be *the* clue.

"I don't know for sure, but Picklemann was working on the Leever deal to buy up land right outside town. You hear about that?"

"Uma told me all about it."

"Well, then, she probably told you Charlie refused the offer. If Charlie didn't sell, the deal fell through, and Bud was sunk. I'd heard them argue about it several times."

Oh, really! The deal fell through if Charlie held out, huh? Maybe Charlie and Bud argued about it again. And Charlie got so mad he gave Bud a whack with a shovel. Not on purpose, but in the heat of the moment. This certainly screamed motive to me.

"I don't like that look much, young lady. Your eyes look like a cat's eyes. One that has a mouse trapped in its sights. You going to chase after Charlie the minute you leave here?"

The minute I left. Nah, it was too late in the day for that. I would chase after Charlie first thing in the morning, of that Walt could be sure.

CHANGER ⫼ NINETEEN

"And now, enjoy the best of Through the Garden Gate *with your beloved host, Paige Turner."*

"This is All Washed Up with a complaint about your advice."

"I want to make sure my callers are happy, so go ahead, All Washed Up. Tell me what's bothering you."

"Well, I tried to follow your step-by-step instructions for putting in a small pond."

"How wonderful. Water gardening can be as fun as digging in the soil."

"Not for me. I got the pond in, but I'm having trouble with the plants. You mentioned one of your favorites is lettuce."

"Yes, water lettuce is great. Although it does flower, the blooms are seldom seen, and that might be your problem, but it does provide much needed shade for any fish you might have added to your pond."

"Like it even floats. I've been chunking in head after head of lettuce from the grocery store, and it don't do nothing."

In case Charlie was still at work, I wandered past the pharmacy. As I'd figured, the pharmacy closed at the usual time of five thirty, and Charlie had left the building. I could stop by his house, but he had a reputation of being exceedingly difficult if he was bothered at night. So I took the cheese pizza Walt insisted I have to my apartment and settled in for a night of computer sleuthing.

With a caffeinated soda and a plate of pizza, I plopped behind the small student desk that was in the apartment when I moved in and turned on my computer. While waiting, I chomped on pizza and doodled on a notepad. Fulcrum. Leever. Were they related?

I took a sip of the cola, and my gaze drifted to the picture sitting on my desk of Lisa and her family. One I'd taken less than a year ago on the Oregon coast. We were all so jubilant and messy after a day of romping on the beach. The girls' hair was tangled and damp, Perry's face sunburned, and Lisa's lips wide with an enthusiastic smile. Her upturned mouth and beaming eyes were so far from the way her face had crumbled during the afternoon debacle. Looking at the picture intensified the episode in my mind, and I wanted to talk with her.

After leaving the bowling alley, I'd called to check up on her. She didn't answer her cell. I hoped she and Perry were working things out, so instead of racing over to her house, I left a message on her voice mail. If I didn't hear from her tonight, I would see her first thing in the morning, no matter what.

But now I needed to concentrate on locating information that could solve this murder. I connected to a search engine and typed in "fulcrum." Although I'd already researched the company itself, I wanted to look up the basic description of fulcrum on Wikipedia to see if something would jog my mind.

I read the words on the screen aloud. "A *fulcrum* is the support or point of support on which a lever turns." Hmm, lever, Leever? A connection perhaps? Did Bud have more of a role in Leever than he let on? Before I could pursue the thought, my cell rang.

"Lisa." I grabbed the phone and saw Adam's name. I didn't think I'd be disappointed to see Adam calling, but a pang of sadness crept over me as I wished it were Lisa.

"Hey," I said with extra enthusiasm so he wouldn't know he was my second choice of caller. "Perfect timing. I was totally bored looking at my computer screen."

"More Fulcrum research?" he asked.

"Sort of." I filled him in on the council's confessions, my conversation with Walt, and my wild thought that there was a connection between Leever and Fulcrum. "I don't have anything that really points at Charlie, but it's a lead anyway."

For a short while, he said nothing, as if choosing his words carefully. "I know you don't want to hear this, Paige, but it's time to hire a professional or tell Lawson what you've discovered."

I sighed. "I don't want to do either one. No telling how Mitch might bungle this."

"*You* might not be bungling it, but with as complicated as this is getting, I can't see how you're going to resolve things on your own."

"Thanks for the confidence in me." My words came out sharper than I'd hoped.

"Paige, come on." His tone was consoling. "This is a murder investigation. Do you really think you have the skills to solve it?"

"Yes, I do. Apparently you don't have faith in me." Realizing this was leading to a fight, I counted to ten before going on. "Did you call for a reason, or just to harass me?"

"I'm not harassing you, and I did call for a reason. Lawson called me. You need to stop by the station tomorrow. He didn't give me a time. Said come in at your leisure, but we'll want to schedule a time when I'm free to accompany you. I'm in court all day tomorrow, so I'll set up an appointment for late in the day. I'll text you with the time once Lawson agrees."

"Why does he want to see me?"

"I questioned him, but he was vague. Rumors are, they've gotten the forensic report on the shovel. Perhaps it proves the shovel was used to hit Bud, and Lawson wants to put a little pressure on you in the hopes that you'll confess to killing him."

Guess this was the forensics report Perry mentioned at lunch. This was not good news. Not at all what I wanted to hear right now. Mitch was moving along nicely in his quest to convict me, while I was coming up empty-handed. I sat back, tears nearing the surface. "This can't be happening. I'm innocent, Adam. They can't send me to jail."

"That's why I want you to hire an investigator. You can't do this on your own."

My ire rose at his lack of faith. "If that's all you have to say, I have to get back to work."

He groaned and let the phone fall silent. I waited for him to speak. After a long and particularly uncomfortable time, I decided to end the call.

"Is there something else?" I asked.

This time a sigh. "No, nothing else. Just think about what I said."

I said good-bye and hung up. I needed to work harder. Smarter. Faster. With a renewed purpose, I focused on the screen and clicked through link after link, page after page, hour after hour. I finished the list of five hundred plus Fulcrum leads, searched county records, googled Leever and Pacific Pickles and all their officers, and finally sat back in defeat.

Maybe Adam was right. Maybe I needed to hire a pro. I was nearly out of clues to follow. I laid my forehead on the cool desk, trying to dig up the energy to plan ahead. I closed my eyes and felt my confidence and drive melt away.

A knock sounded on the door, and I bolted upright. I'd left a trail of drool on the desktop. I must have dozed off. As I answered the continued pounding, I glanced at the clock. Nearly nine. I opened the door and yawned.

"Is it too late?" Lisa asked.

I held out my hand to invite her in then twisted my head and stretched my neck. "I fell asleep in front of the computer. I was hoping I'd hear from you tonight. How are things with Perry?"

She laughed in her normal cheerful way, sending a wave of happiness through me. "With Perry, fine." She sat cross-legged on the worn blue sofa. "With my self-respect, not so good."

I sat beside her. "So the two of you talked?"

"Yeah. He told me he was getting bored at work. He's limited to what he can do here in Serendipity. He asked me if I would consider moving if he found another job."

Move! No. She couldn't leave me here with all the quirky plants of the world. I had to have Lisa around to keep me sane. I tried to keep my angst at the thought of losing my best friend off my face and out of my voice. "Would you move?"

"If it meant Perry was happy, yeah, I would." She laughed again, this time in a more mocking tone. "Besides, after my performance today, we might need to leave town."

"It wasn't *that* bad."

She snorted and swatted a hand at me. "Spoken like the friend you are. I figure the best thing I can do right now is get out in public in normal clothes and show them I'm okay."

"I'd offer to do lunch with you tomorrow, but I'm behind at the shop, and Adam just told me I have to go see Mitch tomorrow." I shared the highlights of my conversation with Adam.

"Adam's right, you know." Her mom voice was now in full bloom. "You have to let go of this, Paige, and let someone else help you."

"Yeah, right. Like you did with Perry?"

She laughed, head thrown back, once again telling me everything with her would be all right. "And you saw how well that worked. If I had turned it over to God, I would never have done something so stupid. So learn from me. Ask for help."

We moved into the kitchen and chatted about her conversation with Perry and of the possible places she might like to live if they moved. I worked on preparing a soothing bedtime tea so we both could get a good night's sleep for a change.

Another knock sounded on the door.

I spun around. "Who could that be?"

"I didn't know you were so popular," Lisa said from a barstool at the counter. "Want me to get it?"

"Please." I continued filling the teapot.

Lisa peeked under the curtain. "It's Adam."

As the door creaked open, I put the pot on the stove. What was Adam doing here? Did he come to argue more? Or maybe he came to drag me down to the station to tell Mitch what I knew. I dried my hands on a worn dish towel and crossed the room.

Wearing a polo shirt and no jacket, Adam stood on the landing, dancing a bit to keep warm. Though we'd had a tiff, the sight of him eased my frustration and helped chase out the chill that whipped into the room. His face was meek and his eyes apologetic.

I opened my mouth to ask why he was here.

He held up a hand. "Before you say anything, I know it's late, but I didn't like the way we left things. So I wanted to apologize in person for not supporting you." He clapped his hands on his arms to stay warm.

"Come in before you freeze," I said with a belligerent tone that was meant to cover up how thrilled I was that he cared enough to drive all the way from McMinnville to apologize. "I'm making tea. Want some?"

"Not a tea guy," he said, his tone clipped and unusually terse.

Maybe I just needed to warm him up. "How about hot chocolate?"

He shook his head. "Just give me a few minutes of your time."

"So, sit then." I held my hand toward the living room.

"Maybe I should go?" Lisa held the doorknob and took a step toward the landing.

I shook my head. "No, you stay."

She searched my face then said, "I'll finish making the tea."

She went into the kitchen, and Adam ambled toward the plaid love seat handed down from my mom. It was worn and sagging, but I didn't want to part with it. The memories from the day she helped me move into my first apartment clung to the faded blue and red fabric like I wanted to cling to her.

I watched Adam lower his body onto the end cushion. This was perfect, the man I was growing to like sitting on one of my fondest memories. But he perched on the edge as if he'd bolt for the door if I said the wrong thing.

Our eyes connected. He opened his mouth then closed and opened it again. I listened to the tabletop fountain sitting on a sofa table behind him and wished I could make him speed up to at least the pace of the slowly dripping water. He was making me nervous.

"Out with it already," I said.

"If you never want to talk to me again, I'll understand. I can even find you another lawyer."

Surprised and confused by his words, I quickly glanced at Lisa, who had her back to me. I dropped onto my favorite overstuffed chair with a big plop. "Okay."

"I know you don't want anyone to take over this investigation. You made it perfectly clear that you didn't want to hire anyone, but I have an investigator who works for me all the time and—"

I flapped my hand up like a crossing guard demanding a driver to stop. "You came all the way over here to convince me to hire an investigator? Un-be-lieve-a-ble."

"Now, Paige, before you get all mad, just listen. I don't want you to hire Frankie. I already sort of did."

"What?" I jumped up and looked to Lisa for support. Her head was buried in the pantry, probably looking for cookies to go with the tea. I turned back to Adam.

His eyes begged me to give him a chance. "Please, just hear me out."

Should I? He'd gone where no man should boldly go, into my control zone. This was the very point in my relationships in the past where I said *adios, amigos* to any guy who survived our first date. His motives might be good, but if I let him take over this area of my life, what was next? And next and next and next?

"Bud Picklemann owned Leever." His words rushed out like racing floodwaters. "He had a scam so big planned it made the pickle factory look like child's play."

"What?" Feeling like I might drop, I fell back onto the chair.

"It's true. He was buying up all that land, but not to re-rent the places back to the tenants. He was going to sell it for a casino." The expression in Adam's eyes changed from hesitant to excited.

"Those people would have been booted out of their homes."

Mine remained wary. "How did you find this out?"

"On my way back home after our lunch, I got to thinking about what you said about the Leever thing seeming suspicious. And Picklemann was involved, so I asked Frankie to check into it. He has access to records and people you could never get to. If it turned out to be nothing, then I could forget about it. If Frankie found something suspicious, then I would have to risk telling you about it, even if you never talked to me again."

Maybe his betrayal wasn't as bad as I first thought. "So you didn't hire Frankie to take over the investigation? Just to check out Leever?"

"Well, and one other thing. I asked him to look into Picklemann's finances. He's working on that right now."

"But you said—"

He held up a hand. "No way you could get that kind of information, and it could be important."

"And that's it. You stopped there, and you'll never do anything remotely like this again without talking to me first?"

"Exactly." He forced a tiny smile to his lips, the scar moving a mere fraction.

I looked at him. Really looked at the man I thought I might be interested in. His eyes neared panic level, and his hands twisted. Could I let him take this one little step? Could I trust him not to dig deeper?

He must have sensed me wavering as he smiled like a little boy pleading for something from his mother, and my resolve to end our budding relationship faded.

I was thirty-four years old. If I ever wanted to enter into a relationship that lasted more than a week, I would have to figure out how to let people who cared about me help with my problems.

And, more to the point in my life right now, I was also going to have to track Charlie down first thing in the morning for sure. Between what Walt told me and what Adam just said, if this was the secret Charlie threatened to expose, he had full motive to stop Bud, any way he could.

CHAPTER TWENTY

*"This is Harly Davison, your host of KALM's
exciting new show,* Wacky World of Motorcycles,
*asking you to join me on Friday at nine o'clock,
when I'll be broadcasting a special show live at
Pickle Fest. And for those gardening fans who'll miss
the regularly scheduled* Through the Garden Gate,
*I say, quit wasting your time digging in the dirt and
get a Hog to do it for you."*

As much as I wanted to talk to Charlie, in all the commotion
the night before, I forgot to set my alarm and had to rush to
arrive at the station on time. With my truck at the shop, I jogged
down Main Street, grooming my hair as I went. I was a mess,
but the show was moving along just fine. Not one wacko had
phoned, and even if one had, my rejuvenated Lisa would have
kept him at bay.

Her usual little finger to her mouth, a silly I-love-my-husband
grin in place, and her thumb to her ear, signaled the next caller
was on the line.

"You're on *Through The Garden Gate* with Paige Turner,
caller," I said, catching Lisa's enthusiasm and concentrating

it into my voice.

"This is Weed Whacker, and this will be my last time calling you." Her tone bordered on bitter and accusing.

What did my parents tell me about things that were too good to be true? I should have known a normal show was too much to expect. "What's wrong, Weed Whacker? You sound upset."

"I am upset. I followed your advice, and what did I get from it? My life falls apart all around me."

I could certainly sympathize with her as my life was disintegrating, too, but I would never admit that on the air. Her problem was another story. She'd called, so I felt no guilt in prying. "Is everything all right with your husband?"

"No it's not, and it's all your fault."

She did it. She killed him, and it *was* my fault. "Oh dear, what happened?"

"Remember I told you I was digging that big hole?"

"Yes, a hole that required a backhoe," I clarified for the listeners, and unfortunately clarified in my own mind that we could be talking about a grave here.

"I did just like you said. I rented the stupid backhoe and made the hole six feet deep. Well, Earl is a sleepwalker, and the night after I finished digging, he wandered into the garden and fell into the hole. He broke his leg and spent the whole night calling for me. I didn't find him until the morning. He was good and mad. Said he had plenty of time to think about things. When I pulled him out, he was convinced that I had no real gardening purpose for such a big hole. That I planned to kill him and bury him there. Have you ever heard such a crazy idea?"

I cut a sheepish look at Lisa, whose eyes were as wide as mine must have been. "In Earl's defense, I can see how he might think that."

206 NIPPED IN THE BUD

"I can't, but it doesn't seem to matter. He said I've become obsessed with gardening. Let it take over my love for him, and he's gonna leave me." She sighed, and her emotions ripped through me.

I wasn't responsible for her murdering Earl, but I had somehow been responsible for ending a marriage. I had to find out how. "So, Weed Whacker, I have to ask. Why did you need to dig such a big hole, anyway?"

"I was just following the notes I took from your show on planting lily bulbs." Her surprised tone took me aback.

Eyes furrowed, I looked at Lisa again, and we both shrugged. As Alice said, this was getting "curiouser and curiouser".

"I think you might be a little confused. I would never suggest digging a hole that deep to plant lilies."

"You did. It's right here in my notes. Word for word. Dig a trench—remember you said it's easier to lay out bulbs in a trench if you have a lot of them to plant?—and dig a hole six feet deep to be sure the bulbs are buried at the optimum depth."

"Wait, Weed Whacker, hold on. I think you made a mistake when you took notes. I said six inches deep, not six feet."

"Oh. . .well. . .I guess that makes more sense." She sighed, sending her pain whispering over the airwaves. "No wonder Earl didn't believe me."

"Listen, Weed Whacker, if it would help get you and Earl back together, please have him call me, and I'll explain about the hole."

After I disconnected, Lisa and I shared a grin that I had to fight from turning into peals of laughter. I no longer felt any responsibility for Weed Whacker's marriage fiasco, and even though I seriously hoped Earl didn't call me, if he did, I would do my best to convince him to go home to his wacky wife. Perhaps

I'd even suggest he listen to the show with her in the future so she didn't make another life-altering mistake.

And speaking of life altering, I left Lisa the moment we went off the air and rushed off to find Charlie. As it turned out, I didn't have to search for him. He and I literally bumped into each other as I ran around the corner of Oak and Main. Happy for the collision, I stepped back and smiled. "Good morning, Charlie."

"Paige," Charlie grunted and moved to push past me.

Wait, what? He couldn't leave so fast.

"Was the fact that Bud owned Leever the secret you mentioned in the park?" I blurted out without much thought.

His saggy eyelids tightened as his eyes grew to the size of headlights on the big SUV parked at the curb. "Picklemann owned Leever?" His mouth dropped open.

So what if Charlie seemed like he didn't know about Leever. I wouldn't stop. I needed one single clue to pan out. Oh, how I needed one. "Come on, Charlie. Fess up. You knew Bud owned Leever."

He searched my eyes for a moment. "I don't appreciate the way you keep trying to make me out to be a killer. I will say that I had no idea Picklemann was up to something with the land deal."

"You fought him on it. You had to know."

"Look at me, Paige." He held his hands out, palms up. "I'm an old man. Too old to change. I'd never let anybody own my house and by virtue of that, own me."

His voice was solid and sure. Even if I hooked him up to a lie detector machine, he couldn't be any more honest. Too bad he didn't lie. The thought of connecting Charlie, who wouldn't ever give me a straight answer, to a machine with current running through it, was appealing. Maybe, just maybe, he'd finally tell me the truth without mechanical means. "If this wasn't the secret, then what was?"

He folded chubby arms across a wide chest. "Tell me about Leever."

I sighed and considered my options. If I told him about Leever, he might feel obligated to share his news with me. It was worth the risk. All through my telling he kept shaking his head, and his face grew so angry and rigid that I was afraid he might have a heart attack or stroke.

Before another man died this week and left me holding the bag, I said, "Okay, so I told you what I know. Now you tell me your secret."

He shook his head and took a step away. "Told Lawson. He's the only one who needs to know."

Man! This guy must never have gone to preschool or kindergarten. He didn't have a clue how to share.

"Please, Charlie, answer one question for me," I called out, stopping him.

He turned, and his face had cleared.

So we would not be overheard, I closed the distance between us. "You won't tell me what the secret is, and I guess I have to respect that. If you told Mitch about it, you must believe this secret has something to do with Bud's murder. Do you?"

He shook his head. "Nope. Just answered Lawson's questions about my visit to the park with you and Picklemann, and my argument with Rachel later in the morning."

"So you and Rachel fought about this secret?"

He gave a clipped nod.

"You said you didn't think the secret had anything to do with the murder. Have you changed your mind?"

"Don't know. I need to think about what you told me about Leever and see if it changes things."

"And then you'll tell me?"

He groaned. "We've been all through this, Paige. It's none of your business." He turned and marched off.

I set out for The Garden Gate. I needed to know what Charlie was protecting, and there was no way Mitch would tell me what it was. I was sunk on that front. I could only wait and hope Charlie rethought his loyalty to the person he promised to keep the secret for.

Heart slightly downtrodden, I gave myself a pep talk. I would not succumb to pity this early in the morning. I still had one ace up my sleeve. The reporter. I guess he was more like a joker at this point, but he could turn into an ace. I hoped for a king at the very least. And who knew, I might learn something more about Stacey that would give me reason to move her up on my suspect list from possible to viable.

Rounding the corner, my cell chirped with a text message. I pulled out the phone and scrolled down the screen. My appointment with Mitch was set for five thirty. Adam would meet me at the police station. I had a whole day to prepare snarky comebacks to what I imagined Mitch might say.

I entered the shop and spotted stacks of containers near the counter. My intuition told me things were coming to a head on the investigation, and I wanted nothing more than to run off to the newspaper office to follow up on the reporter, but I couldn't. Not yet. I had to think positively. Keep believing I wouldn't go to jail, and that meant working at The Garden Gate to keep it running. When the workload here lifted, I'd go.

Between dealing with the customer traffic that always picked up on Thursdays and creating the luscious containers for the

Pickle Fest, Hazel, Teri, and I spent the full day rushing around the shop. Now, nearly five p.m. and closing time at the *Serendipity Times*, I shuffled through the stacks of papers on my desk until I located an advertising bill and my checkbook. I didn't want another day to pass before I investigated Zac Young, and I had just enough time before I met with Adam and Mitch to do so.

I rushed out the back door and headed straight for the newspaper office. I hurried down the street, clutching the checkbook and bill as if they were the lifeline I so needed. I don't know what I'd do if this turned out to be another dead end.

At the door, out of breath and excited to hear good news, I paused.

Deep breaths. Calm down, Paige. Won't do you any good to let the wily reporter see you like this.

When my heart returned to normal, and I was sure I could control my voice, I pushed through the door and into the shop. The strong scent of newsprint and ink permeated the disorganized space. I worked my way through piles of old newspapers and haphazard stacks of boxes. A long wooden counter stained with ink ran the width of the shop. Behind it sat Jack, the paper's editor and one of my mom's dearest friends. His fingers clicked away on a keyboard, and his focus was riveted on a computer monitor.

"Hey, Jack," I said with a genuine smile for an old friend. "I've come to pay my bill."

"Paige, good to see you." He smiled, and his face looked like a road map with all the deep lines running through it. "How are you holding up?"

"Okay, I guess." I laid the bill and checkbook on the counter and scribbled the amount due on the check. "Say, Jack," I said in an offhand manner, "I was reading old council minutes at the library and saw a bunch of articles by a Zac Young. He work for you?"

Jack came to my end of the counter, planted his elbows, and leaned forward. "Sure enough. He was a smart young man. Ambitious, too. Started working for me right out of college. Said he wanted to learn the newspaper business from the ground up and no better place to do it than in a small shop like mine. He did some fine work here. Was sorry to lose him."

I ripped out the check and flipped the register pages until I located a blank line. "I heard he left for the bright lights of the big city."

"You heard right. The *really* big one. New York." Jack's tone bordered on awestruck. "Works for the *Post* covering business news. I see his byline quite often. Sends me a fruit basket every Christmas."

Trying to keep from getting excited over the possibility that Jack knew how to get hold of Zac, I slowly wrote the amount in the register and said, "Sounds like the two of you were pretty close."

"Sort of thought of him as a son. That's why, when he up and left unexpectedly, I made sure we kept in touch."

I closed the checkbook and looked at Jack. "Unexpectedly, huh?"

"That's right." Jack fanned the check as his eyes turned dreamy. "I remember the day like it was yesterday, except it was a Tuesday. Zac attended the monthly council meeting the night before and stopped by late in the afternoon to give me the copy. Said he didn't have another job yet, but he'd made the decision to move on. Surprised me. He never mentioned wanting to leave until he quit. Gave me two weeks and then took off for New York. He musta saved most of his pay when he lived here, 'cause he didn't get a job in New York for almost a year. Of course I don't know what kind of place he was living in. Still, it costs a lot to live in the city."

Hmm, left right after a council meeting. Perhaps the one where Nancy Kimble attacked Bud. Had enough money to live in New York for a year. I definitely needed to talk to the lad. "You know how I can get ahold of him?"

"Well, sure." He grabbed a notepad and wrote down Zac's contact info. "Why all the interest in Zac?"

"Like I said, I'm trying to find out who killed Bud. I figure if I talk to everyone who came in contact with him, I'm bound to find a lead."

"Zac's been gone for over ten years now. How could he have anything to do with Picklemann's murder?"

My first instinct was to share the information I'd learned about Fulcrum and Leever. Jack was a good friend of my mom's, and I was pretty sure he'd keep it quiet. "Pretty" was the operative word here. I wasn't 100 percent certain of his silence, so I had to keep mum. "Oh, I don't think he had a thing to do with the murder. Just might give me some background information about how Bud related to the council members."

"You think one of the council members did Picklemann in?"

"I don't know, Jack. Could be anyone around here. Could be you for all I know."

He erupted with a crackly and gruff laugh. "You've always been such a kidder, Paige. I wish your mom could have lived to see how you turned out. She'd be proud for sure."

Wishing my mom were here, too, I left Jack with a hug and a promise to come to his house for dinner real soon. Neither of us acknowledged the heavy thought that hung in the air. . .*if* I didn't go to jail. And if I didn't want to go to jail for failing to follow Mitch's demands, I best head over to the station for my appointment.

As I walked in the cooling night air, I dialed Zac's number only to get voice mail. I left an urgent message and made sure I had plenty of charge left on my phone in case he called back soon. Stowing the phone, I pushed into the police station.

An officer who looked like he wasn't old enough to shave sat behind the desk that a receptionist manned during regular business hours. I walked up, leaned over the counter, and read his name badge. "Officer Riley, I'm here to—"

"I know why you're here. Take a seat. Someone will be out for you."

"Fine," I said. "But I'm not talking to Mitch until my attorney gets here."

He shrugged and swiveled his chair. "Paige Turner's here," he called into a microphone on the desk.

Lamenting the fact that Mitch's bad manners appeared to be contagious among his men, I sat in a faded armchair next to a table holding a wilting pothos. They sure didn't care for their plants here. If I survived this whole ordeal, I would offer to stop by weekly and tend to them. That might be too late for this parched baby. She needed an infusion of water quick. Barring a call to 911, what could I do? I heard a gurgle and remembered a water dispenser sat just behind the reception desk.

Only my love of plants would send me back to talk to the officer. "Can I get a glass of water?" I asked him.

"Knock yourself out," he said and punched the phone line that had pealed a few times. He greeted the caller then sporadically offered various inflections of a grunt.

Thinking he might be talking to an ape on the other end, I filled two glasses with water and returned to the plant. The arid soil sucked the moisture like a parched man at an oasis. I sat down and poured slowly, letting the water soak in, not run through the hard soil to the tray on the bottom.

"Paige, come on back." Mitch's voice booming from above pulled me back to reality.

"I won't talk to you until my attorney arrives," I said without looking up at him and continuing to pour. "You need someone to look after these plants. The ficus in the conference room is in sad shape, too."

"Excuse me for focusing on protecting people instead of watering plants," he grumbled.

While Mitch fidgeted, I finished tending to the neglected darling. Let him see how it felt to be kept waiting.

"Hey, Chief," Officer Riley bellowed. "That was the ME on the phone. Says he'll finish the autopsy on Picklemann tonight and have the report on your desk first thing in the morning."

The autopsy? Did this change anything? Could Mitch use the autopsy report against me somehow? I looked up to gauge his reaction.

"Well, Paige," he said with a snide grin. "We don't need to have our little conversation after all. Looks like this could be your last night of freedom. I suggest you get out of here and spend it wisely."

CHAPTER ⛏⛏⛏ TWENTY-ONE

"And now, enjoy the best of Through the Garden
Gate *with your beloved host, Paige Turner."*

*"Hi, Paige, this is All Dug Out in Tigard. I'm
having a problem with my container gardening."*

*"Thank you for calling, All Dug Out. I'm
so happy that you've chosen to use containers in
your garden. There's nothing like an assortment of
containers to add color all around the area."*

*"Well, yeah, that's what you said, but I bought
about twenty different containers. I got different
colors and textures, even sizes, and planted them all
over the yard. That was about six weeks ago, and not
a one of them silly pots has bloomed."*

Tears clouding my vision, I left the police station and ran smack-dab into Charlie as I had earlier. This time as I tried to right myself, I kicked a large terra-cotta container filled with pansies and sent it into an earthquake tremble. Unlike our last encounter, though, I no longer felt a need to be diplomatic.

I grabbed the arm of his pharmacy jacket and stopped him from passing by. "Mitch pretty much told me he was going to arrest me in the morning. So, Charlie, please, stop being so pigheaded, and tell me Bud's secret."

"Can't. I promised not to." He shook his arm free and stomped off.

I stood as if someone had encased my feet in the concrete of the sidewalk and watched him and my future walk away. My mouth fell open when he yanked hard on the door to the police station. In a stiff march that reminded me of a funeral procession, he entered the building.

Huh? The police station? What was he up to? Did he have more information for Mitch that he withheld from me? Was this a glimmer of hope I could hold on to? Was he helping to clear my name? If he *were* here to help me, why had he been so closemouthed again? *Simple, Paige. He wasn't here to help. He was probably delivering a prescription.*

I shook off my questions and walked aimlessly down the street. At the park, I strolled straight to the play area for the first time since the day of Bud's death. There was no evidence that I had ever worked or found Bud here. Instead, there were dozens of volunteers hard at work constructing booths for the Pickle Fest. They were joined by children running around and men bantering with one another. The anticipation of the annual fun that would begin tomorrow flowed like an electric current through the air.

· If things were different, I would be excited about the craziness of Pickle Fest, too. Pickle bobbing, pickle eating contests, and everything pickle filled the weekend and brought the town together with all the residents in their best moods.

Not me. Not this year. I would be crabby with a capitol *C*. If I was even free to attend it.

I sat on the square tower in the center of the play structure and tucked my legs under my arms. This was as good a place as any to sink into my own deserved fest, a pity fest. Wrongly accused of a crime, I was going to jail tomorrow. I had earned the right to cry. My cell rang. I pulled it from the clip, and without looking at the caller's identity, silenced the pealing. It was probably Adam looking for me. Why waste my last night of freedom talking? If I were incarcerated tomorrow, talking was the one freedom I would retain.

I turned off the ringer to prevent further interruptions and returned to my pity party. Briny tromped into the mulch with a throng of children trailing behind. I never did hear who they hired to play Briny. Gender was certainly veiled in the beelike abdomen of the pickle that rose up over the head. The long slender legs encased in Robin Hood green tights and almost delicate arms indicated a woman.

The tiny tots invading the play structure didn't care if the pickle was male or female. They screamed and latched onto the costume, sending me in search of solitude elsewhere. I strolled down the long line of booths constructed from two-by-fours and heavy canvas. I nodded at booth occupants, who were stocking their space for tomorrow. Few returned my greeting. I was a pariah. A dead woman walking.

I reached the end of the row where my large stall sat waiting for plants. I entered the space and thought about sitting down to mope. But why? What good would that do? I could choose to wallow in my troubles, or I could prepare for tomorrow and not think about the potential for jail at all. Far healthier. Far easier. I chose work.

Suddenly energized, I rushed out of the space and nearly collided with Briny. Standing as tall as I did, the mascot held his or her ground. Which was it, him or her? I voted for him. A woman had never played Briny before. I sidestepped the pickle and headed for my shop. Briny kept pace, following me like a puppy dog all the way to the end of the park.

At my shop, I gathered signage, tables, and display stands and loaded them into the bed of my truck. I made three trips to the park. Each time Briny rushed forward and in silence—as a giant pickle can't speak—he helped carry items to my booth. On the final trip, I thanked him for his help and told him I could handle things from here. I never imagined a fake pickle could pull an attitude, but he did. With bent head and shuffling feet, he clomped away as if I'd hurt his feelings but remained within eyesight.

I happily arranged laminated cubes by the entrance to my stall, humming and aligning them just so. A commotion down the way erupted, and I looked up. Lisa, Perry, and Adam, in animated conversation, hurried down the main pathway. Near my booth, Briny suddenly leaped in front of my friends and stopped their forward progress. He danced in zigzag steps, keeping them at bay.

Seeing the interest of the onlookers grow, I rushed over to my buddies. "Briny, give it a rest, and let my friends through." I felt like Moses asking Pharaoh to let his people go.

Briny stepped back, and Lisa darted into the opening. She rushed forward like a teenage girl spotting her favorite male celebrity and grabbed me into a hug that felt like a bone-crushing effort for the little sprite. "Where have you been?"

Not waiting for an answer, she released me, and Adam took over. He held me so tight I thought I might explode from the pressure.

"I was worried. When I went to the station and neither you nor Mitch were there, I thought something bad had happened."

"Sorry," I whispered back. "I should have called you."

He drew me closer, and as much as I wanted to hug this man,

the sight of me sitting behind bars and this wonderful man on the other side flashed into my mind, and I pushed back to look at Lisa and Perry. Both faces were tight with worry.

I could understand Adam being upset because I wasn't at the police station, but why were they so concerned? "What's wrong with you guys?"

"We've been looking all over for you," Perry scolded, in his father-knows-best tone that he usually reserved for his girls.

I shrugged. "I've been right here. Setting up for tomorrow."

"Why didn't you answer your phone?" Lisa took on Perry's mad parent tone.

"I was busy."

"Is that the only reason?" Lisa asked.

I waved it off. "Yeah, I'm fine. Really."

"Cut it out, Paige." Lisa grabbed my arm and gave me the look that said I don't believe you. "What's going on?"

"Okay, fine. Stay, Briny." I commanded the pickle as I would an unruly dog and walked back to my booth. Briny complied, and my friends tromped into the space. When we had privacy, I continued. "While I was waiting for Adam to arrive for our appointment at the police station, Mitch found out the autopsy report would be available tomorrow. He said we didn't need to have a meeting and that this was likely my last night as a free woman."

"And you didn't tell us?" Lisa's voice hit the top of the scale.

"It's not like you can do anything to stop him." I shivered at my blunt words.

Adam inched closer and wrapped an arm around me. "You're cold."

I stepped away. "I'm fine."

"Well, I'm not," Lisa said. "We need to talk about this."

"No, really, we don't."

Lisa tipped her head at Briny, who'd advanced on us when we weren't paying attention. "We'll go to your apartment where we can talk without an audience."

"Good idea." Adam once again wrapped his arm around my shoulders.

"I'll stay here and close up for Paige," Perry said to Lisa. "Then I'll pick up the girls and take them home. You go with Paige. Spend the night with her."

"Hey, come on," I cried as they railroaded me. "I don't want to talk about this, and I certainly don't need a babysitter."

"Hah!" Lisa shouted. "Yes, you do. Just look at you. Don't know enough to tell your best friend when you need her. You need a babysitter all right. And I'm not leaving your side."

As if I had no say in the matter, Adam hurried me into the front seat of his car and cranked up the heater. Lisa, for once quiet, climbed into the back. An uncomfortable silence filled the space as we drove to my apartment, giving rise to the feelings I'd managed to stuff down at the park. With the preparation for tomorrow keeping me busy, I'd successfully put the impending arrest aside. Now it was back, nearly suffocating me.

Even when I stepped out of the car at the base of the stairs to my apartment, the air was thick and oppressive. Climbing the steps, an overwhelming desire to flee settled over me. That is if Lisa or Adam, either one, would quit imitating a hovering copter and let me go. We all went into the living room. I opened my mouth to offer refreshments, but Lisa took over.

"Sit, while I make you something warm to drink," she said and went into the tiny kitchen. "I don't get you, Paige. This defeatist attitude is so not like you. You've just given up and think Mitch is gonna arrest you tomorrow?"

"Seems practical to me." I sat on the sofa next to Adam, who seemed more at ease than he had last night. "I've run out of time and clues. I failed."

Lisa glanced at Adam. They shared a knowing look, then she stared at me. "Yeah, you did. Big-time. That's what you get for thinking you can do everything yourself."

"Well, thanks for your support when I'm down. Want to kick me, too?"

She filled a teakettle with water. "I'm just telling it like it is."

"Okay, but I'd like it a lot better if you would do something to help me instead of berate me."

"I wish I could help." She left the kettle on the stove and came into the room. "That's all Adam and I have been talking about while we looked for you. Neither one of us can do anything to keep you out of jail. Just like you can't do anything either." She perched on the edge of the love seat. "I guess, when you think about it, you're right. It *is* time to give up. No one can help you."

It was one thing admitting defeat yourself. Having your biggest supporter give in was another. I looked at Adam, hoping he would take over for my now so-called friend, but he didn't say a word. "I know this seems impossible but—"

"Don't look at Adam. He can't help you either."

"All right, all right," I held up my hands. "You win. No one can help me. I'm sunk. Is that what you want to hear? I can't control my life. Never could. I've just been fooling myself."

There went that knowing look again. I wanted to box the two of them upside their heads.

Adam cleared his throat. "God can keep you out of jail."

"Well, yeah, I know, but—"

He took my hands. His were warm and comforting. "Then

why not give Him a chance. Trust Him to take care of you."

Warm hands could not make me believe something I didn't. "That's oversimplifying things."

Lisa pushed off the love seat. "That's the thing about faith. It is simple. Easy, even. We're the ones who make it hard."

I wish I could report that Lisa's incredibly obvious ploy worked. That I had one of those "ah-ha" moments when everything became crystal clear, and I gave up relying on myself. My behavior was too ingrained to let it slide so fast, so easily. I could, however, agree to try.

"Enough of the sermon, okay," I said. "I get the point. If I trust God, this night will be a lot easier. Even if Mitch comes to arrest me, if I'm trusting God, it will be easier. I'm not ready to give over total control yet. I'll think about it, try it even, but I'm not going to give in just like that. The two of you might as well quit ganging up on me and go on home."

CHAPTER ⫟⫟⫟ TWENTY-TWO

"This is Harly Davison, reminding you that we will be broadcasting live from Pickle Fest today with a special two-hour show. For those Through the Garden Gate fans out there, be sure to tune back in on Monday at nine when your host Paige Turner returns with her sage advice. Get it? Sage, the plant? Sage, advice? Oh, never mind. Come by the Pickle Fest."

Lisa, my unrelenting companion, and I filled my truck bed with multicolored containers, shrubs, and larger plants that we would display at the Pickle Fest. She seemed to sense my need for quiet, or she was exhausted. Either way, we worked in silence, and I let my thoughts wander over the long night. Lisa kept trying to drill into my head that if I finally let go and let God take charge, I'd know peace that was beyond explanation. It sounded good, like something to work toward. And I did. I had tried to trust God through the night. I gave Him the good ole college try. In the end, I came into the shop exhausted from lack of sleep and with a feeling of the guillotine ready to fall.

I had learned one lesson, though. Mitch saw to that. I could not, nor would I ever be able to control all situations that I faced in the future. From now on, I would try to take things as they came and cease striving to be in charge.

When the bed was filled with fragrant blooms, I loaded Mr. T, perched in his smaller cage, into the cab of the truck. Lisa held on to his cage as we drove to the park, where we found other merchants hard at work. I was sad to see the KALM booth, reminding me that my live show from this location had been cancelled. Still, I'd go with the flow. I had plenty of work to keep me occupied. We made several trips from the truck to the booth, much like Monday when Lisa helped me haul tools, only this time we had the added assistance of Briny.

I retrieved Mr. T from the truck and set him on a table inside the booth, out of the sun and away from little children's hands.

"Briny, Briny, Briny," he squawked as Briny moved away with a mob of kids dragging his sorry pickle self down the open area. I had no idea what was with this sudden desire of Briny's to spend time with me, but I was growing irritated. Especially with Mr. T calling out his name. For some odd reason, Mr. T had taken to Briny during the fall festival and loved to say his name whenever he laid eyes on him. Maybe birds have a natural fondness for pickles.

I sure didn't. I wanted to march over to Briny and demand he stay away.

Relax, Paige. Remember the new you. No need to control things.

At nine we opened for business, and Lisa worked alongside me, helping customers, restocking plants, and not glaring at the ever-present Briny as I did, until it was time to pick up her preschoolers.

She gathered her things to leave, stopped, and looked at Briny. "What's up with Briny, anyway?"

"Briny," Mr. T said.

I groaned.

Lisa laughed. "He's been hanging around you like a bad cold. I'm surprised you didn't go over there this morning to tell him to get lost."

"This is the new me," I announced with a bit too much pride in my voice. "If the silly pickle wants to follow me around all day long, let him. I don't have to control things."

She rolled her eyes. "Can't wait to see how long this will last."

Before I could come up with a witty defense for myself, my cell pealed in the ringtone I'd assigned to Adam last night when I couldn't sleep.

"Adam," I said to Lisa then greeted him with a warm tone. He, unlike Lisa, had complied and left me alone last night.

"I just got off the phone with Perry," he said in an unexpectedly cheerful tone. "He has some news from the police station."

"Wait. I'm putting you on speaker so Lisa can hear." I clicked to speaker.

"Perry's source confirmed that the autopsy report has come in and that Lawson is not ready to release the details. He also said that Lawson has no plans to arrest you."

When Lisa's eyes grew excited, I controlled the hope that sparked in mine. "What do you think this means?"

"I don't know. Perhaps the report showed cause of death as something other than the shovel, and he's looking at someone else."

There it was, a spark flaming up. "Do you really think so?"

He sighed. "Honestly? No, but we can hope."

Sizzle, out went the flame, and my face fell. Lisa slipped her arm around my waist.

"Paige, are you still there?" Adam asked.

Adam didn't need to know I was down. "Yeah, I'm here. Will I still see you later?"

"Are you kidding? Keep me away. See you around six."

Lisa dropped her arm and dug into her purse for lipstick and a mirror. "Want to know what I think?"

"Okay," I said cautiously.

She applied a quick coat of raspberry colored lipstick. "I think God sees you trying to let go. So He's keeping Mitch away from you."

"Could be, or could be—" My cell chimed again, saving me from the discussion that Lisa wanted to launch into. I looked at caller ID. "Hey, I think this is that newspaper reporter. I've got to talk to him, and you've got to go." I shooed her away with one hand while flipping the phone open with the other.

She wrinkled her nose at me. "Don't worry, I'll remember right where we left off so we can pick this up again later."

I answered my phone and glanced around to be sure there were no eavesdroppers. Zac picked the perfect time to call. There was a small crowd wandering the midway. Nary a customer lingered at my booth. I moved deeper into the space and sat in the lawn chair. I blurted out everything I knew about Bud and explained why I'd left Zac a message before.

"How'd you find out about me, anyway?" he asked.

"Old newspapers at the library."

"Library, huh? Is Stacey still the librarian?"

"Yeah."

He laughed in a mocking undertone that set my radar to beeping and set me upright in my chair. His laughter gradually stilled. "No one's caught on to her yet?"

"What do you mean, 'caught on to her'?"

"Never mind, I really shouldn't say."

What? Not another one like Charlie, clamming up when we get to the good part. "Look, a man is dead. This could be related somehow."

"She was Bud's chick."

Bud's chick? "Exactly," I said in an even tone, as if this bit of shocking information was common knowledge. "You really should tell me what else you know." I sat back and waved at Hazel, who had arrived for the afternoon shift.

"I dunno," he said.

"Please. The police think I killed Bud. I didn't. This might be just what I need to figure out who did."

"Fine," Zac said then cleared his throat. "I was working at the *Times* when Bud convinced the council to hire Stacey. The council members kept asking why such a qualified librarian would come to Serendipity for so little money. Bud said Stacey wanted out of the city. We all bought his explanation. When I saw her, man! I was like, wow, she's so fine." His voice drifted off as if he were remembering his first encounter with Stacey.

I couldn't blame the guy for his infatuation. Stacey was a beauty, one men couldn't help but notice, but he could think about her later. "And?"

"I asked her out a few times. She told me to back off. Said she had a boyfriend. That floored me. I never saw her with anyone. I kept after her to tell me who it was. She clammed up. Like that would stop me. I'm a reporter. I know how to get answers. I dug around until I found out it was Bud Picklemann. Can you believe it? Picklemann. That didn't seem right to me. Can you see the two of them together?"

"No, not really," I said and didn't even try to picture it lest I have a stroke.

"Me neither. I figured he had to have something on her, or

she wouldn't be with him. So I did a background check on her. She never went to college much less held a master's degree. She never even worked in a library. She was a waitress at the casino in Lincoln City. Must be where Picklemann met her."

I knew she was a fake. "Why didn't you tell anyone?"

Silence ensued. "I really fell for her, ya know? Figured, she was better off in Serendipity with Bud than at the casino."

What did this, if anything, have to do with Bud's murder? Was Bud forcing Stacey to stay here, and she finally snapped? I couldn't imagine her staying with Bud of her own free will. That was just yucky with a capitol *Y* and an exclamation point. When I got off the phone, I'd go see her. Wear her down until she confessed to murder.

"You still there?" Zac asked.

"Yeah, sorry. Just thinking. Were you at the council meeting where a Nancy Kimble told everyone that Bud owned the company that held the land for the factory?"

More silence. I decided to wait it out and hope he'd answer.

"Shoot," he finally said. "Picklemann's dead so what do I have to lose. I was there. Picklemann paid me to forget I heard anything. Gave me enough cash to leave town, come to the city, and chase my dreams."

Yes! "I don't know how to thank you for telling me all of this."

"Don't thank me, thank Jack. He called and said you were good folk. Told me to help you any way I could. Jack gave me my start. Taught me how to be a good reporter. I owe him big time, so when he says help, I help."

Preparing to rush to the library and confront Stacey as soon as we disconnected, I stood. "You'll call me if you think of anything else?"

"Yeah, sure. Hey, one thing before you go. Does Stacey seem happy?"

Good question. "I don't really know her that well, but yeah, she seems to like it here." That is, until I reached the library and grilled her.

"Well that's good then. I want her to be happy." I hung up on his wistful tone before he launched into more praises of Stacey, who I now thought was a killer.

I bolted on Hazel, who was helping a customer. I told her I'd be back in a flash. I hoped to return with the solution to the murder. I ran at breakneck speed, losing Briny in the process. He tried to follow. His big feet were too uncoordinated to keep up with me.

At the library, I rushed through the door and found Stacey setting out refreshments on a long table in the middle of the room.

"Planning a party?" I wheezed out between gulps of air.

"I'm hosting the Read-a-thon. It starts in a few minutes. We're combining our big fund-raiser for the year with Pickle Fest to attract a bigger crowd."

I stopped sucking in gulps of air to say, "I remember attending fund-raisers with my mom. Odd how a librarian has to be trained in raising money, too. Do they teach that at library school? Where'd you say you went to college?"

Her eyes tightened and deepened to a dark blue. "I don't believe I did."

"Did what. . .say or go to college?"

She clamped her hands on her slender waist. "Sounds like you have something to ask me, Paige. I'm not good at playing games. How about you just come right out with it?"

She seemed strong, I'd give her that, but I was more determined.

"Okay, I know you don't have a master's degree, and you never worked as a librarian before here."

A small gasp escaped from between her rosy painted lips. "And what do you plan to do with that knowledge?"

I locked gazes with her. "For starters, accuse you of killing Bud."

"What?" she shouted. "Never. I loved Bud Picklemann. He took me out of the casino and gave me respectability. He gave me a house, extra spending money. Why would I end that?"

I looked at Stacey, really studied her and saw the sincerity in her eyes. As hard as it was to believe and more painful to imagine, she loved Bud. But did he love her? Was he stringing her along, using her as he had everyone else around here? One way to find out. "Maybe Bud had second thoughts. He wanted to end things with you. So you snapped and let him have it."

"No, no that's not how it went. He was gonna leave his wife for *me*. He asked her for a divorce on Sunday night."

"Bud asked Rachel for a divorce on Sunday night?"

"Yeah, that's what I said. He wanted to be with me."

"Why should I believe you?"

She ran to the desk and punched keys on her keyboard. "Look." She pointed at the screen. "Here's his last e-mail to me."

I crossed the room and read the e-mail. She was telling the truth. Between mushy pronouncements, Bud said he was finally free. The letter was written on Sunday night at eleven p.m. He said he would see Stacey Monday morning.

I faced her. "Did you see him Monday morning?"

She shook her head. "I closed up the library and went home. He was supposed to meet me there at eleven with some of his things. He didn't show up so I came back here. Then I heard. . .I heard about his murder."

Stacey's cell phone rang out Billy Ray Cyrus's "Achy Breaky Heart." She let it ring. I wanted to ask her if Bud had left her with an achy breaky heart. I'd settle for seeing if she thought Rachel was guilty. "What about Rachel? She could have killed Bud to keep him from leaving. We have to tell Mitch Lawson about all of this."

"Don't you think I'd already have told Mitch if I thought Rachel killed him? The breakup was amicable. Bud had even arranged a huge financial settlement for her."

"Still, breakups can get heated. Things happen. People lose control. Mitch needs to know."

She looked around at the gaily-decorated room. "Please, not now. Can we do it after this is over? I want to finish this event before I get fired. Please, oh please, Paige. I know I've been really snotty to you, but I was afraid. Your mom was the librarian. If I let you get close to me, you'd see right through me. I couldn't be nice to you, don't you see?"

"Still, Mitch really needs to hear this."

"Fine, this ends at five. After I clean up, I'll go see him." She looked around the room, and tears welled up in her eyes. "I'm gonna lose my job. I love this job, and with Bud dead, it's the only thing I have left. I'll have to go back to the casino. Don't take my last event from me. Please."

Her obvious love for the job that my mom loved, too, made me cave. "Okay. We'll go together."

She flew at me and wrapped me in a tight embrace. "Thank you, Paige. You won't regret it. I promise."

We arranged to meet at my Pickle Fest booth at six. I struck out for the park to finish my shift and wait for Adam. When he arrived, I was certain he'd go with us to the police station.

On my way back, I thought about this development. As

much as I wanted to weigh in on the side of Rachel as the killer, I really didn't believe she killed Bud. If Charlie or Stacey didn't kill Bud, and Rachel didn't either, who did? You'd think I had to stumble upon the real killer soon.

CHAPTER ♯♯ ♯♯♯ TWENTY-THREE

"And now, enjoy the best of Through the Garden Gate *with your beloved host, Paige Turner."*

"Hi, Paige, this is Staked Out in Clackamas."

"Thank you for calling, Staked Out. How can I help you?"

"You remember that show you did on staking plants?"

"Sure do. Many plants grow tall, then flop. They not only hide their blooms, but also fall on top of other plants. That's when you need to invest in quality stakes to hold the weaker stems upright."

"Wait until I tell my husband. I told him we had to buy stakes for the plants. He just kept yammering on about how meat can't hold up a plant."

I held down the fort at the Pickle Fest while Hazel took a quick bathroom break. With the fort customer-less at the onset of the dinner hour, I'd settled into the lawn chair with another Nancy Drew book, *The Secret of the Old Clock*. This mystery was certainly simple. Nancy merely had to find a missing will. If only Bud's death was this simple and related to his money. Stacey blew that idea out of the water when she told me Bud gave Rachel a nice settlement.

As I flipped a page, a flash of green caught my attention from the corner of my eye. Briny had eased closer and stood a stone's throw from my booth with his green arms poised on nonexistent hips. He faced to the east of my booth and remained still as if staring at something. Not that it was odd behavior for him. True to form of the last two days, he'd stayed within full view since I'd come back from the library. I hadn't run out and sent him on his way, but I did succumb to grumbling his name off and on as did Mr. T, only with much more enthusiasm.

I didn't have to wonder for long what drew Briny's attention and made him move closer. Charlie Sweeny rushed up to the front of my booth. "You hear? Stacey was found dead at the library."

"What? Oh no. Not Stacey." I slumped against a rough two-by-four and let my gaze wander the park. This was my fault. If I hadn't allowed her to stay at the Read-a-thon, she might be alive. We would have gone to the station, and maybe she would have given Mitch information that led to the capture of the killer before he struck again. I could only hope she didn't suffer. "Do you know how she died?"

Charlie nodded. "She was whacked with a shovel, just like Bud. People are already speculating you did her in."

Before I could recover from my shock and defend myself, my phone rang.

Thankful for the interruption, I dredged up a dismissing tone and said, "Excuse me."

Charlie walked off, and I pulled out my cell. Why was Adam calling? He was due here any minute. Had he changed his mind? My stomach, in knots from the news of Stacey, clenched tighter at the thought of Adam blowing me off.

"Hey," I said with a hopeful tone. "You still coming or is there a problem?"

"I'm here already. I'm trying to find a parking space, but I thought you might want to hear about this right away. Frankie just called. Told me Picklemann left all his money to Stacey except for a trust fund for each of his kids. The wife isn't getting a penny."

"Oh, my gosh," I shouted, sending Mr. T into a fit of flapping feathers. I told Adam about my conversation with Stacey and her subsequent murder. "It must be Rachel. She must have killed Stacey when she heard about Bud's will."

"We need to call Lawson."

For once, I agreed. "I'll call him as soon as I hang up."

"Keep your eyes open, Paige. If Stacey told Rachel that you knew about their affair, Rachel could come after you." As his dire tone sunk in, a horn honked in the background. "Crazy drivers! Where's a parking space when you need one?" After another warning to be careful, he clicked off.

"'Book 'em, Danno,'" Mr. T squawked.

Planning to shush my feathered friend, I looked at him. My eyes flashed wide. Rachel Picklemann, hair frizzed and eyes wild, stood at the front of my booth. I met her stare and she laughed.

"So you have it all figured out, huh," she said, in much the same tone she used in high school when she confronted me about stealing her prom date. "Well, it won't do you any good." She eased closer and poked the tip of a gun out from under a coat draped on her arm.

I gasped and searched around for help. Briny seemed to be watching, but he didn't take any action. I jerked my head, encouraging him to come forward. Rachel came around the front of the table and blocked my view of Briny.

"Don't do this, Rachel," I begged like a child in a candy store.

"There's no point. You obviously heard my conversation. Others have figured out you killed Bud and Stacey. Don't add another person to the list." I looked at Mr. T, wishing I could somehow communicate my problem to the bird. He wanted to butt in all the time when I wasn't in danger. Now, he watched us with barely any interest.

"Ahh, poor Paige. If only I was as stupid at you think. I have this all planned out." She glared at me. "You killed Bud. Stacey found out. You killed her and then, sadly, so distraught over your behavior, you took your own life." She pulled out a folded piece of paper from her pocket. A quick shake of her hand and it opened. She spread the paper smooth on the table. "I have your suicide note right here. Go ahead. Sign it."

I stood slowly, hoping to delay long enough for Adam to find a parking space and come to my rescue.

"Now." She jiggled the gun.

Certain she wouldn't shoot me right there in full view, I planted my feet with an exaggerated emphasis.

She didn't react as I'd hoped. Instead of looking frustrated over my defiance, she shrugged and said, "Not a good idea to peeve me off, Paige. Unless you want me to leave and go in search of Lisa's precious twins instead of you."

Her lifeless tone and glassy eyes convinced me she was serious. She'd killed two people and had nothing to lose. She would go after the girls, encounter Lisa, who would put up a fight, and I would keep my life but lose the people who made it worth living.

"Fine," I said and crossed the space to scribble my name on the paper. I had no idea what I was signing, but at this point, it really didn't matter. I would sign anything to keep Rachel away from Lisa's family.

She jerked her head toward the rear of the booth. "Okay, step back."

I complied, and she snatched up the paper. After refolding the page, she shoved it back into her pocket. Clamping her free hand on my elbow, she jabbed the gun into my back and gave me a shove. "Let's go. I think a trip to the fun house might be just what you need to cheer up."

The pressure of her gun directed me forward and into the crowd. I frantically looked around for help. Anyone who could help. Wait, Briny. There he was. He might be my last chance. I needed him to see me. His head faced in my direction, but he was surrounded by children and would have a difficult time escaping their clutches to help me. Still, I cut my eyes wildly, trying to signal for him to follow us. He stood fixed in the circle of children, and I had no idea if he saw me.

We wound through the crowd. I dragged my feet. Rachel shoved the gun in more forcefully, surely bruising my flesh. I winced and sped up to her frenetic pace, trying to signal my despair to anyone who looked at me. The few people who did make eye contact cut their gazes away with the speed that told me they were certain I was a killer. You'd think someone would find it odd that I, the number one suspect, was so chummy with the deceased's wife. No one approached. Why leave me alone now? Why couldn't they be nosy as usual?

My heart plummeted to my stomach. I was all alone. No one would come to my rescue.

With a jerk on my elbow, Rachel aimed me to the right, leaving the crowd behind and circling to the back of the fun house. She dragged me through a maze of back hallways until she stopped behind a row of mirrors.

"Here," she said and shoved the note into my hands. "Stick it in your pocket."

While I complied, she searched around, likely needing to

confirm that we were alone so she could kill without an audience. Keeping her gun trained on me and eyes glancing at me every few seconds, she strolled to a far corner.

I let my gaze dart about the room. From the other side of the wide space, I spotted Briny as he entered. I stifled the desire to cry out with joy and flashed my eyes in Rachel's direction.

Briny, the smartest pickle in all the land, slipped behind a wall.

Rachel sauntered toward me as if she were strolling through the park, not coming back to murder me. "Perfect. We're alone. Sit down, and we'll make this quick."

As she fixed the gun on my chest, I panicked. What could make her stop before she killed again? She felt alone, abandoned by Bud. But she still had children. That's it. "Think of your children, Rachel. You don't want them to have to live with the fact that you killed me, do you?"

She appeared to ponder my question as her eyes focused more than they had since she arrived, and her face softened a bit. I risked a quick look at Briny's hiding space. I needed to distract Rachel so he could jump out and save the day.

I opened my mouth to talk when suddenly she shook her head as if clearing out a vision and yelled, "I said sit!" She jerked the gun.

I slowly slid to the floor. Rachel, eyes fixed on me, didn't see Briny hurtle from his hiding place. He crashed his pickled head into Rachel like a ball into bowling pins. Rachel shot into the air. Her arm hit the wall, and the gun went flying.

The pair tussled. I jumped to my feet and retrieved the gun. The sight of a giant pickle fighting with Rachel was enjoyable, and I wanted to let them duke it out. With a sudden surge, Briny's head flew off. He—what?—she could get hurt.

"Enough, Rachel," I yelled and pointed the gun at her. "I have the gun."

My voice cut through their struggle, and they stopped wrestling. Briny climbed on top of Rachel and held up her arm like a victor. I stared at the new Briny. Atop a long neck flowed blond—almost white hair, a stunning face with an aquiline nose, and a big grin on ruby red lips.

"Do I know you?" I asked, though I was certain I'd never before seen this Marilyn Monroe look-alike.

She pushed to her feet and came my way in a swish of the soft Briny body. "Sort of. We've talked a few times."

My mouth dropped open. I recognized the voice. "Weed Whacker?" I asked.

She nodded. "When I heard the real Briny broke his leg and then the show about the killer, I figured you might need my help."

Open-mouthed, I stared at the woman who I thought was a crazy stalker. I laughed, almost uncontrollable peals. As Martha Stewart would say in this case, a stalker was a good thing.

Weed Whacker stuck out her slender fingers. "My real name is Daisy."

I reached out to shake, and Rachel made a break for the door. She disappeared around a corner.

"No," I yelled and ran after her.

At the corner, I slammed into Adam and tottered. Like a Weeble, I wobbled but I didn't fall down, thanks to Adam's strong grip.

"Rachel! She's getting away." I screamed in his face but he held me tight.

"Nah, she's right here." Mitch rounded the corner with Rachel locked in his arms.

Adam gently removed the gun from my hand and gave it to Mitch.

Finger in the trigger ring, he held out the weapon to an officer who rushed into the room. "Bag it and get the equipment in here to process the scene."

Adam ran his hands over my shoulders and looked me over from head to toe. Apparently satisfied with what he saw, he pulled me into a fierce hug.

"Are you okay?" he whispered, his breath tickling the hairs by my ear.

He released me enough to breathe, and I stepped back to ease out my fear. "How did you find us?" I asked, my voice shaky.

His eyes turned sheepish. "I thought you might not call Lawson right away, so I did. He met me at your booth. When I found the booth empty, I knew you were in trouble. As we were trying to figure out where you were, Mr. T kept saying, 'Briny! Briny!' So we went into the crowd and asked people if they'd seen where Briny went. That led us here." He turned to Mitch. "Now would be a good time to apologize for what you put Paige through."

"Nothing to apologize for. Was just doing my job." He snapped cuffs onto Rachel's wrists.

I looked at the man who'd caused me so many problems. "I don't get it, Mitch. You were so bent on arresting me yesterday. Why didn't you?"

"After you left last night, Charlie Sweeny came in and told me about Picklemann's affair with Stacey. Said he was leaving this little lady. Later that night, Picklemann's financial information finally came in. Once I knew Picklemann stiffed Rachel, I figured she might have more cause for murder than you, but we couldn't find her. Have her now though."

Rachel flashed a look of hatred my way.

I ignored her glare and faced Mitch. "So the affair was the secret Charlie threatened Bud with on the day he died?"

Mitch shook his head. "Charlie only found out about the affair yesterday."

"Really?" I glanced at Adam to see if he'd heard this news, but his wide-open eyes told me he hadn't. "So how did Charlie find out something none of us could figure out?"

Mitch's gaze settled on Rachel. "Charlie was delivering a prescription for anxiety medicine to Rachel and found her already a little loopy. He thought she was so distraught over losing Pickleman that she might accidentally overdose. So he told her he'd come back the next day and bring her the pills."

Rachel growled in a low, almost guttural sound. "That man doesn't know how to mind his own business." She paused and let her lips curl in a snarl. "I couldn't let Charlie leave with my pills—I needed them. So I told him about the affair and that I wouldn't do myself in over that cheating weasel of a husband." She puffed up her chest. "But as much as I wanted to, I didn't tell him about killing Bud. I knew if I did, Charlie would never leave the pills with me."

"Instead he came straight to the station to tell me about the affair." Mitch tugged on Rachel's cuffs and handed her off to another officer. "Take her to the station."

Casting a final evil glare, Rachel was led away.

"So what was this secret Charlie was keeping about Bud?" I asked Mitch.

"I'm not at liberty to share that," he answered.

I rolled my eyes so hard, I was surprised they didn't do a full loop. "Oh, come on. You have to tell me."

"All I can say is it has to do with a prescription Charlie dispensed for Picklemann. A prescription that Picklemann wouldn't want people in town to know about."

"Bud really didn't know people, did he? Charlie might be a bear, but he's ethical. He'd never have told anyone about this."

"No, but he wanted Picklemann to believe he would so he would quit pestering him about the Leever deal."

"And that's what they were arguing about in the park," Adam said.

"Yes and at the church, too. Picklemann wanted one last score so he could leave town with Stacey and live in style." Mitch glanced at his men. "Now if you don't have any other questions I have work to do."

"No further questions," I said and slipped my hand through the crook of Adam's arm.

"Fine. You folks need to step aside while we process this scene," Mitch said. "I'll want a more detailed statement about what when down here before you're free to go."

Adam clamped his hand on mine and moved us out of the way.

"Guess what?" he asked as he released my arm and pulled me into an embrace. "I'm no longer your lawyer." He stared into my eyes then settled his lips over mine for our first kiss.

Umm, nice. I could do this all day. Loud kissing sounds came from a few feet away.

Adam and I broke apart and peered at Weed Whacker, who was grinning and making the silly noises.

"This is Weed Whacker," I said to Adam. "She's one of my favorite callers from my radio show."

"About that," Weed Whacker said, her eyes suddenly going all serious. "Earl and I made up, and he's back home. Totally understood my mistake once I explained it. Now he's questioning my next plan. Won't let me get started on it until he hears directly from you. I wanted to implement that deadheading technique you told us about, but I can't seem to figure out where to get those heads."

I laughed. "That'll have to wait until Monday's show." I pulled Adam closer. "I have something far more pressing to do right now."

Susan grew up in a small Wisconsin town where she spent her summers reading Nancy Drew and developing a love of mystery and suspense books. Today, she channels this enthusiasm into hosting the popular internet website TheSuspenseZone.com and writing romantic suspense and mystery novels.

Much to her husband's chagrin, Susan loves to look at everyday situations and turn them into murder and mayhem scenarios for future novels. If you've met Susan, she has probably figured out a plausible way to kill you and get away with it.

Susan currently lives in Florida, but has had the pleasure of living in nine states. Her husband is a church music director and they have two beautiful daughters, a very special son-in-law, and an adorable grandson. In her spare time, you can find her traveling to Oregon to visit her children and grandson, reading, or gardening. To learn more about Susan, please visit SusanSleeman.com.

Other
HOMETOWN MYSTERIES
from Barbour Publishing

Nursing a Grudge

Missing Mabel

Advent of a Mystery

May Cooler Heads Prevail
November 2010

The Camera Never Lies
December 2010